WHO IS SARAH LAWSON?

BY
K.J.RABANE

Who is Sarah Lawson

Copyright © 2012 K.J.Rabane
All rights reserved.
ISBN-13-978-1480160767

Who is Sarah Lawson

ACKNOWLEDGMENTS

My thanks go to retired Police Sergeant Alan Lloyd, MBE, for putting me on the right track, to Nona Evans for her tireless proof-reading, to Rebecca of Rebecca Sian Photography for the cover images, and to my husband and family for their enthusiastic support during the long, and it seems continuous, process of editing this book.

Dear Reader,
If you enjoy reading this please don't keep it a secret.
K.J.Rabane.

Dedication
To Frank

Who is Sarah Lawson

This book is a work of fiction and any resemblance to actual persons, living or dead, is purely coincidental.

Table of Contents
Title
Copyright
Dedication
Chapter 1
Chapter 2
Chapter 3
Chapter 4
Chapter 5
Chapter 6
Chapter 7
Chapter 8
Chapter 9
Chapter 10
Chapter 11
Chapter 12
Chapter 13
Chapter 14
Chapter 15
Chapter 16
Chapter 17
Chapter 18
Chapter 19
Chapter 20
Chapter 21
Chapter 22
Chapter 23
Chapter 24
Chapter 25
Chapter 26
Chapter 27

Who is Sarah Lawson

Chapter 28
Chapter 29
Chapter 30
Chapter 31
Chapter 32
Chapter 33
Chapter 34
Chapter 35
Chapter 36
Chapter 37
Chapter 38
Chapter 39
Chapter 40
Chapter 41
Chapter 42
Chapter 43
Chapter 44
Chapter 45
Chapter 46
Chapter 47
Chapter 48
Chapter 49
Chapter 50
Chapter 51
Chapter 52
Chapter 53
Chapter 54
Chapter 55
Chapter 56
Chapter 57
Chapter 58
Chapter 59

Who is Sarah Lawson

Chapter 60
Chapter 61
Chapter 62
Chapter 63
Chapter 64
Chapter 65
Chapter 66
Chapter 67
Chapter 68
Chapter 69
Chapter 70
Chapter 71
Chapter 72
Chapter 73
Chapter 74
Chapter 75
Chapter 76

Who is Sarah Lawson

Chapter 1

It was Thursday. I remember catching the bus to work, having lunch sitting in the park and at five catching the bus back home in the rush hour traffic. I've gone over it again and again, not only to the police but also to myself and my version of the day's events doesn't change.

I walked down the lane from the bus stop. Next door's cat wrapped itself around my ankles and an ambulance siren wailed in the distance. When I put my key in the lock I had no premonition of what I was to find. The hallway smelled as it always did, of furniture polish and lavender air freshener. I heard the sound of a strange voice coming from the kitchen before I saw the plastic scooter lying on its side at the bottom of the staircase.

"Sally, Jake, tea is ready – wash your hands first remember." I took a step backwards in the direction of the front door. Maybe I'd entered the wrong house? But my key was still in my hand and it had turned in the lock. Then I heard children's footsteps running down the stairs followed by a girl of about eight and a boy who looked a year or two younger. They glanced briefly in my direction then called out. "Mum, Aunty Sarah's here."

At this point I was certain I was dreaming. I pinched my arm and felt a sharp pain shooting up to my shoulder as the kitchen door opened and a woman with brown hair tied in a ponytail and wearing a floral apron looked at me and said, "About time, where on earth have you been?"

I was dumbstruck. Who was she and why was she using my house as if it was her home?

"Do I know you?" I asked.

"Don't start all that again, Sarah. If you want tea with the children you better say so otherwise you're going to make me late. I'm in the middle of cooking dinner."

The woman turned on her heel and walked back into the kitchen from which came the aroma of coffee and baking. It crossed my mind to think that neither smell would be present in my kitchen as I didn't drink coffee and hadn't baked anything since I'd moved in.

When my heart rate slowed to something approaching normal, I found the words tumbling out of my mouth in a torrent as I rushed after her.

"Look, whoever you are, what on earth are you doing in my house? I don't know you or your children and if I don't get a satisfactory explanation, I'm going to phone the police immediately. I'd also like to point out that my name is not Sarah, it's Rowena."

The woman was at the sink. She didn't turn around but in a bored tone said, "I suppose you think that's funny?"

The children looked on open mouthed.

"You're the giddy limit, Sarah. You do realise you could frighten the children with all this nonsense."

The feeling of being lost in the middle of a nightmare swirled around me like thick fog. I sat on one of the kitchen chairs, unhooked the telephone from the wall and dialled 999.

"Emergency services? Police please. My name is Rowena Shaw and I live at 34 Bramble Lane, Lockford Heath."

The woman spun around.

"Sarah, this has gone far enough. How dare you? You know the penalty for wasting police time. I don't understand what's got into you. Is it about Andy? Is that the reason?" She wiped her hands on a towel. "You'll have some explaining to do my girl, not only to the police but to Andy when he comes home."

I sat and stared at the unfamiliar scene – children eating their tea at the table I'd spent hours searching for, the woman preparing a meal for her husband; it seemed an age before the front doorbell rang. I stood up and went to answer it but found that before I could reach the hallway the woman had hurried ahead of me. I smelled Mischief, my favourite perfume.

Through the open door I could see a tall

man getting out of his car in the drive and two police officers waiting on the step. The woman stood back as a WPC stepped inside followed by a stocky policeman and the man whose car was parked in the driveway.

"Miss Shaw?" The WPC looked at the woman first then turned to me.

I sighed with relief. "Yes, that's me"

"Sarah?" The tall man took my arm. "What's this all about?"

I would say he was about six foot two maybe three with thick dark hair curling over his collar. He was wearing a business suit and carrying a laptop case. In the kitchen he spoke to the police officers.

"Look I'm sorry you've been troubled. Sarah is my sister and I'm afraid she's been having some memory problems resulting from an accident."

I was even more baffled. I was his sister? This must be Andy. He looked nothing like me; for a start my hair was the pale blonde shade that people always found remarkable when they knew it hadn't come out of a bottle, in addition to which he had dark brown eyes whereas mine were blue. Nevertheless I couldn't help looking for comparisons, even though logic told me it was ridiculous to do so. I wanted to scream and shout but knew that I would be playing into their hands; how easy it would be to write me off as suffering from delusions.

Gradually my 'brother's' words began to sink

in as I watched the WPC taking notes and what was all this rubbish about an accident?

After she'd closed her notebook the WPC sat down beside me. "Miss. Shaw?"

I could see what it must look like – the children, the husband and wife obviously at home in their kitchen and me the mad aunt. How could I possibly explain that this was my house and that I'd never seen any of them before? The man called Andy was talking to the policeman, his voice was lowered and I saw a look of sympathy etched on the police officer's face. He nodded then spoke to his colleague.

"I'm satisfied with the situation here. I think we should leave Mr and Mrs Lawson to finish their tea in peace."

He didn't look at me. I opened and closed my mouth aware that my sanity was hanging by a thread, unable to find the right words and frightened at the prospect of being left alone in my house with these strangers. As she stood in the doorway, the WPC put her hand on my arm. "If you need any assistance in future, Miss Shaw, please give me a ring." She removed a card from her pocket and slipped it into my hand.

I recognised that under the circumstances there was nothing more she could do so nodded in bewilderment, as the door closed behind them leaving me staring at the tall man who ran his fingers through his hair and sighed. "I don't know what you think you're playing at, Sarah. But if it goes on you do realise we'll have to take you back to Dr. Kilpatrick at the Hermitage." He gave me an exasperated look. "In view of this latest bit of nonsense I think I should take you home right now."

He took my arm and marched me towards the front door. "I won't be long, darling. Just taking Sarah home; put my dinner in the oven, I'll eat it when I get back"

I followed in a daze, part of me intrigued as to where he was taking me and where my 'home' might be, the rest of me wandering in a maze of confusion. The power to shape my own destiny disappeared as I slid into the front seat of his car with an uncomfortable feeling that this was just the start.

Chapter 2

I felt physically sick as we drove away from my home. I had no choice but to wait and see where he was taking me. He drove down the lane and on to the dual carriageway, switched on the car radio and didn't speak throughout the journey. After a while he took a slip road leading to a built up area then turned a sharp left until we reached a block of flats.

"I hope you understand that this finishes now, Sarah." He opened the car door and waited until I was standing on the pavement. "No doubt you've lost your key again." He dug his hand into the pocket of his trousers. "You can have mine, after I've seen you safely inside. Then I'll have to get back. I haven't time to spend listening to it all again this evening."

I looked up at the block of flats. They were unremarkable in appearance, probably built in the middle of the last century and with concrete balconies overlooking a square grassed area where children were playing. I wondered which featureless chicken coop was supposed to be mine. I'd tried getting the police involved and could see that my attempt had failed miserably. There was nothing for it but to see how far they intended to go with this deception and why.

My flat, it appeared, was on the third floor. There were three further floors above, each as uninspiring as its predecessor. A lift smelling of disinfectant deposited us on a landing from which a door led to a covered walkway running outside the building. A row of drab-coloured front doors, each with a brass number plate, stood in front of us reminding me of a motel I'd stayed at in the States some years ago. Andy Lawson stopped outside number twenty-six, inserted a key then handed it to me.

"Right then," he sighed. "I suggest you make a cup of tea and have an early night. I'll ring you tomorrow." He bent to kiss my cheek but I turned away. "OK, have it your own way." He shut the door behind him and I heard him retracing his steps and the door at the end of the corridor closing with a clang.

Leaning back against the front door I closed my eyes. There was a faint smell of paint and something else. Tears slid down my cheeks as I realised it was lavender air freshener. Wiping my eyes with a tissue I felt my shoe catch on something and looking down saw three letters on the mat. I picked them up, walked down the short passageway and in through the door facing me.

The living room walls were newly painted a pale shade of primrose yellow, my favourite

colour; the furniture was nondescript and signs of occupation littered the place exactly as if I'd left in a hurry that morning to go to work.
A newspaper lay on a side-table alongside an empty cup and a plate spattered with crumbs; the television remote rested on the arm of a chair whose cushions showed evidence of earlier occupation. I turned around and saw a digital radio and IPod on top of a waist-high wooden cabinet alongside which a book lay open with a National Trust bookmarker lodged in its pages.

My pulse started to race as I walked into the bedroom. The duvet was rumpled but pulled up. I never straightened mine in the mornings, as I was always in a rush to get to work. An alarm clock blinked at me from a bedside table whilst I opened each drawer of the chest to reveal underclothes, make up bags, toiletries and a jewellery box. Inside the wardrobe the clothes were hung neatly on hangers and the scent of Mischief drifted out from within their folds.

They were thorough, I had to give them that, but what purpose lay behind it all was a mystery and one, which I was determined to unravel. I decided that since my persecutors had gone to so much trouble, I'd accept my new address while I planned what to do next. In the kitchen I put the kettle on and looked out of the window to a block of identical flats and over the top of a row of terraced houses with small square front gardens to a road crammed with parked cars.

The tiny kitchen, with its chipboard units

painted cream, was a far cry from those I'd installed at Bramble Lane. I'd chosen the new fitted kitchen so that it would be ready when I moved in, picked clean bright lines for the cabinets and bought a scrubbed pine table and chairs. Wiping away tears of frustration and confusion, I made a cup of tea and went to open the letters addressed to Sarah Lawson.

The first wasn't really a letter it was a card encased in a plastic envelope announcing that there was a new range of Clarique make-up being previewed at a reception in a local department store on the 28th of this month. I put it to one side and opened the next one, which was from Marks and Spencer sending me a new credit card. It came as no surprise to see that the name on the card was Sarah Lawson. The third envelope looked official, the logo of my bank stamped on the reverse of the envelope. I put it to one side as I finished drinking my tea.

My aunt Fiona died whilst I'd been living and working in London. The day the letter arrived from her solicitors, I was shocked to discover that a relative, of whom I had little knowledge, had named me as her sole heir. She'd left me the house in Bramble Lane together with ninety thousand pounds. It was at a time when things were unravelling between Owen and me, our wedding plans were scrapped and although the details were blurred I do remember feeling that a move to the South coast was just what I needed.

As I struggled with the memory I began to feel uneasy. Something was trying to resurface, a sense that today wasn't the first time I'd heard the name Sarah Lawson. Aston and Cooper the consultancy firm I worked for had numerous clients; one of whom I reasoned could have been her.

I'd intended to transfer to Lockford from London and still keep my position within the company but something had gone wrong. An uneasy feeling, that today had not started out as I'd imagined, crept over me. Where had I been all day? I couldn't remember having been to work, only coming home in the bus.

The cheque from my aunt's estate was sitting in my current account as I'd been planning to buy a new car and have a long break in the sunshine for which I needed to have easily accessible funds. I knew that Aston and Cooper owed me a protracted break from work in view of the Santa Monica deal so maybe I was taking that break. At least I had money available to help me sort out this mess I thought putting my empty teacup in the sink.

The bank statement was on the kitchen table where I'd left it. My bank at least but not my name - Sarah Lawson, yet again. I clenched my fists and bit my lip until I tasted blood then slid the statement out of the envelope and looked at the balance of the account, which stood at a miserable £153.46. So it was not only my name that my persecutors had stolen, predictably of the ninety thousand pounds there was no trace.

Chapter 3

At the bottom of a badly constructed Ikea cabinet I found a half-empty bottle of brandy and poured a stiff measure into my teacup. The events of the day spun around in my head, none of it making any sense. After another brandy then another, anaesthetised I slumped fully clothed on top of the rumpled duvet in the unfamiliar bedroom.

Awaking some time later with a pounding headache, I padded into the bathroom and took two painkillers, which were conveniently waiting on a shelf in the cabinet. My reflection stared back at me, dark circles under my eyes and a worried frown creasing my forehead. My image looked unfamiliar. Splashing my face with cold water I went to answer the mobile phone, which was ringing from the depths of my handbag in the living room.

Hi, Sarah; it's Lyn," an unfamiliar voice announced. "I'm sorry to hear you still aren't well. I just wanted you to know I've finished reading the proofs of *Away with the Fairies* so don't worry about rushing back. Concentrate on getting better and we'll see you when you feel up to it."

For a moment I was speechless. "I don't understand. Why would you think I wasn't well?" I stopped myself asking why I should be reading proofs of any kind, although the title was apt, under the circumstances.

There was an uncomfortable silence for a beat then the woman replied," Your brother called Suzanne in Personnel. We all understand; it must have been frightful for you. Get well soon. Got to go, bye."

This was just too much. Anger fought with fear as I succumbed to a self- pitying bout of tears that left me with puffy eyes and an aching throat. So Sarah Lawson had colleagues that were concerned about her welfare and she was some kind of proof- reader, well that was a start. Next, there was the problem of finances. If I was to discover what was going on, I needed money - one hundred and fifty pounds would be gone in no time.

Afterwards I made an appointment to see the bank manger for the following day in the vain hope that I might be able to access my own account. I sat down and began to make a list. Funds first, then I'd hire a private detective. After that I'd ask around to see if anyone recognised me and, although I hadn't lived in Bramble Lane for more than a month or two, I'd spoken to the old lady who lived in the house with ivy creeping over the front porch and the man living further up the lane who regularly walked his dog.

I began to feel more positive as I placed the notepad in my handbag and made a cup of tea. How was the bank manager going to react when he saw me and not Sarah Lawson I wondered? Feeling confident that this subterfuge was about to unravel before it had a chance to knit together, I opened a packet of biscuits I'd found in a cupboard and had eaten two before I realised they were my favourite kind.

The sun shone through a gap in the thin pink cotton curtains, that I wouldn't have bought in a fit and crept up the duvet cover to my face, making me blink. The previous day had passed without further incident; neither my brother nor sister-in-law had rung so I'd been left to my own devices. What was the reason behind total strangers invading my house and robbing me of my name? The answer was staring me in the face; there was ninety thousand pounds for a start?

In the wardrobe I found clothes that more or less fitted and which were neatly hung and pressed. In the bathroom I stepped into the trickle of lukewarm water spilling out of the showerhead and washed, longing for the cleansing force of my power shower. I imagined Andy and his family using my new bathroom, the children splashing in my outsized bathtub and their mother making up her face in the mirror.

Turning off the apology for a shower, I dried my body with the rough towel that stood on a rack near the bath and began to outline a plan of attack. Selecting a pale grey trouser suit and crisp white cotton blouse from the clothes in the wardrobe, I tied my hair back into a wispy knot, applied make-up and walked purposefully out of the flat.

I'd become used to travelling by public transport since living in Bramble Lane as the journey to town was short and it didn't seem worth using my car and going to the trouble of finding a parking place. Now I had no choice. What had they done with it? Andy had been driving a navy BMW so where had they hidden my silver grey Audi? I felt tears of anger pricking my eyelids.

The bus was crowded. I sat alongside a young man with an IPod earpiece glued to his ear and sighed as two women sitting in front of me coughed and sneezed their germs into the air. Eventually the bus stopped at the bottom of the High Street and I followed the rest of the alighting passengers into the busy street.

Inside the bank a middle-aged woman wearing a name badge showed me into the manager's office. "Miss Lawson, please sit down," he said, and my heart sank as I removed the statement from my handbag.

"I was surprised at the balance of this account," I began. "Perhaps you could look at it for me?"

The manager's nameplate stood on his desk. Mr Briggs looked at me for a moment, glanced at the statement then typed in a command on his computer keyboard. "This appears to be correct."

"Really? Then perhaps it might be possible for you to trace another account for me? Sometime ago I had an account of mine transferred from your Regent Street branch in the name of Rowena Shaw."

He looked at me over the top of his glasses. "I'm afraid, I don't understand."

"It's my business account. I use the name professionally. You'll find it in your records. I'll give you my signature as proof of identity - you must have it on file." I could hear a note of panic creeping into my voice. He'd recognised me as Sarah Lawson, even clasped my hand like we were old friends. He was looking at me now as if I'd lost my mind.

He turned to the screen and tapped the keyboard.

"There should be a balance of over ninety thousand pounds in the account," I explained.

Turning to face me once more, he frowned. "First, let me say Miss Lawson that this is a most irregular request. I've searched our account database for verification purposes only, to see if we carry an account in the name of Rowena Shaw. But I must stress that under no circumstances would I be able to divulge any details of the contents of that account to you; not without strict controls to establish your right of access to the account. A signature alone would not qualify I'm afraid." He looked uncomfortable. "However, as it turns out, no such account in that name exists in our branch at this present time."

Trying to regain an appearance of composure after such news was difficult but I think I managed to sound plausible. "You must think I'm a real scatterbrain, Mr. Briggs. I'm afraid I've let things slide financially. Of course my business account must still be held in London. I'll contact them later. I'm so sorry to have troubled you."

"No problem. Is there anything else I can do for you?" He sounded relieved.

"Er, yes, as a matter of fact, there is. Could you tell me how the rest of my accounts stand at present, it will save me having to queue up at your enquiry desk on the way out."

I was praying that there were other accounts and that Sarah Lawson wasn't quite as impoverished as she appeared to be.

"Of course, now let's see." He turned back to his computer screen. "Ah, yes, your Deposit Account stands at two thousand five hundred and ninety pounds and of course there is a Savings Account with a current balance of three thousand pounds."

I smiled. "Thank you so much for your help. I'd like to make arrangements to close both the

Deposit and Savings Accounts and transfer the balances to my current account, please."

Looking as if he was about to make a suggestion, he stared at me for a moment, changed his mind and opening the top drawer of his desk removed a transfer slip and asked me to 'sign on the dotted line'.

I held my breath – this must be the time he'd see that Sarah Lawson's signature didn't tally with his office records. But he hardly gave the signature a second glance – why would he – he knew me and I was signing the form in front of him, why would he bother to check?

I thanked him and held out my hand.

"Anytime, Miss Lawson. Give my regards to Andy. Tell him I look forward to our game on Sunday and even more so to the nineteenth hole afterwards." He laughed at his own joke and walked me to the door.

Afterwards, sitting in Starbucks my hands wrapped around a mug of hot chocolate large enough to drown in, I pondered on the fact that the bank manager had no difficulty in accepting my identity as Sarah Lawson, the problem only arose when I'd tried to make him accept me as Rowena Shaw. Was it a coincidence that he just happened to be a golfing buddy of the man who was professing to be my brother?

The scars under my hairline began to prickle uncomfortably. Removing my hand from the mug I absent-mindedly massaged them and

Who is Sarah Lawson

gazed into the street.

Chapter 4

I stared through the window of Starbucks and saw a child in a yellow shiny raincoat jumping in a puddle and being swiftly yanked away by a frustrated mother pushing a pram. Rain slid down the steamed up windowpane as I drank the remains of my hot chocolate and wondered if there was anyone in this world who knew me.

Feeling foolish, I searched through the contacts in the mobile phone that belonged to Sarah Lawson. It was a hopeless task as none of the numbers were ones I recognised, until with a shock I saw the name Owen Madoc.

I hesitated and let my fingers trace the number on the screen. One by one I punched in the digits until I heard the ring tone. I waited until a mechanical voice cut in asking if I wanted to leave a message then rang off. He might pick up his missed calls – he might ring – fate would decide if I heard from him again, my courage had run out.

Next, I thought about the money that remained in the amalgamated bank account in Sarah Lawson's name and presumably the sick pay from my phantom job that would still be paid into the account. Not a fortune but enough to hire a private detective and to live on for a short time. Taking the bus back to my flat, I decided to search the yellow pages as soon as I could. I got off at the stop on the main road and walked down the path and across the square of grass.

"What weather eh, Sarah, perfect for ducks?" An elderly man in a shabby raincoat and wide brimmed hat was feeding the birds soggy bread from a plastic carrier.

I lowered my umbrella. "You know me?"

"It's Arthur, love; didn't you recognise me in my old hat?"

The shower turned heavier and before I could reply the old man shuffled away and disappeared into a doorway at the end of the ground floor corridor. I followed but was confronted by a line of faceless doors and short of knocking on every one I had no hope of finding him.

Inside the flat, I shivered and wrapped my arms tightly around my body. The old man had called me Sarah and I had no idea who he was. Before I began my search of the directory for someone, who I hoped would make my world return to normal, I took two pain killers to stop the ceaseless pounding in my temple.

Never having been in the position of having to hire a detective before, I didn't know where to start. Two large advertisements in the yellow pages caught my eye. The first read Drayton and Douglas Associates, divorce, missing persons and burglary cases undertaken in complete privacy, our motto is discretion in all things; the second announcing that no case was too large or too small made me hesitate, until I saw that their offices were on the outskirts of town. Not having any transport I ruled them both out. Then at the bottom of the page I noticed a small advertisement, Richard Stevens, Private Investigator, Hastings Buildings, 23 High Street, Lockford. Perfect, I thought, an address that was on my bus route. I rang, spoke to a secretary who sounded about twelve, and made an appointment for the following morning at eleven fifteen.

It rained all night; I tossed and turned in the uncomfortable bed until finally drifting into a disturbed sleep in the early hours of the morning. After breakfast, I dressed and tried to cover the dark circles under my eyes with make-up.

    The rain had stopped leaving behind a raw wind that had the clouds racing across the sky like Olympian athletes. Shivering in my thin coat, I waited in the bus shelter with something akin to hope. The journey to town took fifteen minutes and the bus stopped a few meters away from Hastings Buildings. In the street, I glanced at my watch; it was five minutes past eleven.

I never liked to be late for an appointment; if nothing else I knew I was always punctual.

Hastings Buildings was a three-storey block of blackened sandstone. Inside the front door a small reception area stood to my left and facing me was a staircase and a number of nameplates screwed into the wall. I ran my finger down the list of names until I found Richard Stevens then followed the staircase to the next floor.

An opaque glass door greeted me through which I could make out a shadowy distorted figure moving about like a ripple on a lake. A bell pinged as I entered. The receptionist was in her mid twenties but the impression of a young girl persisted. She was dressed in a short black skirt and white blouse and looked as if she was on her way to school.

"Rowena Shaw, I'm here to see Mr Stevens," I said.

"Right, Miss Shaw." She picked up the phone on her desk. "Your eleven fifteen is here, Mr Stevens." She looked up at me. "He says to go on in."

Richard Stevens stood up as I entered, walked around his desk and held out his hand. "Miss Shaw, do sit down." He pulled a chair away from the desk so that when he was seated I was facing him, with the desk separating us. He was in his early forties with a lived-in face and lock of thick sandy coloured hair that flopped on to his forehead. Two deep lines etched between his eyes gave him a permanent frown. From his expression, I could see his thoughts flitting over his face like a transparency projected onto a canvas. He was trying to make an instant assessment. He waited for me to speak.

"I need your help, Mr Stevens. Someone is trying to make me believe I'm not me." Aware that the words sounded ridiculous I smiled, but was certain it appeared more like a grimace.

"O...K." He picked up the phone. "Coffee for two, Miss. Smith, one with two sugars."

"Not coffee for me, tea if you have it?"

"Make that one coffee and one tea then, Miss Smith."

He chatted about the weather and where I lived until the drinks arrived then handed me the tea, which was liberally laced with sugar. I accepted it without commenting that I didn't take sugar either and slowly drank the glutinous dark liquid. Surprisingly I began to feel better.

"Now then, why don't you start at the beginning and tell me what this is really about."

Gradually I told him of the events which had led me to his door and when I'd finished he got up, walked over to the window and looked down into the street. After a short while he turned to face me.

"I am able to employ you for two weeks but my funds are limited and after that...?" I began.

"Let's not worry about money for the moment, after all, if I can solve this case there is always your aunt's inheritance to recoup. We can reach an agreement as to my costs then."

I breathed a sigh of relief. "You'll take the case?"

"Certainly. In fact you've caught me at a slack period, professionally speaking; I'll get on to it right away."

Initial impressions are not always reliable but I had the strong feeling that whatever else he turned out to be, I could trust Richard Stevens. It was comforting to know that at least someone was prepared to believe I was not stark staring mad. I left Hastings Buildings with a lightness of spirit that had not been evident upon my arrival. Outside, the wind had strengthened and my hair blew into my eyes.

"Hi, Sarah, fancy seeing you here." A man wearing a business suit and carrying a laptop case bent forward and kissed my cheek. He was a total stranger.

Chapter 5

Richie Stevens watched her walking down the High Street - saw a man bend to kiss her cheek and the look of bewilderment on her face. At first sight she was an enigma, but he had no doubt that the case, like many others, would turn out to be a matter of routine. However, watching the wind whipping her hair across her face, he had to admit that there was something bothering him about her. It was something to do with her face - it didn't suit her. Opening a new folder on his computer he typed in the words, Who is Sarah Lawson? At the end of his investigations he hoped to have the answer.

It was on days like this, when the wind whistled around the building and sunbeams trapped dust like dancing divas that his past begged to be let in. He remembered the day his promotion came through. Lucy had said, "Inspector Richard Stevens of the Metropolitan Police will still have to empty the dishwasher, so don't let it go to your head, my love."

He'd been on the force for over twenty years and was looking forward to retiring in his fifties with a sizeable pension. The kids were growing up and life was good, that was until the night Lucy had gone into town to pick up the twins from a disco. She was on her way home when a drunk driver ploughed into her car. He got three years. It was a joke. Phillip Heaton's name was forever etched into his brain, every slice of the scalpel more painful than the last. He was the scum responsible for the loss of Richie's family; a punk, who drove without either insurance or a licence and who, regularly, ignored his driving ban.

Somehow Richie managed to work through the three years after it happened. But seeing Heaton in the public bar of the Horse and Jockey that Wednesday evening he'd lost it and given him a long overdue beating. Although his colleagues had sympathised and privately applauded his behaviour, he knew that his suspension from the force was inevitable.

Public sympathy wasn't with Phillip Heaton - even the press had gone easy on Richie. But it was no use, he couldn't face living in London. As soon as the sale of the house had been completed, he moved to a flat in Lockford, where he wouldn't be able to see Lucy's face around every corner.

Richie opened the bottom drawer of his desk and removed a plastic evidence bag then gingerly held the teacup with the pink kiss mark around the rim and dropped it into the bag. As he placed it in his drawer he frowned. It would soon join the rest in the small kitchen cupboard, once he'd decided that her fingerprints were of no further use to him. But it was his belief that you should never make snap judgements and he'd learned from experience that a little initial groundwork usually paid dividends in the end.

His mobile phone began to vibrate on the desk followed by the introductory bars of Brubeck's 'Take Five". He glanced at the display. It was Mick.

"How's it hanging?" his voice crackled above the sound of traffic.

"Nothing for you, I'm afraid."

"Sure?"

"Sure."

"I'll pop in anyway as I'm just outside. See you in a mo,."

Mick Parsons worked for the Lockford Heath Courier and was desperate to move to one of the mainstream tabloids. But Richie was pragmatic – divorces, theft and missing persons were an unlikely breeding ground for the scoop Mick so fervently desired.

Having managed to persuade Mick that there really was nothing doing, Richie heard the door close behind him then walked into the outer office where Sandy was busy filing her nails. "Anything new?" he asked.

"Nah. But I've made up a new file for Rowena Shaw. Printed off the computer documents and filed it away under S."

Richie nodded. Contrary to appearances Sandy was efficiency personified. It was a mystery why she wasn't working for the managing director of a Multi-National company, for a grossly inflated sum, instead of sitting behind a desk in his office working for a pittance. He'd asked her once but she'd fobbed him off with some excuse. 'Why kill myself – this suits me; only so many clothes you can wear and I've got plenty, as for the rest, I've bagged me a rich boyfriend. Besides, I like working here.'

"Thank-you, Miss Smith," he said. "Please continue filing your nails. I've work to do, so you can catch me on my mobile if anything urgent turns up. Oh and by the way, take a long lunch hour; I'll be back later this afternoon."

He heard her chuckling as he closed the door. When she first started working for him he called her Miss Smith and she'd laughed saying that he made her sound like a maiden aunt. So from then on it was an accepted 'in joke' between them.

Hastings Buildings had a small underground car park for its occupants at the rear of the property. At the bottom of the stairs was a side door to the basement. Richie inserted a Yale key into the lock and the heavy door swung open to reveal a stone staircase leading to the car park.

He'd bought a new car when he'd set up the business – a Toyota saloon. He remembered the smell of the interior and the thrill of driving it after the battered old Ford he'd driven after the accident. The car was now four years old but it still felt new, even though it could do with a clean and the offside back wing was dented.

He clicked his remote and the car's internal locking system flew open with a flash and a beep that echoed around the car park. After choosing a compilation of jazz classics on his sound system, he drove into the street in the direction of Number 34, Bramble Lane.

Chapter 6

It took Richie nearly half an hour to reach the house; there'd been a delay on the outskirts of town. He left the main road and drove down a wide side road lined with bungalows then took a right turn into a pleasant tree-lined road of large detached and semi-detached houses. Number thirty-four was half way down on the left hand side. It was detached and stood behind a high stone wall and looked quite impressive from his restricted viewpoint. Mature trees lined the driveway and he caught a brief glimpse of a neat lawn bordered by flowers.

Removing a clipboard from the boot of his car and attaching a badge of officialdom to his lapel – they never looked too closely he'd always found – he walked up the driveway to the front door.

It was two-fifteen. He guessed that the children would be in school and Lawson would be at work that just left Mrs Lawson. He rang the bell, which was followed, soon after, by the sound of footsteps. The door was opened by a woman in her mid-thirties with brown hair that hung to her shoulders. She was wearing denim jeans and a white tee shirt. She eyed him suspiciously through the half-opened door.

"Good day. Mrs Lawson?"

She nodded.

"Mrs Hannah Lawson?"

"Who wants to know?"

"I'm sorry. I'm new to this game." He gave her one of his little boy lost looks.

"Eric Bradley." He held up his clipboard. "I'm from the council. We're doing a survey into refuse collection in the area and I wondered if you could spare some time to answer a few questions in order to help us improve the service." She was about to say no. He could see it in her eyes. "I realise this is an intrusion. To be perfectly honest I'd rather be sitting behind my desk right now. I'm hopeless dealing with the general public. But what with the cut backs and all that, well, here I am." He started to turn away from the door, but as he'd anticipated she called him back.

"OK but please keep it short, I'm busy."

He thanked her profusely and began by asking when her bins were collected, was the service efficient etc., After running down a list of questions he finished by thanking her for her time and apologising for any inconvenience. She'd shut the door before he started to walk back down the drive.

Later, Richie parked on the Common and glanced at his clipboard. Refuse collection in

Bramble Lane took place on Monday mornings around eight-fifteen. Hannah Lawson said that she found the timing a nuisance as she was usually backing out of her drive in order to take the children to school. Her annoyance stemmed from the fact that she had to negotiate the pile of bin bags that the bin men had accumulated outside her house whilst waiting for the slow progress of the lorry down the lane.

His brief assessment of her had been of a capable, possibly strong-minded woman. She'd looked at home in the house and gave no sign of recent occupancy of the property. In fact she gave the appearance of having dealt with the Monday morning collection on a regular basis. He thought that her annoyance seemed to be genuine.

Richie sighed; at least he knew when to pick up the refuse sack full of a week's worth of rubbish. You never knew what was lurking in rubbish bags. The contents might reveal a clue as to why Rowena Shaw believed the Lawsons were trying to steal not only her house but also her identity.

He intended to beat the bin men next Monday. Lawson's wife had told him that her husband usually put the bags out on Sunday evenings, but as he couldn't be sure of the timing of this event, he decided that half-past five on the following Monday morning would be the best time to execute his plan.

Entering Hastings Buildings at a quarter to

four Richie heard the sound of voices coming from his office. He raced up the stairs to find Mick Parsons sitting on Sandy's desk, a cigarette dangling from his lips.

"I thought I told you….," Richie began.

"I know, old fruit but I had the urge to see the delectable Miss Smith before I went home to write up copy on a boring visit to the W.I. by a member of the Gardener's Question Time panel." He stubbed his cigarette out in Sandy's paper clip tray. "By the way what are you working on at the moment? Sandy said you were out on a case."

Richie glared at her.

"I didn't say a word."

"Ah, so there is something." Mick aimed a self-satisfied grin in Richie's direction.

"I'll give you the nod once there's something positive to report, I promise. Now clear off and take your fag ends with you. Open the window, Miss Smith. There's a bad smell in here."

Mick Parsons grinned. "I'll be in touch."

As the reporter's footsteps clattered down the stairs Sandy said, "Well?"

"Let's just say, I think we are about to experience the most fascinating case that this agency has ever had on its books, Miss Smith."

"Wow!"

"Wow indeed and if you'd like to bring in your notebook, we'll make a start right away.

Chapter 7

Dawn broke leaching a pale pewter light through his bedroom curtains. Richie silenced his alarm with an annoyed slap and groaning, showered and dressed in his sleep-deprived state. The sky had grown dark; rain-bearing clouds hung over the town threatening a downpour.

He lived in a block of flats overlooking the river and was on nodding acquaintance with his neighbours, who seemed to change by the hour, the flats being generally bought for quick sale investment purposes. But Richie wasn't going anywhere. The isolation suited him; he'd had enough of kindly neighbours to last him a lifetime. After the accident they couldn't do enough for him. Mrs Merchant and Miss Tillett living in the houses next-door made it their business to call on him with casseroles, cakes and kind words, until he'd felt suffocated under a mountain of solicitude.

The janitor, who was cleaning the foyer, grunted a good morning when Richie appeared dressed for jogging in a black lightweight tracksuit then carried on swabbing the floor with a mop.

The morning air was crisp and as he headed for his car he could feel the first spots of rain on his cheek. Inserting his key in the ignition Richie noticed that the light shower was turning heavier by the minute. Good, he thought, there was nothing like heavy rain to keep the early risers indoors. Traffic was sporadic and the drive took him twenty minutes. He parked on the corner of Bramble Lane outside a bungalow that looked as if it had seen better days. He assessed that by the condition of the place an elderly person lived there, as the curtains hung limply at the windows and grubby grey nets grew in abundance.

Tugging his hood over his head, Richie jogged in the direction of number thirty-four. The bin bag stood outside on the pavement. Skirting it, he ran the length of the road to where it petered out into a track that wound through the woods then retraced his steps watching to see if anyone was up and about at number thirty-four. He was wet through, so shaking the worst of it from his hood he jogged back along the pavement picking up the black bag with a fluidity of movement that surprised him. Increasing his pace he reached his car, slid the plastic bag into the boot, and drove back to Hastings Buildings. The office filing room was the place to search through rubbish, not in his flat; you just never knew what you'd find or in what condition, he thought, dragging the bag up the stairs.

After making a cup of strong black coffee and taking a biscuit from Sandy's secret store, he changed out of his wet clothes and hung them in the filing room. Then pulling on the dry tracksuit he'd brought with him, he sat on the floor to inspect the rubbish from the house in Bramble Lane. After lining the floor with plastic sheeting, he opened the small window. The room was not much larger than a store cupboard with shelving units containing stationery and office equipment on either side almost meeting in the centre.

Richie pulled on a pair of rubber gloves, opened the neck of the bin bag then tipped its contents on to the floor. The first thing he noticed was the lack of smell and rotting food scraps. Gingerly he lifted up plastic containers, cardboard packing, empty beer and coke cans but the story was the same. Either the Lawson family permanently ate out or had an efficient food recycling system; he supposed that there was always the faint possibility that they used the house infrequently and ate in another property altogether. He didn't consider the latter premise in depth as it could be easily verified by further investigation.

Picking over the remnants scattered at his feet he noticed a receipt from Marks and Spencer for food, an online delivery bill from Tesco and an empty champagne bottle. What had the Lawson's been celebrating? He was beginning to think he was wasting his time when an envelope caught his eye. It was from Lloyds TSB; he recognised the logo on the back of the envelope. His client's bank account was held by Lloyds and it did cross his mind to consider the possibility that, if what Rowena Shaw had told him was true, then the Lawsons could easily have intercepted letters from her bank along with other relevant correspondence.

Removing the Champagne bottle with care he placed it to one side, re-filled the bin bag and tied it securely. There was no reason why it shouldn't go out with the office rubbish the following day. At his desk he slid the bottle into the bottom drawer alongside the cup bearing Rowena Shaw's fingerprints then opened his laptop and updated his file.

When Sandy arrived, the office bore no sign of its earlier use. Richie was still updating his computer, the kettle had just boiled and apart from the faint smell of wet clothes and his casual attire there was nothing unusual.

It was ten o'clock and Sandy was drinking her second cup of coffee when Richie rang through from the inner office. "Miss Smith would you be kind enough to ring Chief Inspector Norman Freeman at the Met.,? You'll find the number on file."

With her usual efficiency Sandy did as requested and Richie was soon talking to his old mate.

"Good Lord, what a surprise! How are things? Still taking the bread from out of our mouths?"

Richie smiled, Norm never changed. It felt good to hear his voice after so long.

"Business isn't exactly booming but I'm sticking with it. In fact that's why I'm ringing. It's about a case I'm working on."

"I see."

"I don't like bothering you but I've no way of moving forward with this. It's fingerprints; I've got two items requiring identification and elimination. I'm coming up to London in the morning and I wondered if you'd be able to meet me?"

He heard the rustle of paper and guessed that his old friend was looking in his desk diary.

"Drop into my office about ten; your old mates would be glad to see you."

He hesitated, "I know this is a big ask, Norm, and I don't want to make things difficult for you but could I meet you in the Bunch of Grapes at about midday?"

The thought of going to London made him break out in sweat. He could feel it prickling his armpits and hastily wiped his damp forehead with his handkerchief. There were times when you just had to bite the bullet. If Andy Lawson and his wife were petty crims., their details would be held on a nationwide database, similarly if his client had a past, hers would resurface in the same manner

In the storeroom he picked up his damp tracksuit, pushed it into a plastic carrier that lay on a shelf in the filing room, and entered the outer office. Sandy had a single earpiece from an IPod lodged in her left ear.

"Who's flavour of the month?" Richie asked.

"It's a language lab transmission actually, I'm learning Russian." Sandy looked up at him waiting for the smart reply but he just nodded.

"I'm off to London for a bit. I'll see you the day after tomorrow," he said. "Oh and don't forget to put out the bins."

Chapter 8

The man was a stranger. I'd smelled a faint aroma of cologne as he'd kissed my cheek and noticed that he kept looking at his watch as if in a hurry.

"Do I know you?" The question seemed to be permanently glued to my lips.

He frowned and I could see he was making up his mind whether I was serious. "Neil Stafford. We met at Andy's fortieth. How are you by the way? Your brother told me about the accident."

The world tilted once more as I wrapped my arms tightly around my body. Who was this man? How could we have met at Andy's birthday party? In addition to which Andy Lawson was not and had never been my brother. Luckily an answer to his question was not required as he glanced again at his watch and said, "Goodbye then, sorry to dash," before leaving me standing in a daze on the pavement.

Behind me lay the offices of Richard Stevens; he was my only hope. Waiting at the bus stop I tried Owen's number once more only to be met with the inevitable recorded voice asking me to leave a message. This time I declined the invitation.

It was two days later when I saw Neil Stafford again. I'd decided to search the local newspaper archives for any reports of the mysterious accident, the details of which I knew nothing. The offices of the Courier were situated in a side street off Manor Road. A young woman called Catherine led me into a room overlooking the street where back copies of the paper were kept on Microfiche. She spent a few moments showing me how the machine worked then left me alone.

It was a frustrating and monotonous task and I found my gaze returning to the street. Then I saw him. Neil Stafford was leaving a building opposite and was in deep conversation with the man who said he was my brother. They were sharing a joke. Both men were laughing uproariously until Andy slid his hand into the inside pocket of his jacket and removed a thick brown envelope and gave it to Stafford.

There was an air of conspiracy between them. Neil Stafford tapped the side of his nose with his finger and my 'brother' laid a hand on his shoulder. I was certain that money had changed hands and even more certain that it had something to do with me.

I suddenly lost interest in my search. Realising that I was paying someone to do the donkeywork, I decided that for the present I'd assume the identity of Sarah Lawson and live her life to the full. But there was no way I was going to give up on Rowena; I would simply put her to rest for a while, until I could find out the truth.

Leaving The Courier, I walked down Manor Road and turned into Victoria Park where I lay down on the grass in the sunshine and soon fell fast asleep. When I awoke, the sun had moved so that I was lying in the shade. The sound of children's voices drifted towards me from the direction of the play area as I sat up, rubbed my eyes, and focused on my surroundings.

I looked at my watch, a habit that was hard to break. What was there to rush home for now? Empty days stretched before me until I could start work again. I'd already more or less decided that I'd leave my identity crisis in the hands of Richard Stevens so what was the point of getting more stressed about the situation. I knew who I was and where I lived, I just had to prove it.

Standing up, I stretched and walked past the duck pond to the artificial lake where rowing boats and pedalos bobbed on its surface. Two optimists were rowing across the lake to a heavily wooded area with a picnic basket and some teenagers were pedalo racing amidst shouts and screams. I wondered how long it would be before I could be as carefree and knew that until I was back in Bramble Lane and using my own name that would never happen.

There was a large area of green-belt land encompassed within the park, which led to a high point overlooking the town. It was known as The Heath, although it was technically parkland. As I climbed the grassy knoll to the spot where the council had erected benches, I watched the shifting scene below me. The High Street was busy with traffic and shoppers, the side roads fanned out towards the suburbs and in the distance there was the motorway with its constant hum of traffic. Directly below me at the edge of the park was a primary school. It was almost half-past three and a line of cars containing mothers waiting to pick up their children snaked around the perimeter of the park.

Deciding that it was time I went back to the flat, I walked towards the entrance of the park and caught the bus that was conveniently waiting at the stop the driver having left his cab to smoke a quick cigarette. As the bus skirted the school, I noticed Hannah Lawson's car pull out in front of us.

I watched the car as she negotiated the traffic on the High Street and anticipated the direction she would take to arrive at Bramble Lane. She would need to drive out of town on the Milton Road, follow the duel carriageway south until it joined Manor Way and then left into Bramble Lane.

The car was plain to see, its distinctive custard yellow colour making its journey easy to follow.

At the end of the High Street it took a right turn on to Milton Road but contrary to my expectation it avoided the duel carriageway and sped northwards on to the Litton bypass. Due to the rush hour traffic the bus progressed slowly down the bypass before turning into the Crossfield estate and out into the maze of streets in a run-down area known as the Cuttings.

As the bus stopped I watched an elderly couple struggling to manage the stairs with their shopping before making their way down the road. Then I saw it; the custard yellow car. I watched mesmerised as Hannah Lawson closed the car door before she and her children walked up a debris- strewn garden path gradually disappearing from my view. I was intrigued; who she was visiting and why?

Chapter 9

As evening shadows lengthened, I closed the cheap cotton curtains and switched on the television for the News broadcast. The picture flickered on the small screen and once more I felt anger bubbling up inside me. My forty-inch plasma TV in Bramble Lane was a far cry from the flickering image I was being forced to watch. I'd rung Richard Stevens's office as soon as I'd returned to the flat but his receptionist told me that he'd left early and that he'd be in London for a day or two. I left a message asking him to contact me on his return and tried ineffectually to put the sight of the yellow car out of my mind.

I was in the middle of making an omelette whilst listening to the news filtering in from the living room when I heard a familiar voice. I'd missed the initial report but entered the room as a reporter from BBC Wales Television was standing outside a shop in the centre of Cardiff describing a burglary that had taken place on the premises in the early hours. I recognised Glyn Morgan immediately; he'd been a newspaper journalist, when I'd known him, a lifetime ago.

Glyn and I had formed a friendship at University which, after we'd graduated developed into something more. But, as fate would have it, the relationship was destined to become a brief fling as I met Owen and from then on there *was* no one else.

Turning away from the screen, I began to wonder how to contact Glyn. The BBC would have his number I was sure. Deciding to sleep on it and ring first thing in the morning, I ate my meal, searched for something to watch on TV and fell asleep in the middle of a film I thought I'd seen before.

Dreams punctuated my sleep; disturbing, complicated dreams that drifted away like morning mist once I opened my bedroom curtains. A street cleaner sitting on what looked like a converted golf buggy chugged his way down the pavement on the opposite side of the road where the flats showed the same dreary lack of imagination in their construction as the block that housed mine. However, one dwelling stood out amongst the rest. The door was painted a glossy black with a brass number plate situated to the left of the front door. At the windows silver grey metal strip blinds twinkled in the morning sunshine. If it were possible to call such a place stylish then it would have fallen into that category.

 As I cradled my first cup of tea of the day, I wondered who lived in the flat opposite but before I could give full reign to my imagination the black door opened and a woman, in her late twenties with blonde hair swept up into a French pleat, emerged. She was wearing a charcoal-grey dress and jacket and carried a laptop case. My curiosity was heightened when I saw her slide into a sleek black convertible parked in front of the building. It seemed odd to me that she was living in such a dreary location. As if to endorse my theory, the old man, who'd been feeding the birds in the rain, appeared from a doorway, spat into the gutter and then shuffled off in the direction of the river.

    He was another mystery I planned to solve. Why did he think I was Sarah? Who had told him my name? I knew it hadn't been me. What I found unable to fathom was the reason behind it all. Fraud, leapt back at me like a slap in the face. There were ninety thousand pounds and a house in an up-market location to consider. But you'd have to be pretty desperate to concoct such a scenario, as there was always the possibility of discovery. How could Andy Lawson and his wife be sure that there wasn't someone out there ready to back up my story? The odd thing was that, for the life of me, I couldn't be sure who that person could be.

    Owen hadn't picked up my messages, or if he had he was ignoring them. The morning news programme on the television reminded me I needed to contact Glyn. Picking up the phone I rang directory enquiries and asked for the telephone number of the BBC Studios in Cardiff. When I'd eventually been given a number, which I rang with shaking hands, I waited an age until a disembodied voice answered my query saying, "I'm afraid Glyn Morgan isn't available."

"It is rather urgent that I contact him; I wonder if you'd have his mobile number?" I tried to sound less needy than I felt.

"I'm sorry. Mr Morgan is flying to Tokyo today but if you'd like to leave your name and number perhaps he could ring you when he returns."

"Is he likely to be away for a while?"

"I'm afraid I couldn't say."

With a sinking heart I left my name and number as suggested. Putting down the phone I felt like Alice in Wonderland, trapped and falling deeper into the earth but I had no white rabbit to help me find a way out of my predicament and could only hope that my faith in Richard Stevens was not misplaced,

Chapter 10

The rain was a surprise. It fell like arrows out of a seemingly blue sky. I sheltered in the bus stop as dark clouds gathered and a cool wind blew my skirt against my legs. By the time I arrived at my flat the force of the rain had soaked through my clothes. I heard the telephone ringing as I turned the key in the lock. Sliding my arms out of my wet jacket, I picked up the phone.

"Is that Sarah Lawson?

My heart began to beat faster. The voice belonged to a woman with a strong welsh accent.

"Who wants to know?" I answered carefully.

"I won't forget what you did?"

I was speechless for a moment.

"I don't understand," I stammered.

"Don't pretend you don't know what I'm talking about."

"I don't."

The woman laughed; a dry humourless sound that made me shiver. "Well now, let me jog your memory shall I? Friday 27th May ring any bells?"

I was starting to get angry. "Look, I don't?" know who you are but I don't propose to enter into your little game, whatever it is."

"Still pretending it didn't happen then? I thought as much. You can't fool me though and I intend to make you pay for what you've done to my son."

I slammed down the phone in disgust. This was the last straw. I should ring the police immediately. Intimidating phone calls, loss of identity, what next, I wondered. I looked at the telephone, even picked up the handset, but my courage failed me. If the situation sounded crazy to my ears what was it going to sound like to the police? They'd already decided I was deranged after my insistence that I lived in Bramble Lane and that the Lawsons were strangers. Replacing the phone I sank to my knees on the rough carpet. When it rang again, I ignored it. Then I stripped off my clothes, stood in the shower and attempted to wash away the horrors of the last few days. Andy Lawson and his family slid with the soap down the plughole and with the unknown caller filtered through the pipes into the sewerage system.

Later, wrapping a towel around me, I picked up the yellow pages, ordered a Pizza then dressed in a pair of cotton pyjamas. Refusing to think about any of it I opened a bottle of Chardonnay that I'd bought in the supermarket earlier and poured a large measure of the chilled wine into a glass. It's impossible to instruct one's brain not to think; it does so like a disobedient child regardless of instruction.

I kept searching my confused memory banks for the owner of the voice on the telephone but it was a waste of time, I just couldn't remember. However, I was certain that the voice didn't belong to any of my friends but couldn't swear that I definitely hadn't heard it before. There was something familiar about it but, try as I might, it wouldn't come. It just kept circling in the background begging to be pulled into the light. But no illuminating beams were forthcoming.

There was always this possibility that she'd ring again and this time I'd be ready. I had dialled last number recall but the number was withheld. Filling my glass once more I began to relax and, finding a station playing classical music on the radio, picked up my book and waited for the Pizza delivery. Whether it was relaxing effect of the wine or not, I sat up with a jolt remembering the significance of the date – how could I ever have forgotten it – it was meant to be my wedding day.

The sound of a van pulling up in the parking area was followed by the slam of a door and footsteps hurrying across the walkway. I was standing near the door when the bell rang.

The young Pizza delivery boy grinned. "Hello again; having an early night?" He eyed my pyjamas and smiled. "House too big for you was it?"

I'd taken the Pizza from him and was searching in my purse for payment when I suddenly realised what he'd said.

"Excuse me. What did you just say?"

"Sorry. None of my business, I know. Just that the last time I delivered Pizza to you it was in the house on Bramble Lane – great big place – number thirty-four if I remember rightly."

It was a shock. I gulped, stared and then stammered a reply, "You remember me?"

"Yeah course, I never forget a face, it's a habit of mine to remember all my customers – never fails – I've got a knack my boss says."

The veil of confusion began to lift as I remembered ordering a Pizza delivery from the same firm soon after I'd moved in.

"I know this is going to sound odd but you don't remember what my name was, when I made the order from Bramble Lane, by any chance?" My heart was beating faster, at last someone knew me.

He grinned and said, "No prizes for guessing eh; let me see now." He stroked his chin and flipped open an order pad. "Mm not so good with names but orders for 34, Bramble Lane have been booked under Lawson. Says so here in black and white. Don't tell me you've forgotten your own name?"

I stared at him, hope dissolving and floating away on the breeze. "No, it's just some friends were staying with me at the time. I think I owe them some money for the delivery." The explanation sounded ridiculous, even to me but I could feel tears pricking my eyelids and my voice verging on hysteria.

Pizza lad backed away and I realised I must look quite mad, standing there in my pyjamas grinning in an attempt to hold back the tears. I asked his name.

"Tom. Tom Devlin."

I searched in my purse, took out a fiver and handed it to him as a tip. "Thank you, Tom Devlin. Thank you for remembering my face."

He left and I heard him whistling as he pocketed the money and made his way back to the van.

Chapter 11

The Bunch of Grapes was like most wine bars in the city, beech laminated floor, metal tables, black leather armchairs and potted plants that looked so healthy they had to be plastic. Richie sank into the soft leather armchair near the window, put two glasses and a bottle of Merlot on the table in front of him and, with one eye on the street, waited for DCI Freeman to join him.

Norman Freeman was an exemplary cop but one with a human face. Rules were there to be bent as long as the bending fell within the loose letter of the law. He never crossed the line but could be relied upon in an emergency. Richie had found him a good friend when he'd been in the firing line after beating Phillip Hatton to pulp.
Some of his so called mates had shrunk into the background, unwilling to stand up and be counted where he was concerned but not Norm, he'd stood his ground at the disciplinary hearing insisting that there were extenuating circumstances responsible for the attack and refusing to be swayed into taking the easy route out of the situation by having him expelled from

the force. Nevertheless, it must have been with a sigh of relief that he'd seen Richie take the initiative and hand in his notice.

Six foot four, muscular framed and with eyes that missed nothing, Norm opened the door of the wine bar and greeted Richie with a wave. "Sorry, have you been waiting long? I got caught up in something – you know what it's like."

"Not anymore."

"No regrets?" Norm filled the chair opposite him.

"Not one, thank God; my own boss now."

"Yeah; business good is it?"

Richie poured the wine and handed a glass to his friend. "Not bad. I make a living, which is all I ask."

After catching up on news of colleagues and changes at the Met., since Richie's days, Norm said, "What's this all about then?"

"It's this case I'm working on. A woman called Rowena Shaw contacted me insisting that strangers have moved into her house, placed her in a flat she has no memory of ever having lived in, and are trying to make out that she's someone called Sarah Lawson. These strangers are purporting to be her brother Andy and his wife and kids. She wants me to find out what's going on and to re-establish her identity," Richie explained. "There's also a question of the theft of ninety thousand pounds to consider."

"Mm," Norm stroked his chin. "Not your usual divorce case then?"

"That's about the size of it."

"Does she seem like a nut case?"

"No. That's the thing. She seems completely normal; so much so that my first impression was that she was telling the truth."

"Aren't there any neighbours or friends who can corroborate her story?"

"That's the problem." Richie put down his empty glass. "She doesn't know any of the neighbours as she's only recently moved down from London. She says she works for a consultancy firm, Aston and Cooper but when she contacted them, the information they gave her was that Miss Shaw had decided not to transfer to Lockford and they believed she was working for a firm in the States but could give her no forwarding address."

"And where do I come in?" Norm raised his glass and looked at Richie over the rim of it.

"Well, I know it's a lot to ask, but I've removed some fingerprints from a couple of items and need to know if their owners have a record."

"If it gets out that I've helped you, that's my job down the Swanee." Norm frowned. "But as I said on the phone, I haven't forgotten old times. Hand them over. I'll let you know if anything turns up."

Richie slid an envelope across the table, which Norm then placed in the inside pocket of his jacket.

"I really appreciate this."

"We miss you on the force you know."

Richie smiled ruefully. "Glad to know someone does."

DCI Freeman stood up. "Now then, business over, I'll fetch another bottle, I'm taking a long lunch hour and Cheryl is picking me up after work, so no driving. Tell me, what's life is like down south, my friend? I'll be retiring in a year or two and it would be good to move out of the city."

At five past three Richie stood on the pavement outside the wine bar and hailed a taxi to take him back to his B&B in Earl's Court. He could have taken the tube but thought 'sod it' and called a cab instead. He didn't admit to himself that he'd chosen to ride in the taxi so that he could watch the changing face of the city that had been his home for most of his married life. He missed London but knew he'd never return; too many memories lingering within its doorways threatening to jump out at him at the least provocation.

The hustle and bustle of the main streets mesmerised him as he watched shoppers, workers and the homeless jostling down the busy highways, independently existing within the framework of commerce. He could smell the river and longed to stroll from Chelsea embankment to the Tower without remembering that on hot summer days it was a favourite jaunt of the family; his family, the one that had ceased to exist.

"This OK for you, Guv? The road's blocked, accident, I think. I can see a blue light up ahead."

The taxi driver half turned towards him.

"Fine, how much do I owe you?"

Leaving the taxi and walking the rest of way he decided to make the most of his last night in the city. He'd promised himself two nights away and couldn't believe he'd stuck to his resolve. He had his client to thank for that.

The taxi driver had been right. It was an accident. An old man lay at the side of road. It was obvious he was one of the city's underclass, a homeless vagrant. Knowing from experience that his face would be mottled, his nose red and bulbous and he'd be wearing cast off clothes that were far from clean, Richie watched the usual ghouls edging forward, desperate for a peep at someone else's misfortune. The screech of an ambulance siren rent the air followed by the parting of the waves of traffic as a vehicle appeared with blue lights flashing like beacons.

The sky had darkened heralding rain. Richie, acknowledging the fact that the paramedics were no longer needed, made for the relative anonymity of his bed-sit.

Chapter 12

He awoke to the forgotten sounds of the City waking from slumber. The pit-pat of heels on the pavement followed by heavier footsteps, insistent, angry, car horns, the distant hum of traffic; it was a world that had once been as familiar to him as the nose on his face; it was the early morning rush hour.

Norm had said he'd ring him on his mobile number as soon as the search was completed and Richie anticipated it would take a while. He could have spent the night at home and returned the next day but having made the effort to conquer his fear of returning to London, he decided to take the next step and spend the following day visiting a few old haunts. He'd stay clear of the river; he wasn't ready for that yet.

After a hearty breakfast, cooked by a landlady who had three strapping sons and knew from experience how to fill a man's stomach, he threw his overnight bag into the boot of his car, locked it and walked to the nearest tube station.

Rush hour was over. The escalators were easy to negotiate, shoppers, teenagers with nothing to do, and members of the grey brigade, his son's description of anyone over forty, made their way down into the bowels of the earth.

He followed the direction of the Victoria Line along a white-tiled tunnel from which the faint strains of a violin drifted eerily towards him. Turning a corner he saw the musician, a young man in his early twenties, tall and thin with a faint outline of stubble on his chin. He was talented, one of the many whose talent was not necessarily the vehicle to instant success. Richie threw a pound coin into the rapidly growing collection in the violin case.

As he walked away he thought about the young man. A student, he decided, trying to eek out the expenses of living in the city by doing what he did best. There was always the possibility that a few years down the line he'd be dressed in a black tailcoat and bow tie and leading an orchestra in the Albert Hall. Then he felt the dreaded black cloud descending. The young man had a future; it hadn't been smashed away by drunken driver.

Focusing hard on the tunnel in front of him, he concentrated on the minutiae of the day until the cloud dispersed and he heard the rumble of the trains. As he waited on the platform he felt a sudden warm gush of air being pushed out of the tunnels and blowing towards the waiting passengers. There were changes, as in any city, since Richie had lived and worked there but they were superficial; tube stations given an updated look, new department stores, boutiques and wine bars where once had stood grey uncompromising office blocks and shabby apartments decaying under a weight of pigeons' excreta.

Leaving the Victoria Line at the next stop, which was Green Park, he followed the directions for the Piccadilly Line. He could have walked the short distance but relished the chance to use the Tube trains, sucking up the atmosphere like a vacuum cleaner, enjoying every last dusty footstep that he took towards the hive of activity surrounding Piccadilly Circus. The air was warm as he walked down the Haymarket inhaling the scents and sounds of the City. Taking a short cut in the direction of Covent Garden he found a small café with tables and chairs arranged outside in the sunshine. He sat down, ordered a cup of strong black coffee and watched the world go by.

Sitting at a nearby table was a beautiful woman. Describing her as anything else would be doing her an injustice. She was groomed to perfection; blonde hair pulled back off her face and twisted into a gleaming knot, understated make-up, her clothes epitomising City Chic.

Once upon a time such a woman would have sent his blood pumping but now he cast an appreciative glance in her direction then carried on drinking his coffee and continued to watch the passers by. However, the sight of the woman had started a train of thought that culminated in Bramble Lane. It hadn't been too difficult for him to assume the identity of a member of the council enquiring about refuse collections in the area. Similarly his client's features were regular and well formed, there was not a single feature that was out of proportion, her nose was straight and neither too long nor too short, her lips were plump and her blue eyes were well spaced. It would be perfectly possible to alter her hair and make up in such a manner as to resemble the woman at the nearby table for example.

With this thought uppermost in his mind he walked towards the market, which as usual was busy with shoppers. Strolling along the aisles between the stalls with the sun shining through the glass roof of the covered market, Richie decided to look for a gift to take back for Sandy.

He discounted the customary badly made trinkets in favour of a stall that sold handmade jewellery. Its creator, a hippy-girl-woman sat on a stool with a pair of pliers in her hand as she fashioned what looked like a reel of wire and some brightly coloured stones into a delicate necklace. He watched mesmerised at the transformation.

"That's really lovely," he knew he sounded surprised.

The girl noticed. "You didn't think it would be?"

He smiled. "Fair enough. How much?"

"Well to such an appreciative audience, a tenner."

"You are joking?"

"Can't do it for less, sorry." She started to turn away.

"No, no, what I mean is, yes, I'll have it."

"Make up your mind, Sport," she said pulling out a cardboard box from a drawer at her side.

Watching her slipping the necklace inside then placing it in a paper bag with psychedelic swirls looping around her name he asked, "Aussie?"

"Pommy?"

He liked the girl. He'd been used to having to rely heavily on his intuition and it hadn't let him down in the past. Handing her a twenty-pound note he said, "Keep the change. You're underselling yourself you know."

"Ta very much and yeah I do know but what can you do? They won't pay, not now anyway. Maybe when things pick up and the telly stops going on about the recession, who knows?"

Young, talented and street wise – before he could stop himself he said, "Look it's lunchtime, how about you joining me for a meal?"

She looked at him as though he were the village pervert.

"Nah,,,"she started.

"Don't get the wrong end of the stick. It's only lunch on offer. You're young enough to be my daughter."

She screwed up her eyes and looked at him again, made up her mind, closed the stall and said, "Why not? There's an Italian just around the corner – that do?"

"Sure." He followed her flowing skirts, with a spring in his step. It was the first time he'd shared lunch with a stranger of the opposite sex since before his marriage and in spite of himself - it felt good. The part that said, it was because she reminded him of Tess he pushed to the back of his mind.

Chapter 13

Nikki's Italian Pizzeria was obviously popular with the Market Traders. Most of them knew Angie Peters. Richie guessed it was why she'd chosen it – it was safe, if he turned out to be a pervert after all.

He ordered spaghetti bolognaise for them both and they shared a plate of garlic bread. He remembered his student days and for a brief moment the years slid backwards as if he hadn't a care in the world and was sharing his lunch with an old friend.

"So what's this all about?" Angie asked, through a mouthful of garlic bread.

"There's no ulterior motive. I didn't fancy eating on my own and you looked as if you could do with a good square meal, simple as that."

He liked her directness. But he wondered if she would ever realise that the main reason he liked her was his daughter would have been about her age had she lived and it was she whom he missed like losing a vital part of himself.

As if reading his thoughts Angie said, "You

got a family then?"

He thought about lying, about making up the wife and kids he'd lost but just replied, "No."

She didn't question him further and before he knew what he was doing he was explaining why. It was as if the floodgates had opened. He was telling a stranger things he hadn't told a soul, how he'd felt when he'd identified the bodies, what it was like returning to an empty house, getting rid of their clothes, the childhood toys. She waited until he'd finished, looked at him through a fringe of dark brown curls then patted his hand.

"Tough shit," she said as the spaghetti arrived.

She told him that she'd come to London from Melbourne two years previously. She'd studied art in Australia but after she'd qualified she wanted to spread her wings. Her flight had led her to a market stall in Covent Garden. She was keen to set up her own business and had to start somewhere.

"Where d'you live?" he asked.

She hesitated, but only for a second. "I share a bed sit with two girls just around the corner. They're studying music at the Guildhall. They play here sometimes, usually on a Sunday morning."

They talked about her life and aspirations until looking at her watch she said, "Got to get back, earn my living and all that. Ta for the meal, Richie."

"No problem, thanks for the company. G'day, Sport."

She laughed; a loud unselfconscious belly laugh that made him smile. He watched her walk away, the breeze lifting a curtain of hair around her like a curly cloud.

Afterwards, he felt as though a weight had been lifted from him. The burden he'd been carrying was lighter. As he walked in the direction of the Tube station his mobile rang. It was Norman.

"I've got some answers for you. Can you come into my office do you think?"

This time he knew he could. He'd left behind the fear of sympathetic glances from his erstwhile colleagues; it was another step along a road that was the hardest to travel. "I'll be there in twenty minutes," he replied.

Most of the office staff had changed since his days at the Met., but, he recognised a few of his former colleagues who, apart from raising a hand or nodding in his direction, seemed to be busy all of a sudden. Richie understood their embarrassment, but at last felt he could cope with it.

Norman sat behind a desk piled high with files and correspondence. "Sit down, my friend. Sorry I couldn't leave the office. I hope you don't mind."

"No problem. Thanks for sparing the time. I can see you've enough to do."

"Yeah, no peace for the wicked, eh? Of course

you realise that what I have to tell you is confidential.

"Go on."

"First, your client's prints didn't produce a match. But the prints you took from the Champagne bottle told a different story. Amongst the others you provided was a set belonging to Andrew Lawson, which threw out a match on our system."

Richie sat forward in his seat.

"It appears that Lawson was arrested after a disturbance in a bar in the city a while back. A Mr Owen Madoc was stabbed with a broken bottle and taken to hospital after a fight. Lawson was charged but the case was later dropped, as Mr Madoc didn't wish to proceed. But not before Lawson had cooled his heels in a police cell overnight."

"I see. At least that gives me a starting point. I owe you one."

"Who knows, I might take you up on that one day. Stay in touch, remember a good cop is hard to find."

"I will. Let me know if you and Cheryl decide to come down my way and I'll show you around."

Driving back to Lockford, he began to plan his next move. He needed to talk to Lawson first. Then a phone call to Owen Madoc might be in order. He was whistling to himself as he drove into the basement car park of Hastings

Buildings. Sandy was taking a phone call as he opened the door. "Oh, hang on a minute; he's just come in." She mouthed, "It's Rowena."

"Hello, Miss Shaw. What can I do for you?"

"I need to see you urgently. There have been some developments."

He arranged that she should call at the office in an hour. But in actual fact he'd only had time for a quick cup of coffee before she arrived. She told him about the phone call and about the Pizza delivery boy. He decided not to tell her about his conversation with DCI Norman Freeman, there was plenty of time for that later, after he'd talked to Lawson. He appeared to be listening intently but her words floated over his head. He was concentrating on the necklace she was wearing. It was distinctively fashioned from wire and coloured stones. Angie Peters's face swam before him, a reminder that he hadn't given Sandy the gift he'd bought for her.

Chapter 14

I was beginning to wonder if it had been a mistake employing a private detective. There was no movement in my case, no sudden breakthrough. His receptionist had told me that he'd been working in London for the past couple of days - following up a lead she'd said, but there'd been no evidence of it in our conversation the previous day.

I rang Owen's number again but this time there was no message just a low-pitched signal. So that was the way he wanted it? He'd obviously decided not to return my calls and had even gone to the extreme measure of changing his phone number. At first I was mad; what did he think I wanted? We'd been together too long for me to be treated like some kind of stalker. My anger cooled and I was left with a feeling of overwhelming sadness at the death of a relationship that had once showed such promise. I'd remembered that we'd loved each other and were planning to marry, if only I could remember the rest of it.

The sound of children's voices floated in

through the open window and I looked out; they were playing football on the grass and seemed as if they didn't have a care in the world. I shuddered, as if a ghost had walked over my grave. I didn't hold any animosity towards Owen - relationships ended. But why was he refusing to take my calls?

Every door slammed shut in my face. There was nothing left for me but to rely on Richard Stevens's ingenuity to give me my life back. I wasn't expected at Aston and Cooper but people were waiting for me to turn up for work, somewhere. What was I waiting for? Why didn't I do just that? Whatever Andy Lawson had told them, it *was* supposed to be her job and after all people did get better - even if their name was Sarah Lawson. Later, as I slid into bed, I started to feel more positive about the future.

It felt good to be on the crowded bus going into town. I glanced at my fellow passengers. One young woman was trying to read her book squashed up against an overweight man. Two girls in school uniform were comparing homework. A workman in overalls was complaining to a man in a business suit about the failure of his car to start and a few early morning shoppers jostled along with the rest of us.

Classifying myself as part of the human race once more, I left the bus at the main road and walked up the hill towards the office block where Sarah Lawson worked. I'd found the address in her flat; it was on a letter from her latest employer sympathising with her illness, which had been forwarded by a secretarial agency. The main car park was beginning to fill up. I followed a group of women into the foyer.

Two women, one cradling a mug of coffee, were chatting outside an open door through which I could see a man gazing at a computer screen.

"Hi, Sarah," the woman holding the mug said. "How are you? Just popping in for a visit?"

"Not really; I'm ready to start work. I don't need to stay off any longer."

She looked confused and turned to her older companion. "I thought you said..." she began but was interrupted by the older woman taking my arm and leading me away from the doorway.

"There's been a misunderstanding here, I'm afraid." She looked over the top of her glasses at me. "Your agency should have kept you informed. The post has been filled, we no longer require a temp. You will of course be paid at the end of the month."

"I don't understand."

"We explained to your brother that we couldn't keep the post open for ever. I do sympathise, Sarah but things change, you know how it is."

"I think I'm beginning to," I said turning around and walking back to the exit. So now the net was closing in. I had no job and very little funds in my bank account; the situation was desperate.

On the bus back to the flat I began to wonder how much longer I could afford to pay the rent and utilities before I realised that I was being ridiculous. This charade had to stop; I had to confront the man who was posing as my brother and the sooner the better.

Once more the phone was ringing as I opened the front door.

"Sarah?" It was a woman's voice and one, which I recognised. "I know you and Andy are at loggerheads but we *are* family and I'm not willing for this to go on a moment longer. Come over tonight for dinner. What do you say?"

So the mountain had come to Mohammed, I thought, as I replied. "OK. What time?"

"The kids are having a sleep-over at a friend's house. It's not far from you. I could pick you up on the way back. Let's say seven?"

"Fine," I said.

The rest of the day passed in a flash. I was anxious. It didn't escape my notice that the children would be absent. Maybe they couldn't be relied upon not to say something they shouldn't. Children could not be programmed like robots. The memory of the custard yellow car stopping outside a house, not a million miles away from my flat, made my head swim. I had to get to the bottom of it all before I was sucked deeper into this web of intrigue. It was no good simply relying on Richard Stevens; I had to take the initiative. With some careful subterfuge I should be able to beat them at their own game.

There was no reason why I shouldn't become the sister they wanted – at least for the present.

Chapter 15

Waiting on the covered walkway outside my flat, I saw her car pulling into the forecourt. Hannah Lawson wound down the driver side window and waved to me. I smiled, waved back and went down to meet her. To a casual observer it would have appeared that we were at least friends.

She seemed flustered as she backed out of the parking area into the evening traffic. I heard her mutter a curse as she knocked the offside wheel against the curb The inside of the car was less bilious than its outer shell; brown fabric seat covers were littered with the detritus of family life, crisp packets, an empty plastic bottle that had once contained juice, a beheaded power ranger and a pink notebook with a Hannah Montana bookmark spilling out from its pages. I shifted uncomfortably in my seat and waited for this stranger to begin talking.

"There, that's better. I always hate that roundabout, won't be long now, Andy's keeping an eye on the curry. It's your favourite. I thought we might eat in the summerhouse. It's a nice evening, if not quite as hot as it's been."

A shaft of loss hit me like a needle piercing skin – the summerhouse; I'd loved it at first sight. It stood at the end of a well-manicured lawn edged by mature trees. There were shrubs with terracotta pots spilling colourful Busy Lizzies arranged around its perimeter. If I'd any doubts about the house being too big for me the summerhouse had dispelled them, besides I'd already decided to raise our kids in that house. But now there were no kids and no Owen.

The Lawson woman prattled on, how glad she was that I was joining them; she hoped that this latest bit of nonsense was over - perhaps we could all get back to normal - if I felt lonely at all, having finished work - well she could do with a hand - the house was always in a mess with the kids.

I clenched my fists and ground them into the seat cover but smiled as if her request had been a perfectly reasonable one.

Lawson's car stood in the garage. Once again I clenched my fists – where was *my* car and what did they intend to do with my ninety thousand pounds?

"You OK?" She was looking at me intently as she drew to a halt outside the front door. I pasted a look of surprise on my face.

"Fine. Thanks."

"Right then, why don't we take the side door into the garden and surprise Andy."

Oh what good fun, I thought, following her. He was carrying a tray into the summerhouse as we arrived.

"Just in time," he said. "Glad you've decided to see sense, Sarah."

Ignoring his comment I said, "Something smells nice." It was the sort of remark that sounded reasonable, I thought. I was beginning to get used to censoring my words. There was no point ranting and raving, that hadn't worked.

The sun was sinking in the sky casting elongated shadows over the lawn when Andy, leaving the kitchen carrying another bottle of wine, approached me but I found it easier to concentrate on the shadow rather than its initiator.

"How are the children?" I tried desperately to remember their names. "Jack and Sally."

Andy shot a quick glance at his wife. "Jake," he said. "We called him Jake."

"I know that, it was just a slip of the tongue."

Lies piled up like litter. For a moment I was aware of an uncomfortable silence until Hannah picked up her empty dish. "They're fine."

"How long did you say they'd be away?"

"Just for tonight. They might be spending some time with relatives soon though, especially during the school holidays." I didn't miss the look Andy gave his wife. This time it spoke volumes.

I nodded, which seemed to satisfy them.

Later, as night fell, they suggested we move back into the house.

"Why don't you stay over? Your bed is still

made up in the spare room. I've drunk too much and Andy is way over the limit. It makes sense - you don't want to have to pay for a taxi - I'll drive you back home tomorrow morning," Hannah said running the sentences into one as if in a hurry to finish them.

"Right, thanks." I registered the look of surprise on Andy's face. He'd expected an argument, I thought.

I sat with them whilst we watched television. At least, they watched my plasma screen - I watched them. At half-past ten, Hannah offered to make some hot chocolate.

"I'll make it, after all I know where everything is don't I?" I said.

I noticed the hesitation; they missed a beat in unison. Then as if awakened from the same dream, they responded, "Yes, thanks."

In the kitchen I switched on the kettle - my kettle - found the large jar of drinking chocolate that I'd bought in Sainsbury's before this nightmare began - poured milk into a saucepan and waited for it to rise in the pan. Then I tipped an equal measure of water and milk over the powdered chocolate - exactly as they liked it.

Chapter 16

There was no possibility of him posing as another official. It was too risky. He had to find another way of engaging Andy Lawson in conversation without arousing suspicion. Richie, assessing the situation, found that he kept returning to the children. Busy fathers usually spent time with their children at weekends, took them to the park, whilst mothers had a break. Surveillance of the property was required and he knew exactly how to achieve it.

Opening up the Internet application Google Earth he homed in on Bramble Lane then eased the cursor back until each side road and geographical feature lay before him. He saw a heavily wooded area at the rear of the property beyond which lay fields that appeared to stretch in the direction of the house where Sandy's father lived.

He stood up and walked into the outer office where his receptionist was busy filing her nails and applying a coat of peach coloured varnish. "I need Bruce."

She didn't look up. "Surveillance?"

"Got it in one."

"Give me a moment for my nails to dry and I'll ring Dad."

Bernard Smith was in his early seventies and suffering with osteoarthritis, which made walking Bruce, a Golden Labrador, difficult. Sandy helped at the weekends and with her brother Dan made sure that Bruce usually had plenty of exercise.

Bernard was waiting on the doorstep as he drew up.

"Good to see you again, lad. Still keeping that girl of mine in order?"

"Other way around."

The older man chuckled. "Just as I thought. Come in, there's a cup of tea in the pot."

Later, with Bruce at his heels, he left his car in Bernard's drive and headed for the lane leading into the field. It was dry underfoot and Bruce lost no time in chasing rabbits back to their burrows, making the occasional sortie into the undergrowth and returning like a homing pigeon whenever Richie whistled.

The dog was a perfect cover. No one questioned a man's right to roam if he had a dog in tow. He became invisible, no longer a private investigator, but simply a dog walker exercising his pet Labrador. He knew that even if Hannah Lawson saw him from her bedroom window she would never link the man walking his dog wearing an anorak and a baseball cap with the dark-suited researcher from the council carrying a clipboard.

As they neared the woods he called Bruce to heel and attached his lead. A trodden down pathway through the wood led to the houses on Bramble Lane so he followed it until the trees began to thin. Sunlight penetrated the foliage and dappled his shoulders as he walked towards the boundary of number thirty-four. Careful inspection of the property, via his computer, earlier, had given him all the information he required.

Bruce raised his head as Richie removed a small rubber ball from his pocket. The dog barked.

"Ssh, not now; we'll play later, I promise," he whispered throwing the ball high into the air. It sailed over the fence bordering number thirty-four as the dog strained at the lead.

Skirting the rest of the houses until they reached the main road, he pulled the peak of his baseball cap lower and walked back towards number thirty-four. The yellow car was just backing out of the drive so he walked past the gate until the car disappeared down the lane in the direction of town.

It was Saturday morning. Sandy would be locking up the office about now. He glanced at his watch. Hannah Lawson had been alone in the car. A black BMW stood in the drive. As he approached the house he noticed the absence of children's voices. It was a pleasant morning; why weren't they out playing?

Ringing the bell, he waited, Bruce sitting obediently at his heels. After a while the door opened and a tall thin man with thick dark hair stood back in the shadows.

"I'm sorry to bother you. We were walking through the woods and I'm afraid my dog's ball landed in your back garden."

It looked as if the man was going to shut the door without comment but then he said," And you want me to search for it, I suppose?"

Assuming a sympathetic expression Richie said, "I know I'm a terrible nuisance bothering you like this but it's his favourite." It sounded lame even to him. "My kids would go mad if they thought I'd lost it. They love the dog to bits but as usual I'm the one left to exercise him." He took a step back. " I could go around the side - search for it myself - I really don't want to put you to any trouble."

The man sighed. "If you take the side door, I'll join you in the back garden."

"Very kind, I appreciate it," Richie said urging Bruce forward.

The garden was larger than it had looked on his laptop. When his client had described the property she'd told him that a gardener still called to keep it in order, as it was too large for her to manage. The lawn was unkempt and in need of a good trim. The border plants also showed some evidence of neglect, although it looked recent. "Do your children have any pets?" Richie asked as he searched the undergrowth.

"Nah, kids are enough trouble without having animals as well," Andy Lawson replied kicking at a shrub with the toe of his trainer.

"My sentiments exactly. I was duped into caring for Bruce. They conned me."

"That's what kids do."

The conversation about children flowed as they searched.

"Lovely houses these, spacious, my place is bursting at the seams. Been here long?" The question sounded innocent enough

"Here it is." Lawson held up the ball. "It's not one of ours, so must be yours." Handing it to Richie, he replied, "We moved down from Birmingham, a few months ago, to be nearer my sister."

They had reached the back gate.

"Lucky man. Thanks again for letting me disturb your Saturday morning. I expect your kids keep you busy at the weekends?"

The question remained unanswered as the man closed and bolted the gate leaving Richie and Bruce standing on the path. Walking towards the road, he looked back at the house and saw Lawson standing at the window watching him.

Chapter 17

On Monday morning having had the rest of the weekend to think over the case, Richie took the stairs to his office two at a time.

'Kak dela'

Sandy was obviously progressing.

"Spasiba, horošo. A u vas?" he replied.

She removed the IPod's earpiece, and gasped, "You speak Russian?"

He could see her initial hope fading, as he walked to the water dispenser and commented, "That's the lot I'm afraid."

Watching the air bubbles in the bottle glugging into a polystyrene cup, he held an empty one up to Sandy.

"No thanks. Was Bruce a good surveillance dog?"

"Excellent. But I think the time has come for you to do some field work of your own, Miss Smith."

Sandy leaned forward. "About time, I thought you'd never ask."

"First, tell me, do any of your brother's children go to the school on Milton Road?" "Yes, Chloe. She's in the second year reception class and longing for the summer holidays to start."

"And when will that be?"

"Next month around the 24th, I think. Dan's taking the family to Crete."

"Very nice."

"What do I have to do?" Her eagerness made him smile.

"Nothing too strenuous I assure you. Just arrange with Dan that you'll take and pick up Chloe from school, until further notice."

"You're serious?"

He nodded.

"Jane will be pleased; she's got enough to do breast feeding baby Adam morning, noon and night. He's going to be a whopper."

"Your job will be to get to know Hannah Lawson. Her photo should be on file. She has two children, a boy Chloe's age and his older sister; she drives a yellow car, you can't miss it. Put your best socialising skills into operation - get her to invite you back for coffee - you know the kind of thing."

"I'll certainly do my best."

"I've no doubt you will, Miss Smith."

"When do I start?"

Richie handed her the phone. "No time like the present. Give your sister-in-law the good news."

The photo of Hannah Lawson was not a good one. He'd taken it from a distance but he believed that it was clear enough for Sandy's purposes. He wondered idly if there were any photos at number 34 that would hold a clue to this mess. He picked up the phone on his desk and rang his client's mobile. "If you have a spare moment, perhaps you'd call in at the office later this morning, Miss Shaw," he said.

It was nearly lunchtime; Sandy had gone to pick up her niece from school. Richie's belly was screaming for food when his client arrived.

"Is there any news?" she asked eagerly.

"Nothing concrete, I'm afraid." He looked at his watch. "I wonder if you'd like to join me for lunch and we can discuss what I have in mind. I skipped breakfast and I'm suffering."

"Fine," she replied following him out into the street and towards the Sweet Pea café.

"The food here is good. Grab a table near the window and I'll pick up a menu." Richie walked to the counter and removed one from the top of the pile.

They each ordered the smoked salmon salad, Richie with a portion of chips on the side and whilst they waited for its arrival he made a suggestion. "How confident do you feel about searching number 34?"

"Searching?"

The waitress arrived with their food. He waited until she'd moved away before continuing, "Perhaps you had a photograph album somewhere in the house? It might hold a vital clue to your past. We all have photos of relatives and friends hanging about the place. What do you think?"

Uncomfortably aware that this was not always the case and that he'd left his family album in London with his sister, he waited for her reply.

"That's possible," she said slowly. "The only problem is, they might have beaten me too it. They do seem to have been extraordinarily thorough. And for a few years now I've kept most of my photos on computer file. Although where my laptop has got to is anyone's guess."

"Do you still have a key to the house?"

"I do, although I haven't used it since the day I arrived home and found that they'd taken up residence."

Richie put his cutlery down on his plate. "That seems strange. You could have gone in at any time, taken over the place, established residency."

She sighed. "Easier said than done. They are a family, there are children involved, and besides the police already think I'm slightly demented. The thing is I can't prove the house is mine."

"That should be easy to determine via the deeds of ownership, plus there's your aunt's will."

Richie waited. Finally she said, "Again, easier said than done. I rang my solicitor in London soon after it happened and he told me that the firm dealing with my aunt's estate, Rawson and Hodge, are no longer in existence. There was a fraud case brought against one of the partners soon after my aunt died, the business folded and by then the papers concerning the will had been transferred back to Rawson and Hodge."

"The papers must still be on file somewhere." He was sceptical. The excuse was too convenient and he distrusted coincidence.

"I rang the liquidators of the company and they told me that once the case had been heard they'd be able to release the papers. They apologised and said that it was impossible to isolate the documents relating to my aunt's will at the moment but assured me that they would be available at a later date."

"The land registry would have a record of ownership," Richie said wiping his mouth with his napkin. "Although I suspect that it would still be registered in your aunt's name." He sucked in his bottom lip, a sign that something was bothering him. "That's it!"

"What is?"

"If the house is still registered to your aunt – it can't belong to the Lawsons – we just might have cracked it."

"You think so?"

She was smiling. He could see that she was beginning to hope.

"Mm, just in case this is another dead end, what do you think about my suggestion that you try to find your photograph album?"

She looked doubtful. "I'll certainly try. Perhaps I could offer to babysit one evening and when the children were in bed I could start my search."

"Right." Richie stood up.

"And you'll ring the land registry?"

"Of course. I'll be in touch as soon as get an answer."

Chapter 18

Things were moving far too slowly for his liking. Every avenue seemed to lead to a dead end. Richie paced the floor. Sandy was doing the lunchtime run at the school. She'd be taking Chloe back about now. She'd managed to persuade the child that lunch with her aunt was a better option than the school canteen. A week had passed and she seemed to be no nearer befriending Hannah Lawson.

He stood at the window and looked down the High Street then saw a flash of red hair and Sandy's trim figure hurrying towards the office. He was never sure which image she would project when she arrived for work. Sometimes it was the dizzy schoolgirl or sometimes the competent career woman; today it was the busy aunt on the school run. Her hair was now auburn and swung to her shoulders, she was wearing a skirt of flowing material in muted tones, flat shoes and carried a bulging leather shoulder bag.

He heard her footsteps on the stairs and put the kettle on. "Well, Miss Smith, any developments?" he asked handing her a mug of coffee.

Sliding the bag from her shoulders to the floor, Sandy sat behind her desk, caught her breath and opened up a new file on her computer. "I'll type up my report as soon as I have a moment." The edges of the competent career woman's image blurred with that of the busy aunt.

"All in good time. Just tell me the bones of it so that I can decide what to do next."

"I've established contact, at last."

He was beginning to feel like M interviewing James Bond. "And?"

"Apparently, Chloe and Jake have made friends. I did have to promise her a trip to Legoland as a bribe though."

Richie smiled.

"Hannah Lawson asked if Chloe would like to come to play with Jake, after school tomorrow."

"That's great. Perhaps you could have a look around number thirty-four whilst you're there. You know the kind of thing, decide whether the family are behaving as if it's their house or if something doesn't feel right."

"I don't think that will be possible."

"No?"

"The address she gave me is definitely not Bramble Lane - it's somewhere entirely different."

Later, looking at the file Sandy had compiled he saw that the address Hannah Lawson had given was Byron Terrace. Accessing Google

Earth on his laptop he traced the satellite image of the house. It was situated in the middle of a terrace, in an area nowhere near as prestigious as Bramble Lane. As he zoomed out of the district he caught sight of the block of flats where his client lived and noticed the proximity to Byron Terrace - it was no more than a ten minute walk away.

The following day, as Sandy was about to leave the office to pick up Chloe and take her to Byron Terrace, he said, "Give me a ring when you get home, I'll still be here. There are a few loose ends I need to tie up."

The phone call came at five to seven. Richie had ordered a Take Away and the office smelt of Sweet and Sour Pork and soggy chips.

"I'm updating the file on my laptop right now," Sandy said, "but I thought you'd like to know that the children aren't Lawson's. Their father lives in Byron Terrace. I'll give you all the details tomorrow. Got to go now."

That night he dreamed of Lucy. She'd called him to say she was going to pick the kids up from the disco and he'd tried to dissuade her. "Tell them to take a taxi, Luce." He'd kept repeating the words, but it was no use, she couldn't hear him. He awoke drenched in sweat, his heart pounding; the illuminated figures on his bedside clock read five past four. A faint grey light of dawn was seeping in through his blinds, he couldn't stay in bed, he was afraid. Lucy's face hung before him like a fearful phantom and the thought of falling back into his dream shot him into wakefulness.

After clearing his head by showering in tepid water, Richie dressed, got into his car and drove towards Byron Terrace. The morning traffic was almost non-existent. He passed a workman on a bike; a street cleaner humming his way down the road on a miniature electric dustcart and a couple of early morning commuters driving in the direction of Lockford Heath Halt.

The road stretched into the distance, on both sides stood featureless terraced houses that had been customised to a greater or lesser extent by their owners depending on their taste or lack of it; gardens littered with debris, prams, broken bicycles and the detritus of modern-day living spilled depressingly around him. Sandy told him that she'd dropped Chloe off at number fifty-two, which was on the left hand side of the road.

He drove to the end of the terrace, turned around and drove back then parked opposite number fifty-two. Taking a road map from the glove compartment he spread it out over the steering wheel, in an attempt to persuade casual onlookers that he was searching for his destination.

There was little or no movement in the road. Occasionally someone opened their door, got into their car and drove off. But it wasn't until seven o'clock that traffic increased and the occupants began to surface like ants from an anthill.

At a quarter past eight the door of number fifty-two opened and a stocky man emerged, he had a shaved head and was dressed in a red tee shirt with the name of a DIY store written in large navy letters across his chest. Ten minutes later a woman wearing a pair of grey jogger trousers and a grey fleece top opened the door followed by two children whom she bundled into the back seat of battered Ford Fiesta that stood at the curb.

In view of his client's and Sandy's experiences over the last few days, it didn't take a genius to deduce that the children were Jake and Sally Lawson.

Chapter 19

It was odd sleeping at home again, especially with strangers in the house. At least the couple were using the large master bedroom at the front. I'd never liked it, preferring the room overlooking the back garden with its square bay window and upholstered window seat.

Thankfully they'd left it untouched, it was the spare room they said. I was sure I wouldn't sleep a wink but my body had different ideas. I sank into the bed and before I knew it I was dreaming. It was a dream like many others, confused, populated by people I seemed to know and situations that appeared perfectly normal however strange they actually were. I slept until I heard someone knocking on my door and awoke to a room that smelled familiar, was flooded with sunlight and the sound of birdsong drifting in through the open window.

Hannah Lawson stood in the doorway. "Breakfast's ready. How did you sleep?"

"Fine thanks. I'll be down in a sec,." I replied.

Breakfast and the drive home passed in a flash

and soon I was back in the dismal flat. Something made me try Owen's number again; it was probably the dream, he was the only one of my night-time companions that I'd recognised on waking. But there was still no answer just the same depressing answerphone message.

Richard Stevens's suggestion that I try to find my photograph album had given me something to do. First I searched the flat, which took less than an hour. There was nothing hidden, I hadn't really expected that there would be. The place was a shoebox, which had been hastily put together for my arrival. Hiding anything was virtually impossible.

I was beginning to think that spending the night with the Lawsons hadn't been such a bad idea after all, by accepting their lies as truth they might relax and allow me to do some baby-sitting.

I picked up the phone. "Hannah? It's Sarah," I said the name through gritted teeth.

"Sarah?"

"I just wanted to thank you both for last night. I know I've been a bit of a pain lately but I've come to my senses. Put it down to hormones, Andy usually does. Anyway I thought I'd like to make it up to you by offering to baby-sit one night. What do you think?"

I could almost see her face; hear her weighing up my sudden change of heart and deciding what to do about it. In reality all I heard was a slight hesitation in her voice. "Er, yes. Yes that would be great. Thanks, Sarah. I'll have a word with Andy and get back to you."

I mentally patted myself on my back. I only hoped I could keep up the pretence when I came face to face with them both, last night had been quite an ordeal one way and another.

Later that day, it must have been about half – five, I heard the roar of a sports car drawing up. If I hadn't been bored with the book I was reading, I might not have moved across to the window. Voyeurism had become a bit of a habit since I lost my identity.

The car belonged to the Grace Kelly look-alike that lived opposite. I watched as my neighbour slid her long legs out of the sports car. This time she was dressed in a black pencil skirt that rested on her knees and a crisp white blouse with a ruffle at the neck. She was carrying a laptop case.

I was so engrossed in watching her that for a moment I didn't see her companion as he opened the passenger-side door, closed it with a whisper and followed her into her flat. However, I had recognised him as he took the car keys from the woman and locked the car with a flourish exaggerating the gesture to full effect. It was Neil Stafford.

Surely this was one coincidence too far? He knew Andy Lawson, was he also playing a part in this deception? Would that explain why his girlfriend was living in such an unsuitable location? Was she watching my every move? Aware that paranoia was threatening my sanity, I took a deep breath and tried replacing it with logic. But my thoughts were interrupted by the telephone ringing so I dragged myself away from the window to answer it.

"Hannah says you've come to your senses at last."

"Andy!" I tried to put as much enthusiasm into my voice as possible. "I'm sorry to have caused you so much trouble."

The sigh was palpable. It echoed down the phone line and slid like a snake into my ear. "Am I glad to hear it! I gather you're willing to baby-sit?"

"Of course – anytime."

"What about this weekend then? Saturday night all right?"

"No problem. What time?"

"I'll pick you up at seven." Then as an afterthought, he added, "Stay the night?"

After the phone call, I rang Richard Stevens and left a message on his answer phone telling him of my plans for the weekend. Perhaps his strategy would pay off. Only time would tell.

Chapter 20

My house no longer smelled familiar. There was no scent of lavender air-freshener in the hallway, no lingering traces of furniture polish and the fresh smell of clothes left to dry in the utility room. I inhaled the remains of the children's meal and a faint aroma of sweaty socks coming from a linen basket at the side of the sink.

"Jake's in bed, Sarah. Sally's had her bath and she's watching a DVD. We've told her that she must be in bed by eight."

"Is she allowed a story?" I asked placing my overnight bag at the bottom of the staircase.

"The usual, you know what she likes, but no Harry Potter. She always has nightmares that she's being chased by giant spiders or worse."

She was wearing a black shift dress and gold jewellery. Her hair was piled up on top of her head in soft curls. I thought she looked older.

"This is good of you," she said. " We do appreciate it. We won't be late but don't stay up if your tired. Just make yourself at home."

I bit my lip until I felt the blood flow. What else could I do? This *was* my home. Dabbing at my cut lip with a handkerchief, I followed her into the living room overlooking the garden where my 'brother' was giving Sally last minute instructions as to how she should behave.

"You be good for Aunty Sarah now my girl and who knows I might buy you that new Hannah Montana DVD." He was bending down in front of the child and seeing me he stood up. "Hi, Sarah, don't take any nonsense from little Miss Busy remember." He turned to his wife. "Right then, if you're ready, darling, we'll be off."

I watched the end of Sally's DVD sitting next to her on the sofa I'd bought in Marks and Spencer's end of season sale.

"It's time for bed," I said turning off the TV.

"Aw, it's still early. It's not dark." I shook my head and held out my hand. Reluctantly she agreed but with a condition. "Can I have a story though?"

"Of course. Now let's get your teeth cleaned then I'll tuck you up in bed. Be nice and quiet, there's a good girl, Jake's asleep."

We passed a door with JAKE'S ROOM in bright letters written on a balsawood sign. Sally pressed her fingers to her lips.

After a superficial teeth cleaning session she ran to her bedroom, threw open the door and took a flying leap on to her bed. "Harry Potter, can I have a chapter of Harry Potter, please, Aunty Sarah?"

"Um, no, not exactly; Mummy said you

mustn't, not before you go to sleep. Let me see, what else do you like?"

"The Worst Witch."

I smiled remembering my childhood enthusiasm for the same book. I didn't think that there was anything too frightening within its cover. So taking the book from the shelf, I began to read the first chapter.

As I read, the years slid back and I was in Scotland. My parents were alive and the sound of the Dalkeiths arguing next door competed with my father's soft voice as he read to me. Sally's eyelids began to droop and I kissed her goodnight without thinking; it wasn't the child's fault, after all.

Leaving the door open, I went downstairs, and began a methodical search of the living room in an attempt to find my photograph album. I faintly remembered bringing one with me from London. It was an A4 sized album with a butterfly motif on the cover. Inside I'd arranged a selection of photos from my childhood up until the time I started work at Ashton and Cooper. Being an only child there were no sibling photographs just my progression from infancy to school uniform, teenage dances, a succession of boyfriends, culminating in the ones of Owen and me. My holiday snaps I'd abandoned, there were too many and besides I had my memories so didn't need them. At least I think they were my memories.

After an hour of fruitless search, I moved into

the dining room. The cabinet where I'd kept my crockery was full of plates I didn't recognise, well-worn dishes and brightly coloured napkins. I lifted up a linen tablecloth and felt a flat square shape underneath. But after further inspection it turned out to be a cardboard box containing steak knives and forks.

Where had they put it? It wasn't in the flat - it had to be here - somewhere. Night was falling as I stood in the kitchen and switched on the kettle. The grey twilight had deepened into darkness. At the bottom of the garden the summerhouse stood limed by moonlight. Now let's see, I thought. I turned on the garden light and, leaving the kitchen door open, followed its beams down the crazy-paved path to the summerhouse.

The curtains were closed, as were the blinds on the glass doors. I twisted the door handles but they were locked. Remembering that in the third flowerpot to the left of the sundial was where I usually kept the spare key, I thrust my hand into the space between the fronds of the palm plant and the side of the pot and felt around in the compost. I breathed a sigh of relief as my fingers closed around the key. It turned in the lock.

Inside, it smelled of wood. I loved that fresh pinewood smell. Aunt Fiona had installed electricity and for that I was grateful as I clicked on the light. One by one I lifted up the seats to reveal the storage units beneath but it wasn't until I came to the last one that I saw the album nestling under a rug. I could have cried as I sat on the floor cradling it in my arms. But before I could open it, I heard an ear-splitting scream followed by a howl of sheer terror. It was coming from Sally's bedroom. I switched off the light, making a mental note to return later to lock up then ran into the house and up the stairs to her room.

Her face was streaked with tears, "I, I, there was a witch at the bottom of my bed," she whimpered. Thankfully the disturbance didn't appear to have awakened Jake.

I put my arm around her shoulders. "There's nothing to be frightened of. It's just a dream. I'm here, don't worry."

"I want my Daddy," she said quietly.

"Mummy and Daddy will be back soon and don't forget, Daddy said he'd buy you that DVD, if you're a good girl."

"He's not my daddy," she replied cuddling into me. "He's just Andy."

Chapter 21

According to Sandy the children spent every other weekend and sometimes part of the week at the house on Byron Terrace with their father and stepmother. Hannah Lawson had been less than forthcoming with information but Sandy had heard it from Rozanna, another mother at the school, who knew the family.

Rozanna, a garrulous individual, was only too keen to divulge snippets of information at every opportunity. To date she'd managed to disclose that Hannah had been married to Andy Lawson for four years, maybe less. Apparently she'd met him at work when she'd lived in Birmingham. Afterwards, her former husband, an unemployed lay-about called Bill Young, had managed to find work in Lockford and had moved to Byron Terrace. However, Hannah had chosen to stay in Birmingham and she and Andy had moved in together with her children.

Sandy said that Rozanna had been as surprised as anyone when she'd discovered that Hannah had moved into a house in Bramble Lane, which was a far cry from the houses on Byron Terrace.

Richie decided the time had come to tell his client of the latest developments, when coincidentally Sandy rang through on the internal line. "Your client wants to know if she can speak to you."

"Which client?"

"The only one you've got at present," Sandy reminded him.

"Tell her to call in whenever she likes."

Then he heard Sandy say, "Go right in, Miss Shaw."

She was flushed, excited and carrying a photo album, which she removed from a plastic carrier and thrust across the desk in front of him.

"I found it." She stood at his side as he reached across and picked up the album.

He could feel her breath on the back of his neck as she bent forward unable to hide her anticipation. The first few pages showed a baby's progression through infancy, schooldays and teenage years. After establishing the identity of her parents and her younger self, he continued turning the pages until he saw the emergence of what looked to be a boyfriend.

"Who's this?" he asked pointing to a photograph of a man with his arm around her waist and the fuzzy outline of someone standing to one side of them.

"Owen. Owen Madoc."

He recognised the name instantly but showed no outward sign of it. Richie peered at the man standing behind Madoc whose face was in shadow and half turned away. He could have sworn it was Lawson. He hesitated but saw no hint of recognition on her face. When he closed the album, she walked around the desk and sat in the chair in front of him.

"This proves it."

"What exactly?"

"Can you see any evidence in these photos of my brother, sister-in-law or their family?"

Richie was about to say yes but thought better of it, for the moment.

"It proves that I've had a life entirely independent of any of them."

"Mmm, I understand where you're coming from but we need more than a few photos to build up our case."

"Yes of course but it is a start, isn't it?"

Her excitement was fading. He could see her look of disappointment at his lack of enthusiasm. "It is a start. Perhaps you'd let me hang on to it for a bit?"

She brightened. "There's something else. It might be nothing but when I was baby-sitting, Sally woke up after a bad dream and when I tried to comfort her she told me that Andy wasn't her father. I didn't take much notice as she was half asleep at the time."

Before he could tell her about Sandy's discovery, the phone rang. It was Norm.

"Excuse me a moment. I have to take this call," he explained.

"How's the case going?"

"Not sure. Could I ring you later?"

"Client with you?"

"Got it in one."

Richie put down the phone. "Right, well leave it with me, Miss Shaw," he said. "Nothing else is there?"

"Well yes, as a matter of fact there is. Remember I told you about Neil Stafford, who recognised me as Lawson's sister the other day?"

Richie nodded.

"Well, yesterday I saw him enter a flat directly opposite mine. I'd already begun to think it odd that the woman who lives there seemed a bit out of place."

"In what way?"

"Difficult to say really, just that she's very smart, drives a sleek black sports car, and looks as if she should have an address in Chelsea."

"And you say this Neil Stafford was with her yesterday?"

"Yes." She sighed.

"Right, well I'll see what I can come up with regarding Stafford and your neighbour and get back to you."

"I'll expect an answer soon then? " She stood up. "You'll let me have my album back when you've finished with it?"

"Of course."

Later, after talking to Norm who had been in touch with the land registry on his behalf, he learned that Rowena Shaw had sold the property, which was now registered in the name of Mr Andrew Lawson. Richie walked to the window and saw her leaving the building and walking to the bus stop. She'd been excited at finding the photograph album. So either she was a highly skilled actress or she was telling the truth and his instinct was pushing him in the direction of the latter. But, unless she asked him directly about his contact with the land registry, he thought it best to keep the knowledge of the sale to himself for the time being.

After he'd heard all about Sandy's new boyfriend and her continued surveillance of Hannah Lawson, Richie opened the photograph album, found the photo of Owen Madoc and removed it from its cellophane cover. Sliding it into his printer, he lifted the lid of the scanner, slid the photo underneath and enlarged the area showing the man he'd thought bore a passing resemblance to Andy Lawson. The image on his computer screen, although pixelated, confirmed his suspicions. Now why the man Rowena Shaw was going to marry should know Andy Lawson and why she hadn't made the connection in the photograph was a mystery.

Chapter 22

Matlock Rise consisted of three blocks of identical low-rise flats standing like sentries. Each block was six stories high. Between them stood parking spaces enclosing a grassed area and a few strategically placed benches. It was nothing like Bramble Lane.

Richie lifted his tripod stand and his digital camera from the back seat of his car, carried them though a door market Block A then made his way via a lift that smelled of pee to the third floor. Following the walkway he reached number twenty-six.

His client opened the door before he could ring the bell. "Come in. She's not left for work yet."

"Excellent. I'll just get this set up."

He didn't need to be told which flat was the one in question. It stood like an oasis in the desert. Someone with an eye to design had concentrated on making the best of a bad job. It was situated in the middle of Block B and through his camera viewfinder he could see the number 19 in large brass letters on the door.

Picking up his mobile, he rang Norman's number and left a message on his answer phone giving him the address.

"Coffee?" she asked from the kitchen doorway.

"Ta, strong and black please."

"Have you had breakfast?"

"Nah, too early." He finished assembling his equipment and sat on the high kitchen stool she'd placed near the window for him.

"Will toast do? I'm not really a breakfast person."

"Toast is fine"

When she returned with three rounds of toast and a mug of hot coffee, he thanked her and said, "I'm going to be here for the rest of the day but please don't think that you have to stay in. I'm not going to run off with the family silver."

She laughed, a dry humourless sound. "Any family silver I had would be in Bramble Lane, that's assuming of course that I had a family."

He wondered about that. "No one?"

"No one. When I was a teenager my parents died in a fire at our house."

"I'm sorry," Richie sympathised. "Were you injured?"

She fingered the scar on her forehead. "No. I was in my first year at the L.S.E. I didn't know anything about it until the hospital rang."

"So there's no one left?"

"Not now. My aunt Fiona was my last

relative. She's the one who left me the house in Bramble Lane." She walked to the window and looked out. "My parents and aunt Fiona used to send Christmas cards but apart from that they'd lost touch. It was quite a shock to discover that I was her sole heir."

"Must have been," murmured Richie through a mouthful of toast.

She shrugged and walked back to the kitchen. "Right then, I'll leave you to it."

At half-past nine the door to the flat opposite opened and a woman emerged. She was, as his client had described, extremely well groomed and elegant but she'd failed to notice the one thing that to any man was more than obvious. The woman was sexy. From the top of her shiny blonde head to her high-heeled shoes, she oozed sex. He took a series of long shots and close ups then switched on the vid.cam. She disappeared from view presumably taking the lift to the ground floor then re-emerged and clicked her key remote. Lights flashed on the sports car and he focused on the number plate as the car purred out of the car park and into the road.

He'd always hated surveillance, stakeouts the American police force chose to call them. Either way the end result was the same. Sitting and staring into space until your bum got numb and your mind wandered. After the woman opposite drove away, his client told him she was going to the library in town.

When he was alone, Richie phoned his office.

"Any news?"

"Nothing much, except that Chloe has decided she's Jake Lawson's new best friend. Hannah asked me to bring her over for her tea tomorrow afternoon. This time it's at Bramble Lane. She also told me about her divorce. I think she's beginning to trust me."

"Excellent. I wonder why the kids are known as Lawson?"

"I expect it was easier taking their mother's name; could be a little confusing at school otherwise."

"I wonder what the father thinks of that?"

"Bit messy?"

"Could be."

"Oh, I'm expecting a call from the Met; DCI Freeman. Ask him to leave a message. I'm going to be holed up here all day. I'll see you in the morning. Oh and by the way – good work, Miss Smith."

The day passed, as he'd anticipated it would. He got to know the movements of some of the residents, watched an old man in a shabby coat feeding the birds on the grass, saw the mothers bringing children home from school and nursery and later, as rush hour approached, he saw the cars returning like homing pigeons.

His client left him alone for most of the day but reappeared at five o'clock clutching a pasty and a ham roll for his tea. She didn't talk much as they ate and afterwards went into the kitchen and put on the radio.

At a quarter-past six the black sports car slid into its parking space. Richie watched a pair of long legs slide out of the front seat closely followed by the rest of her, which hadn't lost any of its appeal in the interim. Her companion was a man in his early sixties. He was wearing a dark grey pinstriped suit and had a paunch. His hair, what remained of it, was white. He could have been her father but Richie knew that wasn't an option for the simple reason that, as they reached the front door of number nineteen, the man reached forward and stroked the woman's rear end in anything but a fatherly manner.

He didn't need a crystal ball to know what was going on in the flat opposite. As he was packing up his camera equipment the telephone rang. It continued ringing unanswered until the answering machine cut in. No message was left.

"You didn't answer your phone," he said putting his head around the kitchen door.

She was sitting at the table staring into space. She looked scared. Then it dawned on him. "How long have you been having anonymous calls?" he asked.

Chapter 23

Hawkins and Wright Associates ran the Premier Escort Agency, amongst other enterprises, and owned the flat in Matlock Rise; it was one of many they used in which to place their high class working girls.

When Richie was at the Met, the prostitutes he came into contact with were in a different class altogether than the one he'd seen leaving the flat in Matlock Rise. He rang Norm to thank him for the information and once again assured him of his discretion. Then he opened the computer file where he'd stored the photograph of Owen Madoc and Andy Lawson. The enhanced photo of the latter instantly recognisable, he printed a copy and put it in his inside pocket alongside one of his client.

The necklace Rowena Shaw had been wearing bothered him. It must have been bought from Angie's stall. It was too distinctive for it to have come from anywhere else. When he'd questioned her about it, she was vague about its origins saying that it was a present, which she'd lost but couldn't remember who had given it to her or when she had found it. The gaps in her memory were disconcerting and he wondered whether they might not be a bit too convenient.

Sandy was late arriving at the office, which was unusual. She took the stairs two at a time and, out of breath, slumped in her chair without removing her mackintosh. It had been raining all night and hadn't stopped since.

"Sorry, couldn't make it before," she gasped. "Chloe was playing up and wouldn't let me go. I don't know how much longer I can continue to take her to school, she wants her Mum."

He put the kettle on. "How did you get on yesterday?"

"Let me take this off first and have a shot of caffeine then I'll tell you."

Rain pelted against the office window. Richie switched on the light. It was a quarter to eleven on a June day and outside it was as dark as a witch's heart. Sandy wrapped her fingers around her coffee mug.

"The house is great. No wonder they wanted to live there." She pushed a damp lock of hair out of her eyes. "I wouldn't mind a pad like that. Andy Lawson's a bit of a looker too. You didn't say."

"Not my sort."

"Anyway when I picked up Chloe, Hannah invited me in. She made me stay for a cup of tea and a chat and I did my best to discover anything that appeared to be odd."

"And?"

"Nothing, I'm afraid. If I didn't know better

I'd say they looked very much at home there. I just couldn't see Rowena Shaw fitting in somehow."

"So, they've got it all sewn up?"

"Looks like it. Where do we go from here?"

"Where indeed. First, I think you can put little Chloe out of her misery; tell your sister-in-law you've too much work on to continue with the school run. At the weekend I'm off up to London. There's someone I want to see."

Covent Garden on Saturday morning was busy with tourists and shoppers. Richie followed a waving red umbrella and a group of Japanese sightseers as they crossed the pebbles and entered the covered market. He spotted Angie immediately. She was serving a girl with pink hair and a small group had gathered around her stall, which meant there was little opportunity to talk to her.

"Excuse me," he said weaving his way through the group. "Just want a quick word with my daughter, won't be a minute, I promise."

"Daughter?" Angie grinned.

"I need to speak to you. Could you meet me for lunch at one? Same place as last time?"

"Could be a bit late, if this keeps up. Can't turn away business now, can I, Sport?"

"Fair enough. I'll be waiting."

It was twenty to two when Angie finally arrived. He had drunk enough bottled water to float the Titanic and eaten more bread sticks than he'd had in his entire life.

After they'd eaten and talked about Angie's business prospects Richie explained about the necklace he'd seen his client wearing.

"If I show you a couple of photographs, do you think there's any possibility of you recognising a customer? I know it's a long shot. To be honest I don't expect you to remember but what the heck, I needed an excuse to see how you're doing."

"Thanks, Dad, good to see you too. Let's take a dekko at these photos then. Who knows I might surprise you."

She frowned, screwed up her eyes and looked at the images. She didn't answer at once. Picking up the enhanced photograph she inspected it more closely.

"Mm, good looking guy."

"Which one?"

"Do I need to tell you?"

Remembering Sandy's response at seeing Lawson he pointed to him. "Got it in one. And I think your trip hasn't been wasted, Pops."

"You've seen him before?" Richie couldn't quite believe his luck.

"I have. In fact I've seen both of them before."

"You're sure?"

"Sure. Couldn't forget a guy with a face like that for a start but it wasn't just that. These two came to my stall just after I'd started working here, must be over a year and a half ago. I was desperate to build up my business and the shorter one told me that he thought he could find an outlet for me with a friend who sold jewellery in Cardiff. I think he ended up buying a necklace and taking my card, though he never did ring."

Madoc, Richie thought as she continued, "But when they were walking away, a fight broke out nearby and they both went to help the stallholder who was being harassed. I remember that they came out of the scuffle a bit the worse for wear and then walked in the direction of the wine bar."

"I see."

"You do? So your trip hasn't been wasted?" She was smiling at him. A memory of the daughter he was missing sliced through his insides like a filleting knife.

His answer was sharper than he'd intended. "Thanks for your time." He stood up. "Must be getting back or I'll be stuck in traffic."

He left her picking up her hippy-style handbag, her hair a mass of tousled curls.

The words, "Bye then, Dad," drifted towards him like acid on the breeze.

Chapter 24

It had been a shock to think that the woman was a prostitute. Was my supposed brother involved in prostitution as some kind of pimp or had it been a coincidence that Neil Stafford and he were friends? There were too many imponderables for me to consider either premise in detail. I'd leave that to Richard Stevens, I'd begun to believe in him. One day soon he'd find the truth, I was sure of it then I could start to live my life again.

Nevertheless, I was lonely. I missed my friends, my lover. Why hadn't I stayed with Owen? The question troubled me. There were things I'd rather forget about our break up I knew that much, which was perhaps why there were some gaps in my memory. There had to be a reason. Perhaps something traumatic had happened and I'd buried the memory of it completely. I was also beginning to have the oddest feeling that Sarah Lawson and I shared a past, the details of which refused to resurface. I rang Owen's number again, the digits etched into my brain by now, but once again I was greeted by the same signal.

Telling Richard Stevens about the phone call had made me feel I wasn't dealing with it on my own. How the woman could have known my phone number was another mystery, unless of course she was involved with Andy Lawson. At least the 'Lawson family' didn't look quite the secure unit they'd like people to think they were. The children weren't his. They had a father who wanted to see them regularly. How did Andy feel about that?

I looked out of the window; at last the sun was shining. I'd go for a walk later. I was fed up of watching for the prostitute and waiting for the phone to ring. If I took the bus up to Bramble Lane I could call in on my *family*. It was Sunday and most people visited relatives on Sunday, after all.

The bus service was sporadic and I waited nearly an hour for it to arrive. The annoying old man living in the ground floor flat called to me as I crossed the grass. "Sarah, got any stale bread for the birds have you love?" I ignored him. I'd tried asking him about who he thought I was on several occasions but he'd just looked at me blankly and asked if I was pulling his leg. I'd refrained from replying that I most definitely wouldn't be pulling any part of his grubby body, neither now nor at any time in the future.

The bus stopped on the main road and I walked down Bramble Lane in the sunshine. The man at number thirty was cutting his hedge with a pair of garden shears.

"Morning," he said as I passed.

"Good morning."

"You're a relative of the new people at number 34, aren't you?" He kicked a pile of leaves out of my way.

"Did you see me moving in?" I was hoping that he was the kind of neighbour who didn't miss a thing. But he looked confused. "I saw the removal van a while back and the next thing I saw was Mr and Mrs Lawson and the kids. I've seen you visiting though."

I could have cried. Did no one in this road recognise me as being their new neighbour? Had I been that invisible?

Outside the gates of my home I hesitated. Could I stand another hour pretending to be Sarah Lawson? The yellow car was in the driveway but the BMW was missing. The garage doors were open so either Andy had gone off by himself, or the family was out. I opened the gate and walked up the drive hoping it was the latter. Nevertheless, I pressed the bell and waited. When I was satisfied that there was no one in, I took the key from my pocket and slipped it into the lock.

Dust motes shivered in a beam of light from the hall window. There was a faint smell of coffee lingering in the air. My house was beginning to feel unfamiliar. A Bratz doll dressed like Jordan rested against the newel post at the foot of the stairs and the dining room door stood open. I always closed it and was tempted to do so now.

In the living room the Sunday newspapers were scattered over the coffee table and a half completed jigsaw puzzle lay on the mat. Children's fingerprints clouded the glass table on which I'd arranged my favourite pieces of pottery, which were no longer in sight. My legs felt like jelly as I sank into an armchair. I looked around the room taking in every little detail. They had established ownership of my house and my identity to the point at which it was as if I'd never existed.

Mentally shaking myself into action, I decided to make a systematic search of the place, starting on the ground floor before making my way upstairs. I lifted every cushion, probed into each crevice and searched through every drawer and cupboard.

In the kitchen I found the set of saucepans I'd bought in the shop in Lockford when I moved in. The salt and pepper grinders I'd brought with me. They were the ones I had bought with Owen at the craft fair, when we'd lived in the cottage in Wales. But there was nothing that I could establish ownership of that would make a scrap of difference to my situation. The same fruitless search applied to the master bedroom. In the en-suite bathroom, I splashed water on my face and stared at my reflection in the mirrored cupboard. Then I opened it.

The usual clutter greeted me; an unopened packet containing soap, a bottle of shampoo and conditioner, cotton wool pads, four new toothbrushes in a plastic mug, a box of hair dye and on the top shelf an assortment of pills, ranging from painkillers to prescription drugs. I picked up the packet of hair dye. It was for Ash Blondes but Hannah's hair was brown. I put it back in disgust and began to inspect the bottles and packets with the chemist's dispensing labels in the front. Two were for Andy Lawson; one prescription for his wife for the contraceptive pill and in a recess at the back of the cupboard, I found it.

Rowena Shaw, Vitamin B6; the words were like a lifebelt to a drowning man. Putting the bottle in my pocket I closed the cupboard door, went downstairs and let myself out. I'd been careful to put everything back as I'd found it. It was as if I'd never been.

Chapter 25

I couldn't sleep. When I did drop off for a brief moment, it was to dream of Owen. The bottle stood on my bedside table. In the faint light of dawn I could just make out my name. It shone like a ray of hope. That at least hadn't been a dream. The rest was a living nightmare.

Inspecting it more closely I saw that the prescription had been filled in London. But I knew that I had a corresponding, up to date, prescription from Doctor Watkins at the Lockford Practice when I'd first moved here. In the confusion of the past few days, I'd not thought about contacting my doctor. He'd have my details at the surgery. I decided to ring to make an appointment, as soon as the practice opened.

In an optimistic mood I took a leisurely shower and dressed in a blue cotton dress. The sun was up. I ate breakfast and for once was able to taste my food instead of mechanically going through the motions. At a quarter to nine I rang the surgery, gave my name and asked for an appointment with Doctor Watkins. The receptionist told me that Doctor Watkins was on holiday but a locum, a doctor Barker would be taking his patients.

"Rowena Shaw, you said?"

"That's right."

"And you say you are registered with us?"

"That's right, yes."

"Hold on a minute."

I waited whilst listening to the sound of the Entrance of the Queen of Sheba playing in my ear.

"I've checked our computer records and the name Rowena Shaw has been changed to Sarah Lawson. Change your name did you, dear?"

Her patronising voice was the last straw.

"No I did not!" I shouted into the mouthpiece. "Who said I did?" I was furious; my hands were shaking.

"Er, I think you should have a word with Doctor Watkins when he returns from his holiday. He made the changes himself. Perhaps he can answer your questions then. Would you like me to make an appointment for you in three weeks time?"

I slammed down the phone and burst into tears of anguish. How long was this going to last? I was Rowena Shaw and no one was going to make me believe otherwise.

The pleasure of the day had faded. I threw the pill bottle into the bin and left the flat. When I ran out of my current supply, I'd have to buy a new supply over the counter – there was no way I was going to admit I was Sarah Lawson to

Doctor Watkins, whoever he thought I was.

After walking aimlessly for an hour, I caught the bus into town. Andy Lawson worked in an Insurance Brokers office in Broad Street. It was time his 'sister' paid him a visit and invited him out to lunch. Anger fuelled my every step and the more I was knocked back the more determined to find out the truth I became.

The offices of Bartlett and Janes Insurance Brokers and Financial Advisors had an impressive frontage. A large plate glass window displaying their services gave the impression of a well-established firm with years of experience behind them. So this was where he would have planned the investment of my ninety thousand pounds.

I pushed open the front door, which sighed as it closed behind me. Two young women sat behind a reception desk and a man in his forties dressed in a dark suit sat at a desk near the long mahogany counter. He rose to his feet as I approached. "May I help?" he asked with a plastic smile.

"I'd like to speak to Mr Lawson, please."

"May I ask your name?"

"Tell him it's his sister."

His smile became more genuine. "Hello, I'm Peter Bartlett, pleased to meet you at last."

He led me through the outer office, down a small passageway and into a room where Lawson, another man and an older woman were sitting behind desks staring at computer screens.

I could see he was flustered. He stood up, started to walk towards me and thought better of it. His initial shock at seeing me had given way to concern. "Sarah? Is everything alright?"

"Fine," I said. "Just thought it was time I saw where you worked. I wondered if you'd like to come out to lunch."

He looked at his watch; it was five to one. "Er, I, ."

"Of course he'll come," Peter Bartlett interjected. "Nothing here that can't wait eh, Andy?"

"No, I mean, yes. Just give me five minutes."

"No problem. I'll just sit here until you're ready."

As I waited I looked around his office. The woman smiled at me, the man too; Andy still looked uncomfortable which gave me an immense sense of satisfaction.

Later, as we sat in a restaurant on the corner of High Street and Broad Street I realised I could see the offices of my private investigator.

"I'm glad you've decided to stop acting the goat, Sarah. That nonsense has really unsettled Hannah."

I smiled and dug my fingernails into my palm.

"What would you like to eat?" he asked handing me the Menu.

"My favourite of course. You should know that by now."

He hesitated, but only for a fraction of a

second. "And what is your favourite today? You change your mind so often, it's hard to tell."

"Let's see if you can remember. It's really just the same as always." I was beginning to enjoy watching him squirm.

"Still playing games. OK, if that's the way you want it." He called the waitress over.

"We're ready to order now. I'll have the salmon fishcakes and my sister will have the Penne Arrabiata, please."

So, he was good at guessing games. That didn't prove anything. However, it was as if he'd pricked a balloon with a pin, deflated, I waited for the order to arrive. The rest of the lunch hour was unremarkable. He talked about cricket and the people he worked with. I listened.

Afterwards he walked me to the bus stop and when he left I turned and walked back in the direction of Hastings Buildings. I was heartily sick of Sarah Lawson. The time had come to kill her off for good.

Part Two

Before

Chapter 26

The sun was sinking on the horizon leaving dusky fingers stroking the headland and turning the cliffs to indigo. Owen Madoc packed away his easel and paints and headed back to his car. He'd found the cottage on the coast of South Wales six months ago. It was a bit run down but the price had been right and the repairs were superficial. He'd been born in South Wales and knew the area well, in addition to which it wasn't a million miles away from London via the M4.

In the past year his paintings had begun to sell in earnest, so it made sense to be within driving distance of the galleries. Mark Furnish had assured him that his coastal scenes were flying off the shelves; he couldn't get enough of them. The Furnish gallery was small by comparison to some of the more prestigious ones in London but it was situated in a side street off Covent Garden and was a popular haunt of tourists looking for a reasonably priced piece of original artwork.

He walked back up the beach, placed his equipment in the boot of his car and drove the mile and a half to his cottage. He could have walked the distance and had done so many times but never carrying an easel and paints. The view of the coast was magnificent. The peaceful solitude of the location was a bonus. Screeching herring gulls diving to shore woke him every morning as the smell of late summer wafted in through his bedroom window.

Rowena loved it from the start and had insisted on making the interior as comfortable as possible. He'd told her not to bother; he would use it as a studio and a place to rest his head, it didn't need an interior designer. However, that didn't make a scrap of difference to Rowena, once she had the bit between her teeth there was no stopping her. A week after he'd settled in, she drove down with a boot full of soft furnishings, which she arranged in her own inimitable style. It was one of the things he'd first noticed about her, when he'd met her at Tom's party - she had great style.

Owen planned to spend a month or two painting and when the weather deteriorated he'd return to the city. His only contact with the outside world was via his mobile, which he frequently switched off finding the silence more appealing. Rowena came down at weekends bringing with her half the contents of the local supermarket and a breath of London air lingering in her conversation.

He opened the fridge and removed a can of beer then walked outside. The wooden veranda had looked in a sorry state when he'd first seen the place but had soon been restored by a couple of coats of paint. The chairs and cushions were Rowena's idea.

The evening air was warm against his skin. In the distance he could hear the sea sucking at the pebbles on the shore and spitting them out as the tide turned. Salt lingered on the breeze as he closed his eyes and let the evening descend.

It was his habit to get up early to catch the light, work until late morning then take his easel down to the beach and work there for the rest of the day, weather permitting. Luckily it had been a good summer May, June and July had been hot and sunny, August was proving a little temperamental but Owen had completed his groundwork sketches from which he intended to work during the rain-filled days.

He was in his studio, when he heard the sound of tyres bouncing along the gravel in the lane, followed by a screech of brakes as her car drew to a halt; Rowena was a terrible driver.

"Owen, give me a hand, there's a love," she called up to him.

He smiled as he put down his brush. "No peace for the wicked," he muttered with a grin.

She was wearing a blue cotton sundress, her hair shining like waves of gold; he wanted to paint her but knew he couldn't do her justice.

Opening the boot of her car, she picked up two supermarket carrier bags and kissed his cheek as she passed him. "Plenty more, darling."

He smiled ruefully. "I didn't doubt it for a moment."

After the car had been unloaded and he'd placed her weekend case at the foot of his bed, Owen followed her into the kitchen where she was already switching on the kettle. He slid his arms around her waist and turned her to face him. "Missed you," he said kissing her.

"Me too, sweetheart. Now let's have a caffeine fix and you can tell me how you're managing without me."

Later, sitting on the veranda, Rowena, stretching her long legs to catch the sun, said, "I met Mark Furnish yesterday. He thinks it might be possible to stage another showing in September. He was going to ring you about it on Monday."

"If that's the case, wench, you are going to have to stop enticing me away from my work."

"Do you mean that? You won't be ready?"

"Actually I think I'm well on the way to meeting the deadline. I can probably spare the odd weekend to have the pleasure of my beautiful girlfriend and still have enough work to suit Mark."

"I'm dying to see them."

"You know the drill, my angel - only when I'm satisfied that they're finished."

"I could of course slip into the studio wher

you're asleep." She slid her head on to his shoulder.

"But you won't."
"You're sure?"
"Certain."

Having spent most of the next morning in bed, they were sitting outside as the sun rose to its height leaving the veranda in shade.

"Lunch time." Owen stood up. "I think we'll walk to village and have lunch in the pub. Then afterwards we'll see what the view is like from my bedroom."

"We could always skip lunch," Rowena said smiling up at him.

"We could, but this way we won't have to get up because we're hungry and besides the thrill of anticipation makes the pleasure even greater, I always think."

"What a man, he thinks of everything." She held out her hand for him to pull her out of the chair then, leaving the cottage, followed him down the lane.

Chapter 27

A steady trickle of customers slid through the doors of the Mark Furnish Gallery. The initial reception for the press was over and the serious business of selling was in progress. Mark drifted around the room like a galleon in full sail introducing Owen to those people who he knew were likely to buy his work.

This part of the business was the bit Owen most disliked. He hated having to sell himself; the paintings, he reasoned, should stand alone without having to explain where he'd found his inspiration and the reasons why he'd chosen to paint the sky in a particular manner or why he'd chosen water colours in favour of oils for this collection.

However, he answered each question politely, smiled when necessary and thanked them for their kind words and even kinder purchases. He saw Rowena effortlessly moving from one person to another and envied her grace and natural charm. She caught his eye and moved towards him. "Need rescuing?" she whispered as she kissed his cheek.

He nodded.

Turning to the man, who'd been endlessly boring Owen about his own attempts at using watercolour, she said, "Excuse me, I do hope you don't mind me interrupting your very interesting conversation with Mr Madoc but he's required rather urgently on the telephone."

Owen followed her as she led him into a side room away from the main gallery. Closing the door firmly behind him, she turned the key in the lock then slid her hand around his neck and drew his head forward to reach her lips. Her lovemaking was measured, silent and satisfying.

Afterwards she smiled, ran her fingers through her hair and unlocked the door. "Feeling better?" she asked.

"Infinitely." Owen slid his hand down her back to rest on her buttocks as she stepped into the Gallery.

The evening was proving to be a success. Mark Furnish was unable to hide the fact as his Cheshire-cat-grin spoke volumes. He was talking to a tall man with black hair as Owen approached.

"Over here, Owen ducky, there's someone I'd like you to meet. He's just bought Indigo Night."

Owen groaned inwardly. "Very pleased to hear it; thank you so much," he trotted out the phrases with an equable smile.

"My pleasure," the man replied as Mark explained.

"This is an old school friend of mine. Owen Madoc, meet Andrew Lawson."

His hand felt cold to the touch. It occurred to him that Andrew Lawson didn't appear to be anything like Mark's usual friends. His initial impression being confirmed as Mark added, "Andy wanted to buy the painting as a present for his new wife. They've only been married a month. How sweet is that?"

Later when Owen and Rowena were back at his flat she asked, "Who was that man I saw you and Mark talking to?"

"Which one?"

"The tall, dark and handsome one, of course."

He hadn't noticed it before but her description was spot on. Recognising he'd been too quick to pigeonhole him as one of Mark's gay friends, he replied, "His name's Andrew Lawson. He's one of Mark's old school friends. He bought Indigo Night."

"Did he now? Good taste as well." Rowena moved towards him and slipped out of her robe. "Time for bed I think."

The sale of his seascapes went well. Mark was constantly asking when Owen could show more of his work. Whilst facing the prospect of winter and of fading light Owen had doubts about whether he'd be able to fulfil a commitment that felt like painting by numbers.

Aware that his career was at the point of turning into something worthwhile at last he made a decision to spend the winter at the cottage. It was where he felt at one with the elements and although it wasn't exactly equipped for winter weather, he'd make the best of it.

"They call it suffering for your art, darling," Rowena said on one of those, end of summer evenings when winter seems so far off.

"What about you?" he asked her. "I can't expect you to suffer as well."

"No problem. I've got more than I can handle in work at the moment and besides, I'm sure I'll be able to pop down now and then, so that you don't forget what I look like." She kissed his lips. A kiss filled with promise and he wondered how he was going to get through the long winter months without her.

Before he moved into the cottage for the winter Owen was walking down Regent's Street in the direction of Piccadilly when he saw the man who'd bought his painting again.

"Hello, Mr Madoc."

Owen hesitated. "Mr Lawson, isn't it?"

"Andy, please. My wife loved your painting by the way; you'd be amazed how many of our friends have commented on it."

"Very kind, thank-you," Owen churned out the usual reply and prepared to move on.

"I'd be interested to see more of your work. Mark told me you are about to start on a new collection."

"That's true. I'm off to my cottage in Wales to seek inspiration. Whether any will come is debatable."

Lawson smiled. "Let's hope so."

Standing nearby was a woman trying to control a young child, who'd decided he wanted to stay inside the toyshop, whilst an older girl leaned against the shop doorway. The woman was tall, had nondescript features and mousy hair, which hung lankly to her shoulders. Andy Lawson beckoned to her.

"I'd like you to meet Owen Madoc, the artist who painted Indigo Night." He turned to Owen.

"This is my sister, Sarah," he said.

Chapter 28

At the beginning of the week Rowena had been her usual organised self and had stocked the boot of his car with cans, dried food and enough bottles of wine to satisfy the thirst of a raging alcoholic. "It's going to be a long winter. Besides, you know how much I like a glass of chilled Chardonnay before we make love," she promised

"Hope you've packed enough then," he said kissing her.

He supposed that some promises were always meant to be broken. But it had still come as a shock when, the day before he was due to drive down to the cottage, Rowena had hit him with a bombshell. She arrived at his flat flustered and lacking her usual poise. After a hurried greeting she put a hand up to his cheek. "Owen, I …"

He held her at arms length, afraid now. "What is it?"

"I've been seconded to New York for two months. I won't be back until just before Christmas. I can't say no. It's my career on the line here." She ran her fingers distractedly through her hair.

He laughed with relief. "Thank God."

She looked up at him. "That's not quite the reaction I'd been anticipating."

He laughed again. "Come here; I thought you were going to end it - you looked so serious. Two months is nothing, as long as I get you back at the end of it."

She relaxed against him. "As if I could end it. You know how I feel, how I've always felt."

"We'll get through it, you'll see. By Christmas, I'll have a whole new collection ready. Without your distracting influence, I'll be churning them out by the lorry load."

They both realised that he was humouring her. Owen doubted if he could work efficiently without the knowledge that she was only a phone call away, a motorway separating them, and he knew that she could see through his bluff.

"When do you fly out?" He poured two large measures of brandy into their glasses.

"Tomorrow evening. I've been rushing around in a flat spin today getting everything ready."

"You had no idea that this was coming?"

"I'd be lying if I said that it was a complete surprise but nevertheless it all happened so suddenly. I was hoping that it might have come in the New Year and that perhaps you could have come to the States with me for a while. It would have been a chance for Mark to promote you in the American market, especially with a new collection ready."

He smiled. "You're not in P.R. for nothing, sweetheart."

"That's me, always an eye on the main chance. But seriously, it's worth thinking about. Maybe I can put out a few feelers whilst I'm there."

"What am I going to do without you?"

Their lovemaking that night was tender and poignant both of them knowing that this was all there would be during the coming months and when Rowena eventually awoke, it was to see Owen propped up on an elbow drinking in every glimpse of her, as if it was to be his last.

He drove to the cottage later that afternoon. Rowena had insisted that they say their goodbyes in the flat. She hated tearful airport farewells then looking longingly out of the window of the aircraft, as the land below slipped away.

"Don't forget to keep your mobile charged. I'll ring you every day once I've got the time difference sorted," she said, leaving him standing on the pavement outside his flat. The last glimpse he had of her was her hand raised in the taxi's rear window.

The drive down to the cottage was uneventful. The late October weather was reasonably warm. The weathermen forecasted an Indian summer and although the trees looked dispirited, their leaves pirouetting to the ground like aging ballerinas, he had to admire the depth of colours that the autumnal weather had produced. They would look great on canvas.

In spite of the fact that Rowena would be on another continent Owen felt positive about starting his new collection. If the weather continued for just a few more days it would give him a head start. He began to make plans, ideas slowly shifting into formation.

He was whistling as he drove down the lane to the cottage, which greeted him like an old friend. It was nearly two months since he'd left but the rooms smelled of pine and the lavender air freshener that Rowena had liberally sprayed around the place before they'd locked up, and which still lingered.

He unloaded the car, filled the kitchen cupboards and the fridge with food then carried his canvases up the stairs to the studio. The early evening sun had disappeared; the clocks had gone back the previous weekend and the night was eager to begin. Owen switched on the light. The studio smelled of a heady mixture of linseed oil, paint and white spirit. Stacking the canvases in a corner he stood at the window. He'd had the two smaller ones replaced with a larger one soon after he'd moved in and which caught the morning light bathing the room in colour.

The black block of the headland loomed in the distance. Three lights blinked in steady progression across the bay as a boat headed for the harbour. An intermittent patch of light lit the water from the lighthouse that was hidden by the coastline and he thought, if only he could capture the splendour of this night with paint.

He knew he'd made the right decision to come to the cottage. With so many ideas floating around in his head he couldn't wait for the morning to come so that he could begin. Later, opening a bottle of wine, he drank to Rowena's health and slumped into bed pleasantly inebriated. It was the only way he could get through the night without wondering if her plane had arrived safely. The thought that it had not was too much for him to contemplate.

Chapter 29

He awoke with a steady thumping pain behind his eyes and resolved to go easy on the wine in future. Perhaps he'd call in at the store in the village and pick up a few cans of lager instead. Not that he'd planned on spending his days in an alcoholic stupor.

After taking a couple of painkillers and drinking a mug of black coffee and eating a couple of rounds of toast, he took his sketchbook, walked onto the veranda and felt the faint warmth of morning sunshine on his face. The air was crisper than it appeared. He could almost smell winter begging to begin. Sliding his arms into a hooded fleece jacket he jogged down the lane in the direction of the path that would take him across the fields to the coast.

Dew dampened the ground underfoot, his sandals were just strips of leather secured at the ankle and the wet grass stroked his toes. He took a deep breath. It was as if he were alone in the world, except for a few circling gulls that cawed expectantly waiting for scraps of food.

"Sorry to disappoint you, old sons, I haven't been here long enough to have any stale bread. Come back again next week, it might be a different story." Aware that he'd resorted to talking to seagulls, he thought, it's only the first day, what further idiosyncrasies will I develop by Christmas?

The sand was hard underfoot. It stretched from the water's edge to the bank of white pebbles stacked in front of the moss-covered dunes. He began to pace out the shoreline from the headland to the point at which the coastline curved away from the bay in a series of rocky outcrops that rose into a sheer cliff.

As he walked Owen felt the breeze strengthening, bringing with it a distinct autumnal chill. If he was to work in the open air, he had to find some sort of shelter before the weather changed. He was beginning to doubt that he'd be able to fulfil his promise of producing a collection under such circumstances, when he discovered the cave.

Walking across the pebbles to the base of the cliff, he climbed over rocks made smooth by the tide and saw the entrance to a small cave that was large enough to provide shelter and which offered spectacular views of the sea, headland and bay. It was perfect. But before he could take up residence, he had to discover whether the sea at full tide would make the route to his hideaway impassable. He glanced at his watch. It was twenty minutes to eleven. By the look of the level of wet sand, it seemed as if the tide was on the turn, which meant that his route would be clear.

Feeling positive about his hideaway he walked back along the beach until he found the path leading to the village. Tomorrow he would bring his sketchbook to the cave and make a few preliminary drawings. He felt the familiar thrill sweeping through him and couldn't wait to begin. With the breeze behind him and the sun at its highest Owen removed his fleece jacket and tied it around his waist. Gareg Wen was little more than a few houses scattered like children's toys in disarray, a church, general stores and a pub that served food. He headed for the pub.

He'd met Dan, the pub landlord, in the summer and also had made the acquaintance of the vicar and Mrs Llewellyn who ran the general stores. When his eyes became accustomed to the dark interior after the glare of the sunlit road, Owen saw that Dan wouldn't be hard pressed to produce a meal for him at short notice. Most of the tables arranged in front of the curving oak bar were empty. Sitting on a bar stool reading a paper was a man in his sixties wearing a navy Guernsey sweater. He grunted a greeting as Owen approached.

"Pint of lager, please, Dan and the lunch menu," Owen said.

A young girl in her late teens was hanging up her jacket at the back of the bar.

"Lunch menu for Mr Madoc please, Lorna; late again are you? I'll have to dock your pay my girl."

"Oh now don't start, Dad, I only been clearing up your mess in the kitchen and posting your letters."

Dan laughed. "She got an answer for everything that one." He nodded at Owen. "Got to keep her on her toes now, haven't I?"

The man reading his paper looked up. "When is your missus back from her sister's then, Dan?"

"Next week, thank God. Never thought I'd say it though. Women, they're good for some things, even if they nags the pants off a man."

Owen smiled, took his pint and sat at a table near the window. He missed Rowena already and wouldn't mind listening to her nagging him for a bit.

"You're that painter what bought the cottage at Fallow's End," Lorna said handing him the lunch menu. "Do you paint women? Cos if you do, I wouldn't mind making an extra bob or two."

Her eagerness wasn't surprising. What was there to do for a teenager in a place like this? He almost wished he could say yes.

"Sorry. I'm not a portrait painter. But I can assure you that if I was, I'd jump at the chance of having a lovely young girl like you as my model." He could see his reply had satisfied her.

She blushed. "Just let me know when you're ready to order then, sir."

He watched her walking away and wondered whether she'd stay in Gareg Wen or would she be tempted to spread her wings for the bright lights of Cardiff. As she reached the bar, she turned, tossed a lock of her dark hair over her shoulder and smiled at him. There was no doubt in his mind that it would be the latter.

Chapter 30

The nights were drawing in. Owen had made a series of preliminary sketches of the coastline and bay prior to starting work on the canvases but he was restricted by the lack of daylight.

After a day spent in the cave sheltering from a stiff onshore breeze he decided to walk along the cliff path to stretch his legs before returning to his cottage. He packed his sketchbook in his portfolio, closed the zip and walked towards the rough steps leading to the cliff top.

The muscles in his calves were cramped and he stamped his feet on the steps as he climbed. The tide was coming in. He'd been watching the sea whilst marvelling at how it changed from day to day. His imagination had already transferred the images to canvas, the spray rising in the air like a bride's veil, the changes in colour as the sky darkened, the possibilities were endless.

"Hello again." The man, who'd been propping up the bar in the Anchor the day he arrived appeared on the path. He stretched out his hand. "You're that painter fellow, I understand. Duncan Jones; good to meet you."

Shaking his hand Owen introduced himself, adding, "Do you live in Gareg Wen?"

"Not in the village itself. My wife and I bought a plot of land on the cliffs and built our dream home. We've been here six months now. Great place, we love it."

"Lucky you."

"Where are you headed?" Duncan asked.

"Nowhere in particular. I've been sheltering in a cave all day sketching, just thought I'd stretch my legs before heading back to the cottage."

"In that case, why don't you come along with me and join Megan and me in a spot of afternoon tea? She usually puts the kettle on after I've had my walk."

"I'd like that, thanks. You're sure your wife won't mind an itinerant painter landing on her doorstep?"

"She'd be thrilled to bits. But be warned, she'll want to know everything about you down to the size of the pants your wearing."

Owen laughed, "I'll heed the warning."

He wasn't sure what he'd expected the house to be like or whether he'd even considered the thought as he'd followed Duncan along the cliff path. At the highest point the path divided and taking the route that veered to the right they came across a gate in the middle of a low hedge bordering the path. It led to a landscaped garden. However, he could never have imaged the building that stood before him. An architect with futuristic ideas had obviously designed the house, the back of which was divided into two storeys by an aluminium and glass balustrade, a balcony ran along its width. One-way view windows reflected the late afternoon sun like sightless eyes and Owen anticipated that the view from inside would be spectacular.

"Bit of a shock eh?"

Owen nodded. "I should say so."

"I was in the business. I'm a retired architect. This was our dream."

Duncan's wife, Megan was a woman in her early fifties. She wore her curly pepper and salt hair tied back in a ponytail with a coloured scarf that matched her long flowing skirt. Owen could imagine her in Glastonbury in green wellies smoking dope and swaying to the music of a folk band. She seemed vaguely familiar.

When she spoke his image of her dissolved like sherbet on the tongue. "How do you do, Mr Madoc; I gather you're spending some time in the cottage at Fallow's end." Her voice was cultured and deep, with just the faintest trace of a Welsh accent.

"That's right, but please, it's Owen. Mr Madoc makes me feel like my father."

She smiled, "How do you like living in Fallow's end, Owen?"

"Fine, it's just right, plenty of peace and quiet and the views around the coast are awesome."

"Awesome indeed and quite inspiring I should imagine. Now I suggest Duncan takes you upstairs, whilst I make us some tea. I hope you find the view from our Crow's Nest equally as awesome."

He could see why they referred to the room as the Crow's Nest; the view from there encompassed the coast and the endless expanse of sea to perfection. But that was where the similarity to a crow's nest ended. It was a large room, windows taking up the whole of one wall. Light flooded in from every direction and Owen's artistic soul envied them living in such a location.

The sea, now as calm as a millpond, was the colour of liquid gold trickling from an alchemist's jug; the coastline cradling its precious gift in its arms.

"You like?" Duncan asked.

"It's magnificent; truly inspirational."

"That's the idea. It's why we built the house here, for Megan."

"Your wife paints?" Owen asked.

Duncan Jones shook his head. "Not exactly, although she is an artist; she's a writer."

The pieces of the jigsaw suddenly fell into place. Owen's previous musings had not been so very far from the truth. Megan Lloyd Jones was a well-known author who wrote very successful psychological thrillers.

"You must think me a complete idiot."

"Not at all." Duncan sat in a chair near the window and indicated the one opposite. "Please sit down."

"Not to recognise your famous wife at first sight is unforgivable."

His host grinned. "More like a relief. Part of the reason for living out here is anonymity. Since breaking into the American market Megan is constantly pestered for book signings and tours in faraway places. She hates all that razzmatazz, it distracts her from her true vocation – simply being a writer."

"Yes, I can imagine, although I'm still longing to jump on that band wagon in order to have the luxury of avoiding it."

When Megan arrived with the tea Owen felt uncomfortably aware that he should make some reference to her celebrity status. "I'm sorry I,"…he began but she quickly silenced him with a wave of her hand.

" Let's pretend you've never heard of me and we'll get along just fine."

Later, watching the sun sink on the horizon turning the pot of liquid gold to a mirror covered with a gossamer pink veil, Owen sighed, aware that his thoughts were becoming more poetic by the minute.

"If I could only capture that, I'd go back to London a happy man."

"You will, I'm sure of it." Megan joined him at the window. "Please come again, anytime, bring your sketch pad. It's got to be preferable to sitting in a damp cave in November."

Owen couldn't believe his luck. "You mean it? I wouldn't get in the way?" Duncan placed an arm around his wife's shoulder.

"Does it look as if you'd get in the way? This place has more rooms than Cardiff Castle. Like Meg says you're welcome, anytime."

When he reached the bottom of the garden, Owen turned and waved as he closed the gate leading to the cliff path. He was thrilled at the prospect of working in the Crow's Nest and thought how much he would like to take up the Joneses kind offer. It was dark when he walked back down the lane to his cottage. He almost didn't see the woman as she stepped out in front of him.

Chapter 31

Moonlight lit her face in the darkness so that she appeared ghost-like in front of him. Owen wasn't sure who was the most startled as they both spoke at once.

"I almost didn't see you, I'm sorry," he said.
"It's my car; it won't start."
They both laughed to cover their embarrassment.
"It stopped at the top of the lane and I couldn't get it to budge. I saw the outline of a cottage and walked down the lane. I rang the bell but there was no one home," she explained.
He noticed that she was wearing a thin jacket and that a cold wind had suddenly sprung up. "That's my cottage. Why don't we walk back and I'll ring the garage in the village; they're usually open until late. Jim Jackson can take a look at your car while you wait. It's got to be warmer than hanging about here."
She hesitated.
"My name's, Owen Madoc by the way."
"Thanks, I'm really grateful," she said following him down the lane.
Once they were inside and he'd switched on

the overhead light. He thought she looked familiar. "Have we met before?" he asked.

She hesitated. "I think perhaps we have. Are you the artist who painted Indigo Night?"

"I am."

"Then, yes. I'm Andy Lawson's sister, Sarah."

She didn't look the same. He remembered a rather plain girl with lank brown hair. "I'm sorry, I wasn't sure – you look different."

She smiled. "I've changed my hair colour. I often do, but everyone seems to think being blonde suits me so perhaps I'll stick with this."

It wasn't just the colour of her hair, this girl was well groomed – her make up immaculate, her fingernails painted a vivid red. It was later that he realised she'd reminded him of Rowena.

He left her in the cottage whilst he took her keys back up the lane to the garage. After a while Jim returned with the car and said, "Daft piece just run out of petrol."

"And she didn't notice?" Owen asked incredulously.

"Well to be fair, petrol gauge was a bit dodgy. Fixed now though. Nothing a good tap with a spanner wouldn't sort out."

"Right, thanks, Jim. How much?"

"Let's say you can buy me a pint or two in the Anchor on Saturday night."

Owen drove the car back down the lane and parked it outside the cottage. She was sitting in the living room looking out of the window. "All fixed. You were out of petrol. When you get home I'd have someone look at that petrol gauge if I were you."

"God, how embarrassing. How much do I owe your friend?"

"He's going to settle for the price of a pint or two so don't worry I'll see he's OK."

"No, really, I can't let you do that." She fumbled in her handbag but he crossed the room and put his hand on her arm.

"It's no problem. It's my pleasure."

"Thank you so much." She stood up. "I'll be off then."

Owen, watching her taillights disappearing up the lane was sorry that he hadn't asked her if she'd like to stay for a drink. Something had held him back. Perhaps it was a reluctance to share his cottage with anyone other than Rowena. Or perhaps it was because she reminded him too much of Rowena. He wasn't sure.

Two weeks passed before the weather closed in with a vengeance. He'd used the cave most days and had progressed with his sketches until he felt confident enough to transfer them to canvas. He'd hesitated to take up the Joneses offer as he hadn't seen either of them again and was reluctant to impose on their good nature.

It was on one particularly rain-swept day, when he was making his way up the beach, that he saw Megan again.

"Hello, I've been meaning to give you a call.

This weather is set to stay for the next few weeks, according to the forecast. I told Duncan we couldn't see you freezing your butt off on the beach." She tucked her arm in his and walked alongside. "So I've cleared a corner of the Crow's Nest ready for you. Bring your canvases up when you're ready. You can leave everything at our place for as long as you like. Look on it as a second studio. Duncan's off to Edinburgh for a month; he's my manager and has some business that requires his attention and, well, I'm in the middle of plotting a fourth Hardie Bankcroft novel, so you won't be disturbed."

"That's very kind of you. But wouldn't I be in the way?"

"Not at all. Much as I like my own company it would be good to think that I'm not totally alone for the rest of the month."

"In that case I'll take you up on your very generous offer. You'd be saving my butt in more ways than one."

He heard her laughter drifting on the wind as she walked up the steps leading to the cliff path leaving him with the feeling of optimism at the prospect of working in such surroundings.

Megan hadn't exaggerated about the weather. Two days after he'd started work at their house, storm clouds hung over the bay reducing the light to that of dusk before discharging their load amidst an almighty rumble of thunder.

The view was spectacular. Owen immediately began to transfer the pewter sky to canvas in splurges of dark grey, violet and cobalt paint.

The hours passed in a flash as he concentrated on mixing the colours until he was satisfied with the result. Eventually he looked at his watch and realised it was nearly seven o'clock. Three days ago, when he'd arrived with his equipment, Megan had produced a spare key. "I'll be somewhere around but in case I'm in the middle of something it makes sense for you to come and go as you please," she'd said.

He placed his brushes in the leather roll in order to transfer them to his cottage for cleaning. He'd abandoned watercolour as he thought the dramatic changes in the weather would look better in oils. As he walked towards his car, the rain and wind lashed his face and he silently thanked his lucky stars for Megan and Duncan Jones. His previous meeting, with Sarah Lawson in the lane, was totally forgotten.

Chapter 32

Owen had been working in the Crow's Nest for ten days when he returned to his cottage to find a parcel wrapped in brown paper waiting for him on the veranda. He picked it up and read, *To Owen Madoc, My Good Samaritan.*

Carrying it inside Owen put his brushes on the sink drainer in the kitchen then opened the parcel to reveal a box containing a bottle of Fine Malt Whiskey and a card.

Thank you, once again. Sarah.

She must have delivered it herself, he thought. How had she known it was his favourite brand? The thought had barely formed when his mobile vibrated in his pocket followed by a chorus of the Star Spangled Banner that Rowena had so thoughtfully downloaded for him before she left for the States.

"Hello, darling."

"Rowena, sweetheart, how's it going in the big apple?"

"I'm making progress, in fact I think I've got it all sown up."

His spirits rose, "Does that mean you'll be

back earlier than you expected?" He hated the needy tone that was obvious in his voice.

"'Fraid not, in fact quite the reverse. It looks as if I'll be staying here over the Christmas period. I'll explain later, darling, I have to rush. Missing you - love you loads."

He started to reply but heard the disconnected signal as the line went dead. The euphoria of the day dispersed in an instant. He picked up the bottle of Whiskey and went into the kitchen to find a glass.

It was one of those rare November mornings that begin with the sun shining out of a clear blue sky and a crisp white layer of frost coating the ground. Owen awoke with a hangover. Not the worst one he'd ever had, which was a tribute to the distillation process of the fine malt whiskey, copious amounts of which he'd drunk the night before.

In the kitchen he downed a pint of water then refilling the glass started on a second. Contrary to popular belief, he'd found that coffee seemed to make his hangover worse. He opened the front door and drew in a deep breath of the salt tinged air. He'd ring Rowena later to find out what was going on then work like the devil trying to forget that she'd be still away during the Christmas holiday.

His resolve faltered as he showered and dressed. He was going to miss her. If only he didn't have this deadline to keep he'd fly over the Atlantic on the next plane.

He decided to give the Crow's Nest a miss for a couple of hours, at least until after he'd phoned Rowena. Perhaps an early morning walk on the beach with his sketchpad would blow away the remains of his hangover.

The grass crunched under his feet like tissue paper leaving behind the outline of his trainers in the frost. It was still only ten past eight and yet he could feel the warmth of the sun on his skin. Seagulls swooped to the shore where in the distance he could see someone with a carrier bag throwing pieces of bread into the sea.

The image was lost to him as the path dipped and the dunes rose in front of him. A light breeze swept sand over them changing their solid outline into a shivering mirage of liquid mercury in the crisp morning air. Emerging from the path he climbed the shifting sand until the beach spread before him. He was alone. The gulls were left pecking at the remains of the bread floating on the water but their benefactor had disappeared.

Striding towards the headland, Owen felt his spirits lift along with his hangover. Taking deep breaths, he jogged back down the beach in the direction of the cave. If he could capture the shimmering morning before it settled he'd be a happy man.

He didn't see her until he reached the mouth of the cave. She was sitting with her back to the rocks looking out to sea.

"Hello."

"Good Lord, it's you." He was aware that his surprise at seeing her so unexpectedly had made him state the obvious.

"I think so, yes." She laughed.

She was dressed in jeans and a padded jacket. Her hair was the best thing about her, Owen decided. It gleamed like spun gold in the sunshine and she'd done something to her eyes, they reminded him of the way Rowena applied her eye make-up – subtle yet dramatic.

"You were the last person I expected to see this morning." He sat on a rock near the entrance to the cave. "But it does give me an opportunity to thank you for the whiskey. There was no need, but thanks anyway."

"My pleasure."

"Are you staying in Gareg Wen?"

"I might. I decided to come and delivery my thank-you gift yesterday and then on a sudden impulse thought I'd stay overnight at the Anchor. I have to admit that this morning, when I saw the beach and the glorious weather, I phoned work and took a long overdue two-week holiday. So I'll probably stay around for a bit longer."

Owen followed her gaze to the horizon where a container ship sat like a child's toy as if perched on the edge of the world. He opened his sketchbook and took a pencil from his pocket.

"What work do you do?" he asked as his pencil slid over the paper in short sleek lines.

"I work for Fox and Knight, the publishers," she said watching him. She stood up and stretched. "Rocks are not the most comfortable seats in the world. I think I'll leave you to it, Mr Madoc. Perhaps we'll meet again before I leave."

"Sure to; I pop into the Anchor for a nightcap occasionally. By the way, it's Owen."

Chapter 33

It was nearly three o'clock when Owen finally left the beach. The sun was lower in the sky and shone directly into his eyes as he left the path and walked down the lane to his cottage.

He'd left his mobile on the kitchen table. It was ringing as he opened the door. He rushed towards it afraid it would cut to voice mail and afraid he would miss Rowena. It was Mark Furnish.

"Owen, old man, how are you doing? Working hard, I hope."

"It's OK I'm OK"

"Good, good, glad to hear it. The thing is…,"

Owen recognised Mark's tone, when unpalatable news was to follow.

"Well the thing is, Drew Mailer, the art critic from the New York Post, is coming over from the States and he's staying with a friend of mine. You met him at your last exhibition - it's Lew Rockfield. Anyway Mailer was very interested to see more of your work and I sort of told Lew that I didn't think there'd be a problem if we brought the date of the end of January's showing forward."

Owen groaned, "How far forward?"

"Let's say the fifteenth of December."

"Let's not."

"Don't be like that, sweetie. Mailer has the American Market at his fingertips. He knows all the right people. This could be very good for you."

"It will mean me working morning, noon and night."

"I have complete faith in you. You can do it; I know you can."

After he'd put the phone down Owen knew that he didn't share Mark's confidence. Although he was well on the way to fulfilling his original brief, he knew that the creative process couldn't be hurried. You had to allow for inspiration and his was in New York, although if he thought about it, Rowena might be a distraction, a very welcome one, but a distraction nevertheless. Perhaps he could meet the deadline after all. He looked at his watch - a quick bite to eat and then he'd drive over to Duncan's place. Walking would take too long when every second counted.

Megan was in the garden when he arrived. She was smoking a cigarette.

"Filthy habit," she said. "I'd given it up too."

"Problems?" Owen held the gate open with his back, his arms holding the canvases.

"You could say that. My psychotic heroine is showing signs of complete normality. I can't allow that to happen now, can I?"

"Tricky." Owen stood beside her and looked out at the bay. "If only I could capture that, I could make a fortune."

"You sound as if you've problems of your own to deal with." She stubbed out the cigarette on a fence post.

"Deadline's been brought forward. I've to be back in London for a showing on the fifteen of December."

"Christmas in Gareg Wen is out then? Pity." She took his arm. "So back to work for both of us, it would seem."

The month passed without Owen being aware of it; at first he'd resented the fact that he'd be working flat out but, as he became absorbed in the creative processes, he began to enjoy himself. Days passed in the Crow's Nest, each canvas transforming the scene before him into something more tangible.

On the fifth of December Owen awoke with the realisation that he'd be more than able to fulfil his commitment to Mark. And with the emergence of rational thought, came two startling facts, first and foremost he hadn't heard from Rowena in over a week and secondly he'd broken his half-hearted promise to meet Sarah Lawson in the Anchor the previous month.

Rowena, uppermost in his mind, he resolved to ring, taking into account the time difference. His mind, now free from worry concerning his work, he became concerned about her. It was so unlike her not to keep in touch.

He breakfasted in the little kitchen at the back of the house, took a swift shower and dressed hurriedly. There was nothing more he could do to the canvases in the Crow's Nest; the oils needed to dry out and the watercolours were stacked in his studio in the cottage. The day spread before him, empty and devoid of companionship. Then, just as he was beginning to feel sorry for himself, the heavens opened and rain drummed incessantly on the grey tiled roof. By lunchtime the wind was howling around the cottage walls like a banshee. Owen picked up his car keys and drove into the village. He would have lunch in the Anchor and afterwards he'd ring Rowena.

The Anchor was busier than he'd seen it, the incessant rain having driven most of the locals to seek the convivial atmosphere of the public bar. The vicar sat on the window seat, a copy of The Angling Times spread out on his lap. Grouped in a huddle near the log fire were three elderly men in the middle of a heated game of dominos. In a back room he could hear the crack of billiard balls as they shot into the pockets, whilst, above the bar the mid-day news was providing background viewing for a couple of women who wouldn't have looked out of place at a W.I. convention.

"Owen, over here." Duncan was sitting at a table eating fish and chips. "Join me, won't you? Megan's lost in the midst of her latest plot and

I know from past experience that I'm better keeping out of the way."

Owen pulled out a chair opposite Duncan feeling grateful for the company. "I'm at a bit of a loose end myself. Not a lot I can do until the weekend. Then it's just to put a few last minute touches to the collection and that's it."

"So you're high and dry for a day or two, eh?"

"You could say that."

"Fancy joining Ted and me on a fishing trip tomorrow?"

"Ted?"

"The vicar. We've managed to persuade old Bill Jefferies to take us out on his lobster boat."

"In this weather?" Owen was aghast.

"Set fair tomorrow. They know the signs apparently."

"In that case, yes, I'd love to come."

Duncan called to his sailing companion. "Another convert joining us tomorrow, Vicar."

The vicar raised his hand to Owen. "Glad to hear it," he said before returning to his paper.

Chapter 34

As predicted by Duncan the weather was fine. At seven o'clock the vicar and his miniscule flock gathered at the meeting point, Bill Jefferies waving to them from aboard his fishing boat moored at the end of the harbour wall.

Duncan had warned Owen to make sure he had adequate clothing with him, as it was sure to be cold out on the water. Dressed in the waterproof Rowena had bought him when they'd gone on a walking holiday in the Lake District, he followed Ted and Duncan and climbed aboard.

He'd phoned Rowena the previous afternoon but she was too busy to speak for long. She'd told him she was fine, work was a problem, there weren't enough hours in the day and before she'd rung off she told him that she loved him. He'd have to make do with that. He'd noticed that there'd been no mention of how long she was going to be away or how she planned to spend Christmas.

The bay was shrouded in early morning mist, the air so crisp it almost crackled. But Bill

Jefferies assured them that the sun would burn off the mist in no time and the sea was set to be calm, except for the currents they would encounter around the headland. "We calls them the Cherry Stones - have to hang on to your breakfasts round there, you mark my words."

He hadn't been kidding, Owen noted, as the boat, after gliding through the still water out of the harbour and around the coast, suddenly encountered the aforementioned currents. It lurched and tossed about like child's bath toy but neither the vicar nor Duncan appeared to be the least bit perturbed by this occurrence. Owen swallowed hard to hold on to his breakfast.

The lighthouse stood on a rocky outcrop hidden from view by the headland. Leaving Gareg Wen far behind them and thankfully the treacherous Cherry Stone currents, he joined Bill in the wheelhouse whilst Duncan and Ted discussed the merits of fresh water fishing.

"How long have you been a lobster fisherman?" Owen asked as Bill steered the boat around the coast.

"Couple o' years now. Back a spell, I fished the sea like the best of them bringing back a good catch but times have changed. It's them fancy restaurants in Cardiff what pays the good money for lobsters and the like."

"So you find it worth your while?" He wondered how many he must catch to make a living.

"Aye lad. I'm mostly retired now. I'm sixty-six - now you wouldn't think that, would you?"

Owen agreed wholeheartedly, although Bill's face was weather-beaten with deep lines etched into its surface like linocuts, he moved with the speed and agility of a man half his age.

"The important thing about fishing for lobsters is to keep the location of the pots a secret." He grinned. "You can't let them know where they are see. They steals the lobsters as good as look at you and all you find is empty pots."

"You don't mind me knowing?"

"Nah, you bin approved by the vicar and Duncan, that's good enough for me, ain't no better recommendation in Gareg Wen"

The boat began to rock in the swell as it rounded a point in the coastline known locally as The Devil's Claw.

"Always gets a bit tricky here," said Bill. "That's why I always sinks the pots hereabouts."

He steered inland then threw the anchor, so that the boat bobbed up and down and nauseatingly from side to side. Owen felt his stomach somersaulting again and went to sit on the bench outside the wheelhouse, while Bill made his way to the back of the boat where the winch was situated.

"Want a hand, Bill?" Duncan asked.

"Nah, you're alright. Tide's easy; piece of cake."

Owen watched spellbound as Bill raised the winch with as little effort as if he were pulling up a clothesline. The lobster pot broke through the surface of the water spilling a waterfall of seaweed and mussel shells in its wake. Bill hauled it on to the deck with a swinging motion. Two fair-sized lobsters stared glassy eyed at Owen as Bill quickly opened the lid of the pot and skilfully bound the creatures' claws with elastic bands before loading them into a square tank full of salt water.

"Keeps 'em fresh and my hands in one piece," he explained to Owen, who watched entranced as the procedure was repeated. Afterwards, when Bill was satisfied that he'd exhausted his catch, he chugged a mile or so around the coast and using the same strategy continued as before.

The vicar turned to Owen. "That catch alone will keep Bill in beer throughout the winter I shouldn't wonder."

Duncan nodded. "Not tempted yourself then, Ted?"

The vicar laughed. "With my physique? Carrying a stack of hymn books and landing the odd catch in the river is about my limit."

"Mine too. What about you, Owen?"

Owen smiled. "I'm with the vicar."

Later, when the boat returned to the harbour, and Bill had landed his catch, the bar of the Anchor seemed to be the best place to discuss the events of the day. Owen relaxed as he listened to their tales, which became longer in direct proportion to the amount of beer he consumed and for the first time in weeks put

Rowena firmly to the back of his mind.

A week after the boat trip, Owen shared afternoon tea with Duncan and Megan prior to leaving for London along with his completed collection.

"I can't begin to tell you both how grateful I am for you allowing me use the Crow's Nest and for being such splendid company."

"Nonsense, our pleasure." Megan handed him a slice of freshly baked sponge cake.

Owen held it up for inspection. "Does this mean, what I think it means?"

Duncan nodded. "It does. Megan's finished the final draft. Went off to the publishers this morning."

"Congratulations," Owen said, adding, "By the way, if you're both at a loose end on the fifteenth, I'd be honoured, if you'd be my guests at the Furnish Gallery. I'd like to show you the result of my endeavours."

Megan glanced at her husband then answered. "We'd be delighted. Wouldn't we, Duncan?"

"I should say so. Now let's forget about tea and celebrate with a glass or four of our finest champagne," he said walking towards the kitchen.

A short while later Duncan raised his glass. "To success," he said toasting each of them in turn.

Chapter 35

On the morning of the fifteenth of December an email arrived from Rowena. It read *Good Luck, darling, I'll be thinking of you,* and Owen felt absurdly deflated by the lack of ingenuity or genuine sense of feeling in the words.

The paintings had been collected days ago and Mark Furnish had expressed his delight. "Totally amazing, Mailer's going to be knocked sideways."

The previous day Owen had been surprised at how good the collection looked as he'd inspected the display. Maisie Dalton, Mark's display co-ordinator, had a good eye for detail and had arranged his work to the best effect.

As usual, when he'd been absorbed in fulfilling a deadline, and once his work was completed, Owen, instead of feeling relaxed, felt aimless. He'd wandered around his flat for days before the exhibition, missing Rowena more acutely than he'd thought possible but avoiding calling her in case he ended up pleading with her to come home. It was a hopeless situation. He wanted to fly out to join her for Christmas but as she'd made no suggestion that he should do so, he'd hesitated in making the call.

Mark Furnish was in his element. He reminded Owen of a bee, flitting from flower to flower extolling the creative ability of his artists in a voice loud enough to be heard a mile away. Owen's work was being shown alongside a relatively unknown artist Liv Dickinson who concentrated on using black and white images reminiscent of childhood drawings. She was building up quite a reputation and Maisie Dalton had designed the settings for both collections in such a way that the contrast between both mediums did not detract from either.

Liv, was a woman in her early forties with dark brown hair escaping from a knot on the top of her head. She was dressed in a brightly coloured Kaftan and wore heavy make up. In no way resembling her creations she glided through the gallery like an exotic colourful bird in full plumage, her Kaftan billowing behind her.

"Owen," she greeted him. "Love your collection."

"Likewise," Owen replied with sincerity.

"Mark says, he's expecting hordes this evening." She took a glass of champagne from a tray offered to her by one of the staff.

"That's Mark for you." Owen shook his head, refusing a drink. He'd drunk enough over the past few days to anaesthetise him.

The Exhibition followed the usual format,

press photographers jostled with reporters and Owen, Liv and Mark joined critics and patrons to give interviews and pose for photographs. After the official opening the guests mingled, commented on or arranged to buy the exhibits. Frequently praised by critics and patrons alike, Owen churned out his stock set of replies and thanks then seeing Megan Lloyd Jones left the melee and went to join her.

"So glad to see you managed to come. Where's Duncan?"

"Not here, I'm afraid. He had an accident on Bill's boat. Nothing too serious but he's sprained his ankle and can't walk far. He said to tell you 'Good Luck.'"

"That's a shame. You're not driving back to Gareg Wen tonight?"

"No. Someone at my publishers has booked me into a hotel on the Strand. I hope you don't mind, I suggested she come along, as Duncan couldn't make it."

"Not at all."

"Good, oh here she is now."

Owen turned as the woman approached.

"Sarah, come and meet Owen."

"Hello again." She was wearing her hair up in some sort of pleat and once again he was reminded of Rowena."

"You know each other?" Megan looked from one to the other.

"We met in Gareg Wen," the woman explained. "I'd called to see you about the proofs, I'm afraid my car ran out of petrol and Mr Madoc was my good Samaritan."

"Well, what a coincidence. Good Lord there's Gordon Jessop, an old friend of Duncan's. Do excuse me for a moment, I really do have to go and say hello."

Owen remembered that he owed the woman an apology. "I think I owe you a drink," he said. "After we last met, I had a call from Mark bringing forward the deadline for this exhibition. I'm afraid the Anchor lost my custom for weeks after that."

She smiled. "Never mind. It did cross my mind that I'd offended you in some way though."

"Look, perhaps I could make it up to you. After this is all over, why don't you and Megan join me for dinner? I know of a great little restaurant that's not far from here."

She looked uncomfortable. "I'm not sure. There's really no need."

"Nonsense, it would be my pleasure."

"Well, in that case, thanks." She looked around. "I don't suppose I could ask you to show me some of your work. I'd like to buy something small for my flat."

"Of course. But it does rather depend on whether you are looking for a traditional piece or something a bit unusual and I'm afraid the prices are a bit steep. Liv Dickinson's work might be more to your taste and she is really rather good."

"You do realise you are in danger of losing a sale here, Owen." She laughed and he was aware that it was the first time he'd heard her call him by his Christian name."

The crowd had thinned as the gallery prepared to close. Owen had lost sight of both Megan and Sarah. He still hadn't had a drink and decided he was both ravenous and in need of fortification as Mark approached.

"Mailer just loved your collection. He assured me he'd contact his paper with a favourable report. Think of the influence he has on the American Market. You could be in the money, darling," he enthused as Megan joined them, having bought Moonlit Memories. It was the view Owen had painted from the Crow's Nest after a storm.

"I gather you've invited Sarah for a meal. I'm glad; she could do with a break. I'm away to my bed; it's been a long day." She kissed Owen's cheek. "Don't forget us, at Gareg Wen, will you? You're always welcome at our place."

He walked her to the door feeling uncomfortably aware that he would now have to dine alone with Sarah Lawson, who was waiting for him in the foyer. Silently cursing his impulsive invitation, he pasted on a smile. This was not how he'd anticipated spending the rest of the evening. He could only hope that he could make an early exit.

Chapter 36

The restaurant was a popular venue for what Rowena called the 'in crowd'. Admittedly artists and writers of his acquaintance could often be found taking advantage of Luigi's excellent food and wine, sold at prices struggling members of the artistic fraternity could afford.

That evening, as usual, the atmosphere was welcoming without being intrusive. Owen held the door open for Sarah as Luigi, being always keen to welcome his customers personally, approached.

"Good to see you again, you are in luck, your favourite table is free. Mario will attend to you." He was obviously in a rush and hurried away hardly looking at either of them.

Owen, uncomfortably aware that this was where he often took Rowena, thanked Luigi and without introducing his companion followed Mario to a table in an alcove.

"This is nice. I don't think I've been here before. I thought I knew most of the restaurants in this area."

Mario took her coat and she sat down. It was where Rowena usually sat and he suddenly felt like running out into the night and booking the first flight he could find to New York.

"Owen, are you alright?" She looked up at him.

"I'm fine. Sorry, I suppose it's just been a long day. I'm still amazed at how well things went." He picked up the wine menu.

"If you'd rather not stay, I'll understand." She looked uncertain whether to pick up the menu or not.

Feeling a complete bastard, he smiled. "Of course not. We're here to celebrate after all." He raised a hand to Mario. "A bottle of your finest champagne." He turned to his companion, "You do like champagne I presume?"

She grinned, "Does a cat like cream?"

The first two glasses on an empty stomach lifted Owen's mood to such an extent he began to think she was quite good company. She certainly made him smile. Her conversation was light and amusing. He'd spent worse evenings and besides, Rowena was probably out enjoying herself, he reasoned, why shouldn't he.

As if reading his mind she said, "You're missing your girlfriend?"

"That obvious?"

"It's understandable. She couldn't make the showing?"

"She's working. She's in New York."

"I see. Will you be spending Christmas with her?"

"No."

She didn't probe any further, for which he was grateful and quickly changed the topic of conversation to his friendship with Megan and Duncan Jones.

"Their house is something isn't it?" she said, making short work of a plate of garlic mushrooms.

Owen smiled; her enthusiasm for her food was in direct contrast with Rowena's habit of pushing it around her plate with the end of her fork and sending most of it back to the kitchen uneaten. They chatted about his work and touched on her relationship with Megan and two bottles of champagne followed by a large measure of cognac later, he'd stopped thinking of making an early exit and began to enjoy the evening.

Leaving the warmth and comfort of the restaurant Owen was shocked to see that a stiff wind had sprung up carrying snowflakes towards them with increasing ferocity.

"I'll get us a cab," he said.

"No, really. I live ten minutes away. We can walk."

Owen put an arm around her shoulders, partly to steady himself and partly because her coat was too thin to afford her any protection against the cold.

She shivered. "I should have worn something heavier but I didn't anticipate being out as late as this."

"No problem, I'll keep you warm."

She nestled into him as they walked the short distance to her flat.

Fumbling in her handbag for her key she said, "You will come in for a coffee, at least."

He was vaguely aware that it was a statement rather than a question as he followed her into the lobby and they took the lift to the first floor.

The flat was cosy and warm. It was typical of the type built between the wars. The rooms were well proportioned and Sarah had furnished them tastefully, favouring comfort and colour rather than stark minimalist design. "This is nice," he said settling into the folds of a crimson sofa.

"That's it, relax, kick off your shoes, you'll soon warm up. In fact let's forget about the coffee. I've a bottle of Remy Martin that I've been waiting to share with someone and after all it is nearly Christmas."

The sound of a street cleaner awakened him. Owen looked around at the unfamiliar surroundings and slid out from under the duvet. He must have passed out. He was lying on the sofa, thankfully fully clothed; she'd covered him with the quilt. His mouth felt dry and his head was pounding. Staggering towards the window he opened the curtains. It hadn't been a street cleaner - it was a snowplough. The pavements were thick with the stuff. He vaguely remembered it snowing on their way back from the restaurant.

He watched as the road was cleared, and traffic began to move; pedestrians inched their way along the icy pavements like greenhorn skaters. She must have heard him moving about.

"Do you feel as bad as I do?" she asked. She was wearing an orange dressing gown. The colour made his eyes hurt. "Mm," she nodded, "I can see you do. Two pain killers and coffee coming up."

After his headache receded, he even managed to eat the breakfast she'd cooked for him.

"Look, I really appreciate the trouble you've gone to, Sarah but I must get back. I hate to eat and run but I've wasted too much of your time already." He was beginning to feel uncomfortably aware that the ambiance created by the champagne and cognac had worn off.

"I've been thinking," she said. "You are on your own at Christmas and so am I. At least I can go and spend it with relatives but like you said last night it's no picnic spending Christmas watching the under fives tearing off layers of Christmas wrapping paper only to become fractious and over-excited for the rest of the day."

Had he said that? He couldn't remember.

She hesitated, and then as if taking her courage in both hands she blurted out, "You could spend the day here. I'm not a bad cook and we could always drown our sorrows. You'll be missing your girlfriend and me - well I can always dredge up some sorrow that requires a good drowning."

He smiled and began to think that there could be worse ways of spending Christmas day than getting drunk with Sarah Lawson.

The main roads were clear of snow by the time he decided to leave but she insisted on driving him to his flat a short distance away. Stopping her car in the car park outside, she stretched across him, opened the glove compartment and removed a business card and ballpoint pen. Turning the card over she wrote down her name and her home telephone number.

Later, when he'd showered and changed into jeans and a sweater he glanced at the card propped up against a book on a side table. He picked it up and turned it over to read Sarah Lawson, Editorial Assistant, Fox and Knight, Publishers.

Chapter 37

Aware that he'd had but the briefest contact from Rowena since his exhibition, Owen began to feel justified in accepting Sarah Lawson's invitation to spend Christmas day at her flat. Why shouldn't he, he argued? She was a friend, at least she could become one, although at the moment acquaintance might be more to the point.

He hadn't heard from her since the night of the exhibition, except for a brief message that she'd left on his answer phone telling him that she'd expect him around one o'clock on Christmas Day.

Like most men Owen had left his Christmas shopping until Christmas Eve and the stores in Oxford Street were thronged with last minute shoppers buying presents for loved ones and those who'd given them unexpected gifts. He moved from one store to another hoping for inspiration. He didn't know her well enough to be familiar with her taste in ornaments or whether he should just turn up with a bottle. He wandered around in a haze of indecision, being jostled by the crowds of shoppers snaking along the pavements, until it occurred to him that he had the very thing in his flat, a watercolour view from the Crow's Nest. All that was required was to buy a suitable picture frame and the job was done.

He found what he was looking for in a department store and, after eventually reaching the front of the queue at the pay desk, left with a spring in his step. He hadn't relished the thought of shopping for a gift in the first place, his heart wasn't in it but it seemed churlish to turn up for Christmas lunch empty handed.

He thought about the Christmas gift he'd bought for Rowena months ago; he'd known exactly what to buy then. It was the weekend before he'd gone to the cottage. He'd bought the ring in Tiffany's on Old Bond Street and had planned to surprise her with his proposal of marriage when she returned from New York for Christmas. Her inability to fly home for the event had left him with, amongst other things, a feeling of anti-climax and he began to wonder if he'd ever recover his previous enthusiasm for the idea. He hated the thought of her enjoying herself without him; hated the fact that there had been so little contact between them since last month.

Carrying the picture frame under his arm, he decided to have a drink and a bite to eat in a wine bar before taking a taxi back to his flat. The Vineyard was busy with Christmas Eve drinkers, office workers having finished work at mid day mingling with husbands who had left their wives to shop, whilst assuring them that there would be a drink waiting for them when they'd finished.

It hadn't snowed again since the night of the exhibition but a cold wind swept down Oxford Street as Owen shivered waiting for the next available taxi. He noticed that there was a buzz of expectancy in the air that was almost tangible. The festive spirit swept along the pavement towards him but somehow managed to pass him by. There was an ache in his heart that only the sight of Rowena could relieve. He hadn't heard from her for days and he began to wonder what she would think when she rang his flat tomorrow to find that there was no answer.

A group of revellers spilling out from a pub opposite the taxi rank caught his attention and he watched them threading their way through the crowd of shoppers. It was then that he thought he saw Sarah. She was holding the hand of a young child, a girl, and they were hurrying in the direction of a toy shop which had a large teddy bear dressed like Father Christmas standing in the shop window. As she approached a man who was holding a young boy by the hand stepped out of the throng and kissed her cheek. Owen recognised him as Andy Lawson.

The children were excited; he could see their flushed cheeks and the way they eagerly pulled their father and aunt into the toyshop.

Christmas was about being with your loved ones, nothing else mattered; he was spending his with a virtual stranger and with whom, he thought, would Rowena be sharing that special day?

It was late when a taxi finally drew up; the driver grunted when he realised that his fare would be minimal.

"Couldn't walk it, could you mate?" he asked with a frown.

"Bah humbug," muttered Owen to himself not wishing to antagonise the man into refusing to drive the short distance to his flat.

He had no premonition as he slid the key into his front door; no feeling that the flat wasn't exactly as he'd left it that morning. Even when he walked into the darkened living room, he wasn't aware of anything unusual. Then he flicked on the light switch and she got up from the sofa and slid her arms around his neck. Rowena's perfume filled his nostrils as her lips sought his.

"Don't look so shocked, darling. You didn't really think that I wouldn't move heaven and earth to be with you tomorrow did you?"

She stroked his cheek. The picture frame slid from his grasp and slipped under the sofa. Suddenly Owen knew the true meaning of Christmas and he couldn't wait for it to begin.

Chapter 38

How could he have doubted her? Owen, whistling a chorus of Jingle Bells, put a couple of artistic finishing touches to the breakfast tray on which stood hot buttered toast, Champagne and orange juice. The Champagne had been courtesy of Rowena, as had the food, which now filled his fridge. She'd arrived in the early hours of Christmas Eve and, knowing that he was unlikely to have anything palatable to eat in his flat, had shopped before arriving later that afternoon.

"Happy Christmas, darling," he said, the tray his only adornment.

Rowena smiled a slow sexy smile that made his pulse race. First things first, he decided putting all thoughts of what was uppermost in his mind firmly out of reach.

Sitting in bed, his thigh resting against hers, Owen raised his glass. "To us," he said reaching across to the bedside table and opening the drawer to remove a small box.

"To us," Rowena echoed. "What's this?"

"It's your Christmas present."

"Really? I was sure you wouldn't have

bothered, as you didn't know I'd be back in time." She took the box and opened the lid.

"This present has been waiting for you for months." He touched her face tracing the outline of her jaw with his fingertip. " Rowena, my darling, will you marry me?" The words, so often rehearsed, seemed strange and awkward on his tongue. He waited for her reply unaware that he was holding his breath. The silent seconds lengthened with every tick of his beside clock.

"I, this is such a surprise. I mean, of course the answer is yes, but I had no idea."

He bent forward and kissed her gently. "Yes, is the only word I needed to hear; we'll discuss the details later. God, Rowena, I've missed you so much."

Breakfast abandoned, they celebrated their engagement with a hunger that could only be satisfied by lovemaking and apart from a desperate dash to the fridge to consume a cold Christmas lunch, the rest of the day followed the same pattern.

Boxing Day dawned with a layer of frost turning London into a sparkling crystallised city whose deserted streets beckoned them. Dressed in warm running suits they pounded the pavements, Rowena's engagement ring gleaming in the crisp morning sunlight.

The City was starting to wake up properly by the time they returned to Owen's flat. It was the day when sports fans up and down the country immersed themselves in their favourite pastimes having spent the previous day fulfilling their family commitments. Normally Owen would have joined his mates at their rugby club on the outskirts of the city before watching the match but nothing would drag him away from Rowena side that day.

She was making them a hot drink in the kitchen when he saw the edge of the package under the sofa. Removing the frame he'd bought for Sarah, he exclaimed, "Shit!"

"What is it?"

"Nothing, I…. sorry - there's something I've got to do urgently. I'll be back in a tick."

He rushed into the spare room he used as a small studio, removed the watercolour from his desk, slid it into the frame and wrapped it in the Christmas paper he'd bought on Christmas Eve. "I've got to pop out for a while; won't be long." He kissed Rowena's cheek.

"No problem, I'll be soaking in the bath and dreaming of our wedding," she replied. "God, Owen, you stink of sweat. Don't be too long my love; I'll keep the water warm for you."

Driving to Sarah's flat Owen couldn't think of how he could apologise. It was unforgivable not to have phoned to let her know he couldn't make Christmas dinner.

He waited for lift to take him to the first floor. Outside her door he stood like a guilty child in the headmaster's study then summoning up his courage, he pressed the bell.

She'd been crying. Her eyes were swollen and red-rimmed. He'd thought he couldn't possibly feel any worse about letting her down but now realised he could. "Sarah, look, please don't close the door. I'm so sorry."

"You had my number. You could have rung." She spoke to him through a gap of three inches refusing to open the door any wider. A stale smell of vegetables, long overcooked drifted towards him and he wondered how long she'd kept the meal hot, waiting for him.

"Please, could you let me in? I need to explain."

"There's no need." She started to shut the door.

"Please, Sarah, please,"

Relenting she stood back to let him pass. Through the dining room door he saw to his horror that the dinner plates containing yesterday's meal still remained untouched. It reminded him of Miss Haversham waiting for the lover that never arrived. She was still wearing her dressing gown. The one she'd worn on the morning he'd slept on the sofa. He took her hand in his.

"It was unforgivable of me. I am truly sorry. My fiancée arrived unexpectedly and the shock of seeing her made put everything else out of my mind. It's no excuse I know but it's the truth."

"Fiancée?" she repeated.

"Rowena. She's agreed to marry me. I'd bought the ring a while back and proposed to her yesterday. That's one of the reasons I forgot about our arrangement."

She raised her eyes to his, her expression unreadable. "I see."

He handed her his gift. "Please accept this, I expect you want to throw it at me but I'd like you to have it."

She didn't open it, just laid it down on a side table.

"I promise I'll make it up to you, Sarah. Perhaps we could get together in the New Year; maybe we could share another meal at Luigi's? " He didn't know why he said it, unless it was because he felt so bad about letting her down.

"That would be nice." It was said in a monotone. "You have my number." She held the door open and as he left, said, "Congratulations."

Afterwards, as he drove home he wondered if he'd ever make good his promise to make it up to her. Somehow he doubted it. He was starting to think that he was destined to let her down.

Chapter 39

Owen's assumption that Rowena's work in the States was finished for the time being was incorrect and it came as a shock to hear that on the second of January she'd be returning to New York to fulfil the rest of her commitments.

"I'm so glad I came back for Christmas," she said twisting her ring towards the light. "At least we have a whole week left to make up for lost time. I should be finished in New York by the end of January then we can discuss our wedding plans."

"I'm going to miss you," Owen hung his head, aware that he was giving her his 'little boy lost look' that she found irresistible.

The week passed in a flash, as he anticipated it would. The day before she was due to leave, Rowena tidied his flat, made an appointment to see her doctor to make sure she had a new supply of Vitamin B6, and stocked his kitchen cupboards and fridge with enough food to last a lifetime. Her doctor had advised her that, although it was possible to buy the vitamins over the counter, he would prefer it if she called in to the surgery for a blood test before each prescription renewal, as he wanted to monitor her condition. However, her anaemia was well controlled, as she was scrupulous in following her doctor's orders.

They drove to her flat on the outskirts of the city to pick up a few additional items for her trip. The flat smelled of abandonment, as it had been empty since September. "I'll have to get rid of this place some time soon," Rowena said absentmindedly straightening the cushions. "Two can live more cheaply than one, I understand."

Sliding his arms around her Owen turned her towards him. "How am I going to exist without you for four whole weeks?" He kissed her neck and then her mouth.

"You'll manage, we'll manage, and then, I promise – they can offer me all the incentives they like – I'll not be tempted, not for a second."

Satisfied, Owen released her to continue her methodical tour of the flat as she placed a few essentials in a black leather bag. Rowena was efficiency personified; she was an employers dream, a beautiful woman with a brain and a deep well of enthusiasm that was bottomless.

They made love that last night as if each were trying to take away part of the other that they would keep until they met again. Owen slept fitfully and during his wakefulness watched her every movement, drinking her in like an alcoholic savouring his last drink.

The next day they said their goodbyes in his

flat and he watched her taxi disappear in the melee of rush hour traffic. For most workers it was the first day back after the Christmas holiday and from his bedroom window Owen saw commuters scurrying like ants around the city. He envied them their purpose. Melancholia hung over him like a shroud, the rest of January stretching interminably into the distance.

He hadn't given Sarah another thought, not since his Boxing Day apology and half- hearted promise of making up for his behaviour. He might never have seen or thought of her again if it hadn't been for Duncan Jones.

Three days after Rowena's departure his telephone rang. Owen rushed to answer it.

"Owen, it's Duncan. I'll have to keep this short and to the point, Megan's about somewhere and I don't want her to hear." He lowered his voice. "How are you fixed at the weekend? Megan is sixty on Saturday and I'm planning to surprise her with a little get together at the house."

Owen hadn't been looking forward to the weekend. He knew he'd have to pull himself together soon but he could still smell Rowena's perfume in every room and his body ached for her. "Yeah, that should be fine."

"Stay over, there's plenty of room and it's not worth you opening up your cottage for one night. Oh, look out, I can hear the Missus on the warpath; seven on Saturday then?"

"I'll look forward to it."

There was no doubt in Owen's mind what gift he would give Megan. She'd loved *September Sun over Gareg Wen* and he was pretty sure that it was still unsold. He rang Mark Furnish and asked him to remove it from sale and that he would pick it up later that day.

When he arrived at the Gallery Mark met him at the door. "Owen, darling, I've just heard from Mailer. Thanks no doubt to a glowing report of your work Nigel Bostock is keen to organise a showing in New York later in the year."

Owen frowned, "Much later I hope."

"Nonsense, sweetie, you've loads of work lying around your studio that you can knock into shape."

"I wish I shared your optimism," he sighed.

"Oh I get it. Rowena's left you again, has she? How long this time?"

"Four weeks."

"Right then, ducky. You are coming to Luigi's with Drew and me tonight. We can't have our favourite artist down in the dumps now can we."

Mark and Drew were waiting for him when he arrived. They'd been a couple for as long as anyone could remember; Drew tall and taciturn with a dead pan wit and Mark shorter, fairer, with a head for business that was not always apparent by his demeanour. In Owen's opinion, they made a perfect pair.

Luigi approached their table.

"Mr Owen, not with the young lady tonight?"

"His lady's left him for a while," Mark explained. "Skipped off to the big apple again three days ago leaving him bereft."

Luigi hesitated. "But that cannot be surely?"

"Why," Owen looked up from his menu.

"'Cos she was in here yesterday having dinner."

Owen caught the sidelong glances exchanged by Mark and Drew.

"You must be mistaken, Luigi."

"I don't think so, she ask for you. She say, 'Have you seen Owen, Luigi?'"

The penny suddenly dropped. "You mean the woman I was with after the exhibition?"

"That's right, Miss Rowena."

The lighting in the restaurant during the evening was always subdued, Luigi's fondness for candlelight had been a joke between them and although the resemblance between the two women was superficial, it was just possible that Luigi had made the mistake of thinking it was Rowena.

"I wasn't with Rowena that night, Luigi; it was a friend," he explained

"I'm sorry but yesterday, as the lady booked the table in the name of Miss Shaw and, as she asked for you, I assumed ...."

Reassuring Luigi that there must have been a mistake, Owen returned to his perusal of the menu with the uncomfortable feeling in his gut that he hadn't seen the last of Sarah Lawson.

Chapter 40

During the drive to Gareg Wen, Owen tried to think of a reasonable explanation as to why Sarah had booked a table at Luigi's using Rowena's name but could think of nothing that made any sense. As he drew nearer the coast the weather deteriorated. A bitter wind howled through the trees lining the road carrying with it a shower of snow. He was grateful for Duncan's offer of a bed for the night, especially as the temperamental heating system in his cottage would take days to reach an ambient temperature having being unused for over a month.

Reaching the sweeping drive at the front of the house, he saw it was heaving with vehicles. He noticed Duncan's four by four and Megan's Mercedes and managed to park alongside an Audi convertible with inches to spare. It seemed to Owen that Duncan's description of 'just a few friends' had escalated, an impression that was confirmed as soon as he stepped into the hall.

"Owen, good to see you, come in, come in." Duncan led him into the room overlooking the coast that sat directly under the Crow's Nest.

It ran the length of the property and, like the room above, had large windows facing the sea. The view was magnificent but not quite as spectacular as from the elevated position that had been his recent workplace.

Megan was talking to a large man with a florid complexion so he raised his hand to her. She beamed, left her companion and walked towards him, "Owen, this is a lovely surprise. It's so good to see you." She swept her arm in a circle. "I had no idea about all this."

"The old man managed to keep it a secret then?"

"He certainly did."

Owen gave her the painting, which was badly wrapped in paper covered with bows and balloons. Megan put her drink down on a side table and gasped as *September Sunlight* was revealed.

"Oh this is too much," she said.

"Not at all, it's my pleasure," Owen said, bending to kiss her cheek. "Happy Birthday, Megan."

"Thank you, my dear, thank you very much." She signalled to a waiter carrying a tray of drinks. "As you see Duncan's thought of everything," she laughed. "Caterers and waiters, good book title that, don't you think? I'd never have thought him capable of such organisation. Now let's see who do you know?" Megan surveyed the room. "Ah yes, follow me."

She led him to a corner where a woman with

pale blonde hair worn in a French pleat was talking to two older women. She had her back to him.

"At least you know, Sarah," Megan said as Sarah Lawson turned to face him.

He couldn't avoid it, he gasped. He'd never have recognised her. It was like looking at his fiancée. The resemblance was inescapable. It was as if she'd studied every feature and replicated it.

"Owen," she said, "good to see you again.

Even her voice sounded different.

"Sarah," he managed to form the words without choking.

Megan grinned. "He likes the transformation, Sarah dear. I can tell. Do enjoy the evening children," she said, as yet another guest arriving demanded her attention.

"Do you?" Sarah asked?"

"What?"

"Do you like my make-over?"

He didn't know how to answer. He thought it was grotesque, a preposterous metamorphosis that couldn't possibly emulate the original. Yet some part of him wanted to hold on to the image in spite of it.

"I, er, it's certainly a surprise," he replied.

She smiled, "You don't have to be kind, darling." The breathless tone of her voice unnerved him. If he closed his eyes it could be Rowena. "I was in town, just after Christmas and feeling a bit downhearted decided to take advantage of an offer in one of the stores."

Remembering the possible reason why she was feeling downhearted and how badly he'd treated her, he said, "You look lovely, Sarah, it was just such a surprise that's all. Now let me get you another drink and you can tell me all about the world of publishing."

He knew he was drinking too much and that part of the reason was sitting in front of him. At midnight he'd even begun to think that he could pretend, if just for a while. By half past two, he'd decided he'd succeeded. Most of the guests, had departed, even the ones who were staying overnight and Megan had long since said goodnight.

"I think it's time we went to bed," she said, looking up at him. He could smell Rowena's perfume. He must be well and truly pissed he thought following her into the room where he was to spend the night.

He awoke to the smell of bacon cooking which made him retch. His head felt as if it didn't belong to him.

"Hangover, darling?" She emerged from the en-suite bathroom wrapped in a towel.

He must still be dreaming, Rowena was in New York, what was she doing in his bedroom? He shook his head as Sarah Lawson came towards him, let the towel fall to the floor and kissed his forehead. "Tablets are on the shelf in the bathroom. I'm going to get dressed. See you downstairs, later."

He closed the bathroom door and leant against it holding his head in his hands. What had happened last night? He couldn't remember. Rowena's face swam before him then Sarah's. He only just managed to reach the pan before vomiting the contents of his stomach into it.

A cool shower, two pain killers and a pint of water later, Owen tentatively left the bedroom and went to join the others at breakfast. Thankfully Sarah was nowhere to be seen.

"You look the worse for wear, my old fellow," Duncan slapped him on the back. "Get some breakfast down you, best thing for a hangover, I've always found."

Duncan was right; he did feel better after breakfast. And there was still no sign of Sarah. Megan joined them as Owen was drinking his second cup of coffee.

"Ah, just the person I wanted to see. Sarah asked me to tell you, she's had to go back to London but she'll be in touch."

He nearly choked as the coffee hit the back of his throat.

"I'm so glad you two hit it off, she's such a nice girl. Works hard too, it's a pity she's in such a dead end job."

Owen looked confused. "Surely an editorial assistant for such a prestigious publishing firm couldn't be called a dead end job?"

Megan snorted. "Where on earth did you get

that idea? Sarah's the office dog's body. She drives all the way down here with my proofs, sweet girl, an invaluable co-ordinator, but she most certainly is not an editorial assistant.

Chapter 41

After his conversation with Megan at breakfast, Owen decided that a walk across the beach would help him to think logically about what had happened. Megan wanted him to stay for Sunday lunch, they were all going to the Anchor, but he made an excuse. A quick walk and then he'd pick up his overnight case and leave before he could make matters worse than they already were. Guilt sat on his shoulders like Pinocchio's conscience even though he didn't have the faintest idea what had happened during the night. However, he didn't need a brush to paint the finer details, Sarah's demeanour had said it all. He wondered how much Megan and Duncan knew.

Leaving the house by the back gate he took the path that led to the beach. He was alone except for a couple of dog walkers. The wind was bitingly cold making his ears ache and his fingers numb as he strode across the sand with every intention of putting as much distance as possible between himself and the events of the previous night.

Gulls screeched overhead then dived towards

the shore where a woman with a black Labrador was throwing bread into the water.

Spots of rain began to fall so lightly at first that he wasn't sure whether it was sea spray. As the shower intensified he jogged towards the cave and sat on the same flattened rock he'd used to sketch the coastline some months earlier.

"At least we're dry in here."

Startled, he turned around to see a shadowy figure sitting in the darkness at the back of the cave, "Sarah?"

"Sorry, if I made you jump. I didn't feel much like breakfast so decided to go back to London. But something made me take one last walk along the beach and as you see the rain started and I ended up here."

Inwardly cursing his stupidity in making for the cave, his anger erupted. "So," he said, "Who are you?"

"I beg your pardon?"

"Well, are you Sarah, the Editorial Assistant of Fox and Knight or are you the Sarah, who booked a table in Luigi's under Rowena's name?"

"What on earth are you talking about?"

When he'd finished explaining, she sighed.

"I see. Firstly, I didn't give you my business card; I gave you a card with my address and home telephone number. The card was conveniently to hand but it was simply a joke."

"Forgive me if I fail to see the humour," he snapped.

"Let me finish. I'm a general office worker, a gofer, if you like, but I love my job and work really hard at it. My co-worker Joe is always telling me to slow down and work at the same pace as the rest of them so, as a joke, he printed a bogus business card from his P.C. then left it on my desk. It was a pure coincidence that it was the first thing that came to hand that morning when we were making plans for Christmas Day."

Feeling distinctly uncomfortable, not only for his outburst but having been given a reminder of his thoughtlessness on Christmas Day, he took a defensive stance and asked again about Luigi's.

"That's a bit of a mystery. I phoned to book a table and they said that the place was full up. So I mentioned that it was a pity because you and I had eaten such a great meal there. As soon as I mentioned your name they said fine. They didn't even take my name. Perhaps the guy I spoke to knew that your girlfriend was Rowena and thought I was she – it sounds to me like a simple case of mistaken identity."

Owen put his head in his hands; he'd been only too ready to think the worst of her and what had she done to deserve it, offered him a bed for the night and a meal on Christmas Day. "I'm so sorry. How can you ever forgive me? It seems that all I do is treat you badly, Sarah, please, again, accept my apologies."

"Of course. Oh look the rain has stopped. Goodbye then, Owen, I must get back to

London, I've got a busy day tomorrow. Perhaps we'll meet again sometime soon."

She hurried away leaving him feeling that this time he really did need to make it up to her. He wouldn't follow her now. He'd give her time to drive away before returning to the house.

During the drive back to London he couldn't stop wondering what must she think of him. He'd insulted her, mistrusted her and made her out to be some kind of nut. Rowena would have told him what she thought of him but of course he couldn't tell Rowena about Sarah now, last night had made that impossible. The roads were quiet; a dismal Sunday afternoon in January wasn't everyone's idea of pleasant driving conditions.

When he arrived at his flat, he poured a large brandy, partly to thaw out and partly for a 'hair of the dog' as his headache had returned with a vengeance. Then as if to make matters worse, as he took a glass from the shelf in the kitchen he noticed Sarah's bogus business card propped up against the tea caddy. He turned the card over taking a last look before he transferred her number to his mobile. Her writing was neat and precise but below her address and telephone number was a logo in the shape of a swan. He held the card closer to inspect it in detail then frowned. Was he being paranoid? The logo was a printer's mark. The card hadn't been printed from an office computer printer, he recognised the firm's mark – a company specialising in stationery had professionally produced it. He remembered that they had business premises next to Rowena's Gym. He hesitated, then after punching in Sarah's details on his phone, threw the card in the bin. He was done with suspicion. He'd just have to trust her.

Chapter 42

New York was hit by the worst winter in decades. Television news reporters stood in snowdrifts announcing that the city had come to a standstill; overnight temperatures had dropped to a bone-chilling twenty below. Rowena told Owen that she couldn't wait to come home at the end of the month and he agreed that, as soon as they were reunited, they'd make plans for their future. In the meantime he worked sporadically, his inspiration, temperamental at the best of times, was now abandoned. Nevertheless, Mailer's positive report on his December collection had produced a certain celebrity status. A reporter from the local rag came to see him with a photographer in order to do a centre spread for the weekend edition followed by a guy from Radio London and then a reporter from the BBC news programme.

Later, he took a call from a representative of one of the smaller, but nevertheless prestigious, art galleries in London who arranged to meet him on Saturday morning.

This time he didn't forget his promise to Sarah. On the Thursday evening she agreed to meet him for dinner. Deciding it might not be the best idea to book Luigi's, Owen picked her up at her flat and drove out of the city to a small pub he knew that provided excellent meals in a convivial atmosphere.

She was waiting outside her flat when he arrived. He briefly wondered how long she'd been standing on the pavement shivering in the cold. She was wearing a black coat not dissimilar to the one Rowena had been wearing when she left for the States at the beginning of the month and he shivered. Every time he saw her, the metamorphosis was becoming more complete.

The Plough and Harrow stood on the banks of the Thames, the river shining like quicksilver in the moonlight. Owen parked the car. "You'll soon warm up; there's always a roaring log fire in the bar in the winter," he assured her as a cold wind swept towards them.

A welcoming buzz of conversation greeted them as he held the restaurant door open and pointed to a table near the fire. "Let me take you coat and I'll fetch the drinks and a menu. White wine is it?"

"Thanks, yes." She smiled and shook her hair loose from the confines of her scarf, exactly as he'd seen Rowena do a thousand times before.

Returning with their drinks, Owen explained

that this time he'd make sure she wouldn't have to give him a bed for the night. He held up his glass of orange juice. "There'll be no drunken bum to put to bed tonight."

"I wouldn't mind if there was," she said, and the memory of the night he'd spent in bed with her slid between them like a spectre, even though his was indistinct.

Over dinner he explained about his forthcoming proposed showing.

"I'm so pleased for you. You deserve to be recognised, too many talented people fall by the wayside. I've seen it happen over and over in publishing as with so many other art forms."

The rest of the evening produced no nasty surprises. He'd not been aware that he'd been on his guard but the conversation flowed easily with no uncomfortable topics surfacing. When the time came to drive Sarah home, he even went so far as to say, "I've enjoyed tonight. We must do it again some time."

"That would be nice." Even her reply was innocent of any guile. The sort of thing friends might say to each other so he didn't see any problem with arranging for them to meet the following Friday.

The next day the temperature in the capital being several degrees warmer than in Gareg Wen and his appointment with Harry Lincoln not until two thirty, he decided to walk the short distance to Covent Garden where he intended to amble around the covered market looking for a little trinket to buy Rowena then grab a bite to eat. He was inspecting a line drawing of the Houses of Parliament, with a jaundiced eye, when he felt a hand on his shoulder.

"Owen?"

Turning around he saw Andy Lawson.

"I thought so. Good to see you again."

Putting the drawing back on the stand, Owen shook Lawson's outstretched hand.

"My sister's been enjoying your company, I understand."

Owen looked confused for a moment.

"Sarah."

He felt his cheeks redden.

"I've been in London on business for a day or two and thought I daren't return home empty handed." Lawson explained.

By this time, they'd walked towards a stand which displayed jewellery behind which sat a young girl, her face framed by clouds of curls as she meticulously added crystals and beads to a length of wire which she twisted into a bracelet. Owen glancing at the display saw a necklace made from pale blue stones, which matched the colour of Rowena's eyes. "How much is that one?" he asked the girl.

She hesitated. "A tenner do, mate?"

She had an Australian accent and her uncertainty as to the price of the item made Owen aware that she was new to the game. He handed her a twenty-pound note. "Keep the change, it's worth it."

"Thanks a bunch."

She seemed genuinely pleased, although whether it was because of the money or the compliment Owen wasn't sure. Andy Lawson picked up a bracelet. "I'll take this. Then I only have the presents to buy for the kids." He turned to Owen. "You think this is kosher?"

"I do; it's unique." He winked at the girl. "Worth twenty of anyone's money, at least. In fact I know someone in Cardiff who'd love to sell this stuff."

Lawson sighed as he handed her the note. "I can see I'm being stitched up here but what the heck!"

Owen picked up one of the business cards from the counter. "I'll pass this to my friend, he'll give you a call I'm sure."

They were starting to move away when a row over the price of goods for sale on a nearby market stall started a fight between a burly man with a stud in his nose and the stallholder. Owen and Lawson intervened, their combined strength managing to restrain the man who mouthed a couple of obscenities, pulled away and rushed off into the crowd.

"Look, I don't know about you but I think I need a stiff drink. What d'you say?" Andy Lawson asked whilst dusting off the arm of his jacket.

" I'm with you on that one."

They walked towards a wine bar as two opera singers began to sing the love duet from La

Boheme. Sitting at a table watching the performers as Rudolfo kissed Mimi's hand, Owen became uncomfortably aware that he knew very little of Sarah Lawson, except the conflicting bits of information that had reached him over the past few days. Now, with her brother sitting opposite him, would seem to be the best time to clear up a few misconceptions but somehow he couldn't bring himself to mention her name.

Chapter 43

His meeting with Harry Lincoln had gone better than he'd expected. Owen had agreed to send him an outline of some of the ideas he was planning for his paintings, which should be ready for a showing sometime later in the year. Lincoln wanted a few representative samples of his work and was willing to place five or six canvases in a prominent position in his gallery

He arrived home at seven o'clock on Sunday evening to find that there were three messages on his answer phone. The first was from Rowena saying she hoped that everything was going well for him in London time and that because of the time difference she was leaving a message, as she wouldn't be able to speak to him until the following afternoon.

The sound of her voice made him long for the weeks to pass until they could be together. The second call was from a contact of his who worked in The Orchard Gallery in Bloomsbury. It seemed he'd heard that Owen was set to break into the American market and The Orchard would be happy to showcase in a representative collection of his paintings and he'd be grateful if he could contact him as soon as possible to discuss the matter. Owen smiled 'breaking into the American market' was a slight exaggeration but one which he intended to capitalise on at every opportunity. He wasn't sure how Mark Furnish would take the news. The smile wavered as he listened to his final message and heard Sarah's voice.

"Owen, it's me, Sarah, I just wanted to wish you all the best for your meeting with Harry Lincoln. I'm going to be busy for a day or two, things are a bit hectic in work at the moment so I don't think I'll be able to see you until Friday. I know you wanted to take me out for a meal but I thought perhaps we could stay in. There are a couple of new recipes I'd like to try out on someone soon and it looks like you're in line to be my guinea pig. See you at half seven on Friday then."

Owen walked over to the sideboard and poured a double measure of brandy into a glass. His hands were shaking. The message from Sarah had rattled him. It was the sort of message Rowena might have left. From where had she got the idea that he wanted to meet her during the week? In addition to which her suggestion that they spend Friday evening at her flat was beginning to sound way too cosy for his liking. He was in a difficult position. He couldn't just stand her up again; after all it was he who had suggested taking her out. He'd have to make an excuse – tell her he couldn't make it. Whilst he was arguing the pros and cons and making no headway with either, the telephone rang.

"Sorry to bother you again. It's Sarah. Just wanted you to know that I've spent the weekend stocking up my fridge for next Friday, as I won't have time to shop mid-week. Everything's organised, menu all planned but then I suddenly thought what if you're allergic to oysters? You're not are you, Owen?"

"Er, no, but look here, Sarah. I…" He didn't know how to finish his sentence. He'd been about to make an excuse but the thought of her sitting alone in her flat eating a meal she'd bought especially for him made him lose his nerve. "No, I'm not allergic to oysters but I don't want you to go to so much trouble, we can always eat out."

"Oh, that's alright then. No trouble, it's my pleasure. By the way, did your meeting go well?"

"Yes thanks. Oh and I met your brother, in Covent Garden."

"Got to go, my mobile's ringing," She replied leaving him wondering why he hadn't heard the sound of a ring tone in the background.

He wasn't looking forward to Friday night; in fact he was dreading it. He decided that this was going to be the last time; he would put a stop to any further meetings between them. It was obvious that Sarah was looking for more than he could give from their relationship. As Friday approached, he wished he'd never suggested that they should meet.

She opened the door to him with a flourish. "Bang on time, do come in." She stood aside and held out her hand. "Give me your coat and go and sit in the warm; the temperature has really dropped. They said on the news that we're due to have the bad weather that's been hitting the States."

Owen sat in an armchair, purposely avoiding the sofa where he'd spent the night. She handed him a glass.

"Champagne?"

"Really? Are we celebrating something?"

"Do we need a reason? OK. let's think of one then. I know let's celebrate our friendship."

He took the glass she'd filled for him and with every sip felt like a man digging his own grave. Sarah didn't seem to notice his discomfort; she flitted between the kitchen and living room, chatting and not giving him the least reason to think that there was anything more sinister behind her invitation.

The meal was delicious and although, as before, conversation flowed easily he still found it difficult to relax. She made no reference to his meeting with her brother, in fact Owen realised that during other conversations the subject of her family had never been raised. He knew very little of her background and what he did know was clouded in a mist of conjecture and misinformation. But he kept telling himself that none of it mattered; he didn't need to see her again after tonight.

To be fair, she'd made the best of the evening. She'd been a perfect host and had gone out of her way to ensure that his glass was filled, the food was to his liking and the atmosphere was light and welcoming. Under other circumstances he would have relaxed and enjoyed himself but this was going to be the last time, he was determined of that. However, a niggling feeling at the back of his mind wouldn't go away. As he gave her a perfunctory kiss on the cheek and thanked her for the evening, he realised what had been bothering him. He was certain that she wouldn't let him go without a fight and the thought terrified him.

Chapter 44

In the taxi, Owen breathed a sigh of relief. That was the end of it; it was over. But he could still feel her fingers stroking his face as he'd thanked her for the evening and planted a brotherly air-kiss on her cheek before leaving. He could also still smell her perfume on his clothes, it was Mischief, Rowena's favourite, and he wondered whether that was by pure coincidence or something more. She hadn't made a fuss either, when he'd said that he and Rowena were in the throes of planning their wedding and he hoped she'd understand and that it would be impossible for him to meet her again.

He slept fitfully that night; his dreams plagued by a woman, who was a mixture of both Sarah and Rowena dragging him towards a bed of quicksand. He awoke with relief, showered the worst of the dream away and was sitting in his kitchen watching the early morning news when the telephone rang.

"Hello, Owen, I'm sorry to ring you so early,

old man." It was Duncan Jones. "I think you ought to come down to Fallow's End right away. There's been a fire; it's your cottage I'm afraid."

Driving to the coast Owen put all thoughts of Sarah Lawson out of his mind. If she had some sort of crush on him, she'd soon get the message that he wasn't interested. He'd left a text message on Rowena's phone to let her know that he wouldn't be home to take her call but would ring later; he didn't mention the fire, just said he was visiting Megan and Duncan and thought he might stay over for a day or two. Duncan was waiting for him in the Anchor. He wanted to show him the damage personally and thought it might be a good idea if Owen had a drink before they made their way to the cottage.

"That bad, is it?" Owen asked raising his glass.

"It's not good. No one noticed until the fire was well underway, it's a bit far down the lane for anyone to see it clearly from the village, as you know. But apparently Arthur Conroy was walking his dog along the dunes and noticed the smoke."

"I see."

Duncan hadn't been exaggerating; the cottage was little more than a shell, the thick stonewalls of the original structure being all that remained intact. The roof had collapsed and the wooden veranda reduced to a pile of charcoal. Owen ran his fingers through his hair. "Thank God for insurance – this will take some re-building. Luckily I'd removed the canvases. I wonder what started it?" He walked the perimeter in hope of enlightenment.

Duncan frowned. "I had a word with Gordon Thomas."

"Who?"

"Chief Fire Officer Thomas. He said that there would have to be a formal enquiry but he suspected arson."

"Good grief. Who would want to burn this place down? What on earth would be the point? I'm not aware of having ruffled anyone's feathers locally."

Duncan stroked his chin. "We may never know the reason – apparently arsonists are a breed apart. They do it for the thrill, I understand. But there have been no Welsh language activists in this part since the seventies." He put a hand on Owen's shoulder. "You'll stay with us?"

"I'd be grateful, thanks. I'll need to sort out this lot and have a word with the fire officer but I promise it won't be for more than a day or two."

"Stay as long as you like. We'll be glad to have you. Megan is always restless when a book has been completed. I think she's tied up today, someone from the publishing house is coming down to pick up the last batch of proofs but after that she's as free as a bird. Anyway, when you've finished up here come on over to the house."

Duncan told him that the fire officers had made a thorough sweep of the interior early that morning but the area was still cordoned off.

The upstairs, where his studio had been, no longer existed. The charred mass at his feet bore no resemblance to anything he could identify.

The sky was beginning to cloud over as Owen drove back into the village and took the road leading to the main fire station on the outskirts of the nearest town. Gareg Wen was too small and insignificant to warrant a fire service of its own, especially as the main depot was less than five miles away.

Chief Fire Officer Thomas stood up as Owen entered his office.

"Mr Madoc, what a business," he said indicating a chair. "Sit down, please."

"Duncan Jones told me that you suspect arson." Owen came straight to the point.

The man hesitated. "In my experience of such things, at first sight, yes, but you must understand the lab has to give us the results before I can confirm it."

"I understand. But surely you must have some idea?" Owen raised his eyebrows. "Just give me your opinion, off the record of course."

Gordon Thomas gave a wry smile. "It's my considered opinion that there is no doubt that someone started the fire up at your place, Mr Madoc. As you say, I've been around a long time, I recognise the signs. Is there anyone you can think of who might have had a reason to commit such a crime?"

"I've been trying to think of an answer to that one on my way over here but I'm at a loss to know why anyone would do such a thing."

"Once we can confirm our suspicions we'll be handing the details over to the police and when they've finished their enquiries you should be free to plan re-building in tandem with your Insurance Company. That is of course once they've established the fact that *you* were in no way to blame for starting the fire."

"That's not difficult as I was in London at the time," Owen replied.

"Got an alibi all ready I see, Mr Madoc?" Gordon Thomas quipped as he opened the door.

Leaving the Fire Station, Owen suddenly realised that the only person who could provide him with an alibi was Sarah Lawson.

Chapter 45

Entering the public bar of the Anchor, Owen was greeted by an avalanche of sympathy. The landlord had a pint waiting for him on the bar and the vicar told him that the church was always open should he need to talk things over with his maker. Duncan beckoned Owen to join him. "How did things go with Gordon?"

Sitting alongside Duncan on a bar stool Owen outlined his discussion with the Fire Chief."

"Good God, he wasn't serious about you providing an alibi, I hope."

Owen raised his glass. "No, but it looks like I'll have to provide one for the police, once they've established that the fire was started deliberately."

"But what would be the point of you torching your own place?"

"For the insurance, I suppose. It's been done before."

"Have you eaten?" Duncan picked up a menu from the bar.

"No."

"Right then let's join the vicar and make an afternoon of it. He was just telling me about a fishing trip he's organising along the coast."

The rest of the afternoon passed in convivial company until the landlord decided he'd had enough of them. "Off home with you all now lads, me and my missus need to put our feet up for an hour or two before the tea time crowd arrive."

Duncan grinned. "He always makes the same crack knowing the tea time crowd is likely to be just us and the post mistress."

Outside Owen realised he'd had far too many beers to drive. "I'll leave my car here and walk over the fields to your place."

"As you like, I'll meet you later, there's a book I have to pick up from the vicarage first."

Walking down the lane to a stile that led into the fields bordering the cliff path, Owen heard the sound of a car approaching. Flattening his body against the hedge, he felt the twigs dig into his back. He held his breath somehow knowing that it would be her. When she drew level with him she stared straight ahead, not acknowledging his presence, and he was left with his hand half raised in greeting. Feeling like a fool, he watched the car disappear in the distance and was certain she was watching him in her rear view mirror. What was she doing in Gareg Wen? Had she followed him? He considered the possibilities but managed somehow to avoid the obvious.

Megan was in the garden when he arrived. "I saw you crossing the fields. You've just missed

Sarah, she came down to pick up my proofs."

"I thought it was her car. Duncan's stopped off at the vicarage."

"I know, he's just phoned. When those two get together time stands still. Come in out of the cold and I'll put the kettle on."

Sitting opposite him at the kitchen table cradling a mug of tea, Megan said, "I was so sorry to hear about your cottage. Duncan told me Gordon thinks it's arson?"

"Looks like it." Owen lifted his mug to his lips. "Yes, well I expect he also told you that I might be called upon to produce an alibi for myself."

"Ridiculous."

"Quite," Owen agreed.

"Can you?"

"Provide and alibi? Yes." He frowned. "Bit tricky. I was with Sarah actually. She'd invited me to her flat for a meal."

"What's tricky about that? She'll confirm it and that will be that. Or are you worried about Rowena finding out where you spent the evening?"

"It's not that. You see, I made it more than plain to Sarah that I wouldn't be seeing her again, even as a friend. The thing is. I'd begun to suspect that she might be making more of our relationship than it actually was.

"Really?"

"Why do I get the impression you don't agree?"

"None of my business."

"Megan?"

She hesitated before replying. "Well, let's put it this way. The night you both stayed over after my party there was only one set of sheets that needed washing. But as I said before it's none of my business."

Owen shook his head. "I know what it looks like but I can assure you, as far as I'm aware nothing happened – I was too rat-arsed, to coin a phrase."

Megan stood up and walked to the window. "Sarah's such a vulnerable creature, Owen; I wouldn't like to see her hurt."

"That's just the point. It's why I had to make things clear to her once I realised that she was making more of it."

The front door slammed in the wind as Duncan blew in bringing with him a selection of dead leaves and caked mud.

"Put those boots in the outhouse at once, Duncan Jones," Megan said, then turning to Owen added, "the man's incorrigible."

The topic of conversation had been diverted by Duncan's sudden arrival and Owen was grateful for the intrusion.

The following day the local police force arrived in the shape of Constable Bryn Williams. Megan, Duncan and Owen were sitting in the room where the party had been held, which now seemed like a lifetime away.

"How's Jean, Bryn? Tell her to give me a call. The book's finished and I'm ready for a bit of female conversation."

"I will, Megan. I'll be sure to tell her as soon as I get home."

"Right then, I think Duncan and I might have some pressing business in the kitchen. Duncan, let's give Owen and Bryn some privacy."

Bryn Williams looked uncomfortable as he opened his pocket book. "It's about the fire up at your place, Mr Madoc. The Fire Department has let it be known that arson is suspected, so naturally we have to make some enquiries regarding the matter."

Owen could see that the man felt awkward no doubt partly because when they'd last met they'd spent an afternoon enjoying the hospitality in the Anchor to such an extent that they'd both become the best of friends for an hour or two.

"I understand, Constable." Owen replied, taking his queue from Bryn, who'd addressed him formally.

"Can you provide us with an alibi for the night in question?"

It was a reasonable enough request but Owen didn't have the first idea how to answer it.

Chapter 46

Chief Fire Officer Thomas's investigating team had established that the fire had probably been started between five and six a.m. ruling out the necessity for Owen to produce an alibi. It hadn't taken him long to inform the police that Mr Duncan Jones could confirm that he'd rung him at his flat at a quarter to seven and that there would have been no possibility of him reaching Gareg Wen and travelling back to London within such a short time frame; the details of the phone call could be traced via his phone record, if necessary.

After the Insurance Company had been advised of proceedings, a convenient appointment was arranged for one of their assessors to meet Owen at the remains of his cottage the following Friday. Duncan and Megan had insisted that he spend the rest of the week with them and he'd gratefully agreed. There was nothing dragging him back to London and he welcomed the thought of putting as much distance as possible between himself and Sarah Lawson.

Walking along the beach one morning, when

the tide had receded leaving behind a bank of hard sand drying in the sun, he considered who would have had a reason to start the fire. It wasn't until he reached the cave that he realised that there was one person who definitely had a motive. He remembered seeing her emerging from the back of the cave on the morning after Megan's party. There was something decidedly odd about her behaviour, something as tenuous as gossamer was slipping through his fingers and for the life of him he couldn't catch it.

Her motive could have sprung from anger, jealousy and rage after his conversation with her during the meal at her flat and which was cut short by his speech about not having time to see her again, even as a friend. He could understand it; she'd gone out of her way to make a pleasant evening for him and he'd repaid her with a metaphorical slap in the face; but to start a fire?

The question remained, would she have been sufficiently annoyed to warrant a frantic dash down to Gareg Wen with the precise intention of starting the fire? Then he remembered her saying that she would be busy that week. She must already have been planning to take the proofs down to Megan. It was therefore a feasible proposition that she could have travelled down in the early hours, started the fire and afterwards arrived at the Megan's place mid-morning as if nothing had happened.

Watching the tide turn in the bay he became certain that it was she who was responsible; it made perfect sense. However, he lacked the necessary proof and knew that he couldn't mention his suspicions to anyone. It was all too complicated and besides he had to admit that his feelings of guilt at the way he'd treated her made him feel partly responsible.

When Friday arrived, he met the Insurance Assessor as planned. Alan Morris was a wiry man in his early forties with greying hair and ponderous manner. He made copious notes on a pad as he inspected the property then turned to Owen. "I'll make my report and the Company will advise you of the result." He was a man a few words.

"Any idea how long that will take?" Owen asked as the Assessor walked towards his car.

He shrugged. "Four to six weeks approximately, it depends on the amount of work we have at present and the availability of the latest reports from the police and fire brigade - shouldn't be much longer, in my opinion."

Watching his car disappear in the distance Owen took a last look around the remains of his cottage before closing the garden gate, which had been left remarkably intact. He'd walked across the fields from Duncan's house and was about to return the same way when something in the hedge caught his eye.

Devoid of its summer foliage it was now a thicket of intertwining twigs and brambles against which the wind had deposited a few plastic carrier bags and the odd scrap of paper. But lodged on the end of a sharp twig was a scrap of material, insignificant in itself, but one, which Owen thought looked familiar. Removing it and placing it in his palm he examined it more closely. It was a tiny scrap of purple and pink patterned silky material torn from something much larger. Sarah Lawson had been wearing a scarf of the same material the night they'd dined at Luigi's. He'd commented that he'd thought the colour suited her. Now he was certain as to the identity of the arsonist and equally certain he could do nothing about it. Holding the scrap of material up to the wind he watched it float high into the air along with his conscience as a gust carried it over the fields to the coast.

Later, having thanked Duncan and Megan for their hospitality and promising not to leave it too long before returning to Gareg Wen, he drove back to London with the express purpose of putting the whole sorry incident behind him. He could hear Rowena's voice telling him that he'd asked for it, a sentiment with which he wholeheartedly agreed.

The central heating in his flat having been switched to the timer, Owen anticipated a warmer welcome than he actually received. The rooms were chilly due partly to the fact that the heating switch had been knocked to the off position and partly because two of the windows stood wide open. Owen shivered and leaned forward to close them. What was going on? He might have made an error with the heating switch but he was certain that he'd shut the windows before he left. In fact he hardly ever opened them during the winter months, preferring to keep the bitter winds firmly at bay.

Bewildered and confused he picked up the telephone and rang the security warden's desk on the ground floor. Jack Moorcraft kept a watch on the place at weekends; it wasn't a permanent arrangement, the flats, not being 'posh' enough to warrant a permanent concierge. Nevertheless Jack was a reliable sort who took his work seriously and if he'd been on duty Owen was sure nothing unusual would have escaped his notice.

"Jack, yes hello; it's Owen Madoc here, flat number 16. I wonder if you could help me?"

"What is it, Mr Madoc?"

"I've been away for the past week and I wondered if you'd noticed anyone hanging around my place."

"No, sir, I've been at my desk most days this week as my old lady's off visiting her sister in Glasgow and I had some spare time on my hands."

"So nothing unusual then? It's just that I felt someone had been in my flat when I was away. Some windows were left open."

"Nothing unusual, sir, no. Your girlfriend called sometime midweek. She had some food for your freezer, she said."

"My girlfriend?"

"Yes sir, the lady with the lovely blonde hair."

Chapter 47

Owen put the phone down and sank into an armchair. How had she got in? She must have had a key cut. He closed his eyes then thumped his forehead with his palm. She could have made an impression of his keys anytime she chose. There had been more than one occasion when he'd drunk more than he should. Cursing himself for what an idiot he'd been, he vowed yet again to steer clear of the brandy bottle, which he recognised had played a significant part in the events of the last couple of weeks. He switched on the kettle and made a mug of strong black coffee then rang a locksmith.

Later, he made a systematic search of his flat. The thought of her opening drawers, examining photographs and delving into his private life gave him the creeps. Rowena's last letter was on his bedside table, the rest stored in the drawer underneath; he couldn't be sure but he thought. one or two of them might be missing. In the spare room that he used as a small studio, three finished canvases stood on the floor against the wall, thankfully they looked intact but on the table where he kept his notebooks and sketchpad he was sure he'd left the last batch of sketches he'd made at Gareg Wen. They were missing. Owen walked around his flat in a daze. The mess he was in was of his own making and there was nothing he could do about it without having to admit his part in it to Rowena.

After the locksmith changed the locks and had given him the new key, Owen removed the old one from his key ring and replaced it. Whether the action prompted an association of ideas or not he suddenly remembered the duplicate keys to Rowena's flat that he kept in his bedside table. He broke out in a cold sweat. He knew that Sarah had looked in that drawer and removed one, if not more of Rowena's letters; she must have seen the keys.

In the bedroom, he pulled open the drawer and threw it on the bed. The keys were missing. Owen sank to his knees at the side of the bed and pressed his face into the folds of the duvet. He knew now was the time he should ring the police, but how could he – it was all supposition – he had no proof that Sarah had entered his flat, he couldn't even be certain that the letters were missing – he could have mislaid them and as to the missing keys, there was nothing to prove that he hadn't misplaced those either.

He stood up; what would she do to Rowena's flat? He had to get over there right away. As he drove across the city, visions of Sarah cutting up Rowena's clothes, destroying, and generally trashing the place vied for supremacy. Pulling into the car park he looked up at her window.

Her flat was on the top floor of the block with an uninterrupted view of the park. At least flames weren't leaping out of the upstairs window, he thought, entering the foyer.

"Too late, Mr Madoc, you've just missed her." The concierge gave him a rueful smile. "In a bit of a hurry too, if I'm not mistaken."

"I beg your pardon," Owen replied fearing the worst.

"Miss Shaw, I saw her leaving not ten minutes since. She didn't even have time to stop for a chat, most unlike her."

"I've forgotten my keys, Tom, Miss Shaw asked me pick something up for her and I wondered if you'd be able to let me in," Owen said.

"No problem, just give me a moment, and I'll be with you."

After Tom had opened the door with his master key, Owen waited until he heard the lift door close then entered the small hallway. The first thing he noticed was the smell – it was Rowena's perfume and it was fresh. In the living room, everything was as usual; nothing seemed to be out of place. His heart rate slowed to something approaching normal. In the bathroom he opened the cupboard above the sink, checked the bath, the shower, no damage in either. Then he opened the bedroom door. The smell of her perfume was stronger in here. He felt certain that Sarah wouldn't have been able to avoid looking in the wardrobe. He opened the door.

The smell nearly knocked him backwards. Every item of clothing had been doused with her perfume; the empty bottle lay on the wardrobe floor. Owen covered his nose with his handkerchief, picked up the bottle, slipped it into his pocket and flung the doors wide. Rowena wasn't expected home for a week or two, the smell should have dispersed by then and the emptied perfume bottle could easily be replaced. Next he rang the locksmith. He would explain to Rowena that he'd lost his keys and as a precaution had the locks replaced.

When the man arrived, he looked at Owen as if he was insane. "Make a habit of losing your keys do you, sir?"

"Something like that. Is it a problem?" Owen asked.

"Nah. All in a day's work to me, mate."

Driving back to his place, he sighed with relief, perhaps this would be the end of it. The locks on both flats had been changed. He'd broken all ties with Sarah Lawson; he could thank his lucky stars that nothing worse had happened. Rowena would be home in two weeks time and he couldn't wait.

At six o'clock that evening he received a telephone call from an art dealer in New York, who wanted to know if he had any completed work for sale. Owen thought of the three finished canvases in his studio and confirmed that he did.

"Well, that's just fine. I don't suppose you'd like to bring them over. I'd make it worth your while."

"Certainly." He felt his spirits begin to lift. "I'll make the arrangements and get back to you." At last he felt he could forget the whole sorry mess of the past few days. He was on his way to New York. He'd see Rowena sooner that he'd expected and he couldn't wait.

Chapter 48

She met him at J.F.K International airport and as he kissed her he smelled her perfume. Bile rose up in his throat.

"What is it, darling?" Rowena took a step backwards.

"Nothing, just a bit tired. Give me a moment to recover, I've been dozing on and off throughout the flight."

She slid her arm through his. "This is such a great surprise. I can't believe that you're here. I've missed you so much."

"Me too. I've spent weeks counting down the hours and now I can relax at last." Owen handed her a small package.

"What's this?"

"I picked it up on the plane. One of the air hostesses was wearing it and I thought you might like a change from your usual brand."

Rowena opened the paper bag and exclaimed, "Perfume, how lovely."

"I hope you like it. Of course you don't have to wear it. I just thought …." He hesitated not wanting to appear too eager for her to accept the change.

"No, that's fine. It will be nice to try something different. I'll wear it tonight."

Owen was more relieved than he could imagine. He believed that he would never again inhale the scent of Mischief without thinking of Sarah Lawson. He shuddered at the thought.

"Are you sure you're OK?" Rowena asked.

"I soon will be. Once we're alone." Owen kissed her cheek as they stepped into a taxi.

Two days later, the New York art critics were calling Owen the brightest talent to emerge from the U.K. in recent years. Buyers, wanting to own an original, besieged the Gallery where his paintings were being shown and the television news reporters descended on him like vultures picking over every scrap of information they could find. A young woman reporter from Sky News was the last of the flock to interview him, insisting that his fiancée join him in order that they could film the two of them together while they discussed their forthcoming marriage. "It's an angle; our viewers love romance. Celebrity loves a good wedding," she explained as she asked Owen to slide his arm around Rowena's waist.

The interview began with the usual questions about his work and his future plans regarding his next showing. Would he be spending his time working exclusively in the U.K. or had he thought about setting up a studio in the U.S. Then the questions changed emphasis to their forthcoming wedding and Rowena's ideas on the subject.

"We hope to marry as soon as possible," she said, looking at Owen for confirmation.

"The sooner the better," he added smiling into the camera lens.

"Cut, that's great. This will go out on the late evening news stateside and in your country at breakfast time. Thank you both for your time; oh and good luck with the wedding."

At the end of the week following the interview Owen and Rowena were on a plane heading home. The scent of Mischief no longer in his nostrils Owen began to hope that their new life together would be free from the ghost of Sarah Lawson. Surely she'd get the message when she saw the news of their wedding, which apparently had made the headlines in most of the tabloids. His phone hadn't stopped ringing since and he was uncomfortably aware that there might be more reporters waiting for them once they landed.

Making their way through the arrivals gate at Heathrow they were soon met by a small group of reporters. "I wonder how long we'll have to suffer this, before they get fed up and move on to another poor soul," Owen said, pasting on a smile for the cameras.

"Just grin and bear it, my love. Think of it as money rolling into your bank account. No publicity is bad publicity remember."

How could he know then that those words

would come back to haunt him?

Rowena insisted that the taxi drop her off at her flat. "I need to unpack, tidy up, etc. Give me a day or two then we'll get together and think about where we'd like to live and which property we should put on the market first. I'll ring you tomorrow, after we've caught up with the jet lag." She kissed him and waved as she stepped into the foyer.

Owen could see Tom, the concierge, rushing forward to pick up her bags as his suggestion to see her inside had been met with the words – 'You look done in, I'm a big girl now remember, go home and get to bed.'

His flat was reassuringly much as he'd left it. His answer phone bleeped the red light flashing 16. He groaned and pressed the button. The first call was from the London Gazette requesting an appointment. A few similar calls followed; a hospital radio station, the local television news, Mark Furnish and a couple of well-wishers. By now the red light flashed 9. The rest of the calls were from her, although she left no message. It was beginning to look as if his worst fears were about to be realised. Once he'd cleared his head and resurfaced after a good sleep, he'd change his telephone number, something he should have done weeks ago.

Surprisingly, he slept without interruption until eight o'clock the following evening when he heard his mobile ringing on his bedside table.

It was Rowena.

"I thought I'd ring your mobile then you could see it was me. No doubt reporters have been pestering you? Did you sleep well, my darling?"

"Yeah, and you?"

"Not really. But I'm used to that. It will take me a day or two to adjust. I've been unpacking and generally sorting things out. You know what I'm like – always a bit hyper after a long flight."

Owen groaned.

"I know you're thinking, you'll soon cure me of that. As I said, I've been sorting through a few things. I don't suppose you've seen that necklace you bought me from Covent Garden have you? I was sure it was on my dressing table. I usually keep it on that porcelain ring hand because I love the way the light catches the glass beads. But now it appears to be missing."

Owen sat up. "Anything else missing?" he asked.

"Er, no, I don't think so. You sound worried? What's the matter? You don't think someone broke in to steal my necklace do you?" She sounded incredulous. "It's lovely and you know I adore it but it's not Cartier."

He took a deep breath. "No of course not. I'm still a bit sleepy that's all. Don't take any notice. And don't worry about the necklace, I'm sure it will turn up."

Replacing his phone Owen thumped his fist

on the bedside table making his mobile jump.

He knew exactly where Rowena's necklace was and he was certain who'd be wearing it.

Chapter 49

The week passed in a hectic rush of appointments and it was four days later that Owen realised he'd done nothing about changing his telephone number, partly because his contact list was long and partly because there had been no further calls from Sarah Lawson.

Rowena was working flat out, as, having secured the American contract she was formulating advertising procedures and arranging corporate lunches for the executives involved. There had been little time to concentrate on wedding plans but she'd promised him that she'd take time out at the weekend to inspect a couple of possible venues that he'd managed to line up. Neither of them favoured a church wedding preferring to combine both events in one place.

They met up after Rowena finished work on Friday evening and dined at a restaurant tucked away in a back street that served excellent food and afforded a certain amount of anonymity for which Owen was grateful having found his sudden celebrity status unnerving.

"It will pass," Rowena assured him. "The hype will soon die down."

"You think?"

Rowena laughed. "Lie back and enjoy it."

"Is that an offer?"

"I don't see why not."

Owen lifted her hand from the tablecloth and kissed each finger. As he raised his head his eyes strayed to the street. Sarah Lawson was standing on the pavement facing him. She held his glance until he looked away without acknowledging her presence.

"Owen? Whatever is it?"

Rowena turned to see what had taken his attention. He held his breath and looked again. But the street was empty. Fearing that paranoia was setting in, he decided that the sooner they arranged their wedding, the better.

The next day he picked Rowena up at her flat at ten thirty. They had a busy day ahead of them but he was optimistic that they would find a suitable venue for their wedding before the end of the day.

Rowena answered the door to him saying, "I won't be a minute. Do you know, I was sure I had a spare bottle of my vitamins in the bathroom? I remember picking up the prescription before I went away, now it looks as if I'll have to give the surgery a ring on Monday and get them to issue a new one. I was certain it was in the cabinet. Come here, look, you can see the space where I left it." She frowned and shook her head in bewilderment.

Owen, inspecting the shelf, saw that there

was a definite outline of a circle left in the fine layer of powdered dust. But why would Sarah remove the bottle of vitamins? What did she hope to achieve? Unanswered questions swirled around in his head like an icy wind. "Strange," was all he managed to utter.

"Never mind, let's get going. I'll sort it out on Monday." Rowena took his arm. "Excited?" she asked.

Owen swallowed. "Of course," he said.

"Well, let's go then. Hang on a minute." She bent down to pick up an envelope from the mat. "The post is early. I'll have to open this one, it's from a firm of solicitors."

Perching on the arm of the chair he watched Rowena's facial expression change from one of curiosity to pure joy.

"This day just get's better by the minute. Look!" She handed him the letter. "I didn't realise I still had an Aunt Fiona, apart from a vague recollection of Dad talking about her when I was young, I thought she'd died years ago. Now it seems I'm her sole beneficiary."

"I shouldn't get too excited, she's probably left you a moth-eaten moggy to look after."

Rowena smiled. "I'm sure you're right. I'll give them a ring later. Come on then, let's get started."

The first two places on their list were unprepossessing and they hastily struck them off with a flourish. But the third, The Celtic

Cross Manor House, had definite possibilities. Brandon Harrison, the wedding planner and event arranger was a Scot whose mother was from Ohio. He spoke with an affected American burr that failed to disguise his Glaswegian roots. Somehow both Owen and Rowena found him endearing and soon fell into the swing of things, carried along on a wave of enthusiasm that appeared to be genuine, as Brandon extolled the advantages of marrying in a Manor House of such distinction.

Inspecting the overnight accommodation some time later, Rowena decided that the honeymoon suite was elegant and romantic enough for her wedding night and Owen seeing the sparkle in her eyes agreed.

It was six thirty when they drove down the winding drive leading to the main road having booked the Manor for the twenty seventh of May, which gave them nearly four months to send invitations, buy the wedding dress, arrange cars, etc., ready for the big day.

Rowena sighed. "Next week I'll persuade Noreen to trawl around the bridal departments for a dress."

"I'm guessing Noreen won't take much persuading. When's she emigrating by the way?" Owen asked, steering the car into the overtaking lane on the motorway. The headlights of the car travelling behind him flashed momentarily in his rear view mirror as the vehicle followed him in the overtaking lane then slid in behind him. Owen's heart began to beat wildly. He risked another longer look in his mirror and was certain he hadn't been mistaken. He increased his speed overtaking a lorry carrying food for online supermarket deliveries then overtook a coach and a family car travelling at speed.

"July. Mike starts his new job in Sydney in August. What's the hurry?"

"Nothing, just getting a bit peckish, that's all. Let's not bother with dining out. Why don't we pick up a take-away?"

"Suit's me. Just get us there in one piece," Rowena replied.

Owen put his foot down on the accelerator, his speedometer reaching ninety-five. The car behind fell back. He kept in the fast lane until his exit appeared then slowed his speed to seventy and slipped into the inside lane at the last possible minute. Rowena didn't comment but he could see her giving him an enquiring look that he chose to ignore.

When he was certain that he'd given his follower the slip, he settled down to a steady speed. However, as he turned on to the dual carriageway leading to the city he saw her again. Her car was sitting behind a four by four that was directly behind him. Sarah Lawson was tenacious, of that there was no doubt. But it was becoming obvious to Owen that he'd have to do something about this and sooner rather than later. She was stalking him and there was nothing left but for him to confront her face to face.

Chapter 50

As he drove to the Indian Take Away, Sarah's car was thankfully nowhere in evidence but the experience had unnerved Owen and he was even more determined to put a stop to it once and for all. Rowena slept at his place overnight but left after lunch the following day as she wanted to drive to her friend Noreen's house in the suburbs. With the rest of Sunday free, he drove to Sarah Lawson's flat. His anger at her behaviour increasing as he drove through the city's streets; he wondered what her reaction would be? He was certain that she'd entered Rowena's flat in her absence and that she'd removed the vitamins from her bathroom cabinet also taken the necklace. Similarly her presence on the motorway had prompted him to place her firmly in the category of a stalker, if not a complete nutcase.

When he arrived at her block, he took the stairs two at a time not bothering to wait for the lift to arrive. With a balled fist he banged on her front door; Andy Lawson opened it. "Hello. Good to see you again. Come in." The man didn't seem in the least bit surprised to see him.

Owen followed him into a room where the rest of the Lawson family were seated. The children were watching a cartoon on television and Hannah Lawson was reading the paper.

"Sarah, it's Owen."

She came into the room carrying a tray on which stood three mugs of coffee. Her hair, he noticed, was now the same colour, as her sister-in-law's, a dark brown but somehow the resemblance to Rowena lingered.

"Hi, Owen, I wondered if you'd find time to pop in. Andy's just been singing your praises."

"I have indeed. Indigo Night has become quite an investment, thanks to you. Now tell me, what's this I hear about your latest success in New York?"

Owen recognised that he was trapped. There was nothing he could do about it. He couldn't make his accusations, not in front of her family. Her brother kept asking him about his work, which he answered with a fixed expression that veered from deadpan to vaguely interested. He couldn't stop his gaze wandering to Sarah, who was now playing a board game with the older child. He was at his wits end to know how to deal with the situation, when her brother stood up.

"Right then, kids, pack up your things. We must be off, leave you two lovebirds alone. I've taken up far too much of Owen's time as it is."

He waited until the door closed behind them then said angrily, "Lovebirds? I think you have some explaining to do."

"In what way?"

She was cool; he had to give her that.

"What way do you think?" His anger was resurfacing. "You've been following Rowena and me around, you gained entrance to her flat, and removed items and I'm beginning to suspect you started a fire in my cottage at Gareg Wen. How's that for openers?"

She walked past him to the window and raised her hand to wave. "Andy would be furious if he could hear you talking to me like that."

"Is that a threat? Perhaps you'd like me to explain to him what you've been up to?"

She turned to face him. "You made me believe that you cared for me." She lowered her head and the fight went out of him.

"Look, Sarah, I'm sorry if I've given you the wrong impression. I thought we were mates. You were kind enough to give me a bed for the night but that's all it was."

She looked up at him. "What about after Megan's party?"

He shook his head. "I don't remember. I was drunk. I don't remember any of it."

She began to cry; silent sobs that made her shoulders shake and squeezed tears from her eyes. "It was the best night of my life," she said. He put an arm around her shoulders, aware that this was not how he'd planned it should be.

"I apologise. I didn't mean to hurt you, but

you must understand, I love Rowena and we are getting married in a few months time. There was never anything between us and I'm sorry if you thought so."

She turned then, her eyes blazing with fury, banging her fists against his chest she said, "Get out; go on, get out."

Driving back to his flat he felt bad about the whole situation, which he'd mishandled. He hadn't meant to lead her on; after all, he'd never said he had any feelings for her. It all seemed to centre on that night at Megan and Duncan's and he couldn't for the life of him recall any of the details, but at least he'd put her straight now, he thought parking his car and returning to his flat.

As he put the key in his front door it occurred to him that he was still no nearer finding out whether it was she who'd started the fire in Gareg Wen. Her tears had effectively stopped any further questioning on his part. However, she'd obviously given her family the impression that there was an intimate relationship between them. Surely Lawson had seen the newspaper and television reports about his forthcoming wedding?

Owen poured a double measure of whiskey into a glass, sat down and picked up the Sunday paper that Rowena had been reading earlier. On the society and arts pages was an item about his recent trip to New York and his wedding plans. The photo accompanying the piece showed himself and Rowena smiling at the camera. He was facing the lens but Rowena was turned slightly away. He read the report noting with dismay that Rowena was simply referred to as his fiancée and at no point was her name mentioned. He seemed to remember that previous reporters had been also interested in the story of his recent success rather than in Rowena herself.

With a sinking feeling he inspected the photograph more closely and was distressed to see that there was a distinct resemblance between the photograph of Rowena and Sarah's previous re-incarnation. The woman was like a chameleon. The image in newspaper could have belonged to either of them.

Chapter 51

Mark Furnish arranged to meet Owen at eleven-thirty in the wine bar at the corner of the road near his gallery. He was waiting at the bar when Owen arrived. "I've got a proposition to put to you." He carried the drinks over to a table near the window. "How do you fancy putting in a couple of weeks work on a mural I'm commissioning for the Gallery? It's to be a compilation work by our more prominent clients, into which category you most definitely fall."

"Flattery always works, Mark, as well you know."

"Well?"

"I don't see why not. Weddings are expensive businesses, I can't afford to turn down work at the moment."

"Oh yeah?"

"Yeah. Wives are even more expensive, or so I've been told."

As if on cue, Owen's mobile rang. It was Rowena, "I've just received a letter from the solicitors dealing with Aunt Fiona's will. Apparently it's correct, I am the sole beneficiary.

What d'you think of that?"

"Sole beneficiary? Don't get too excited; remember that moth-eaten moggy."

"You could be right. Anyway, I've arranged to see them tomorrow to discuss the details."

Owen put the phone down and raised his glass. "To Rowena's Aunt Fiona," he said.

The phone call came when Owen was sketching a few ideas for the mural. Mark had assured him that it would only take a week or two, which was why he'd agreed. Rowena would be busy and it made sense to keep a low profile considering recent events. She could hardly speak with excitement. "Darling, no moth-eaten moggy after all. It's a house and ninety thousand pounds. I still can't believe it."

"Good Lord, a house? Where exactly?"

"It's in a place called Lockford, on the South coast. I can't wait to see it. I thought I'd drive down tomorrow. Any chance you can come?"

"I'll make sure of it."

The sun shone out of a clear blue sky, although a layer of frost coated hedgerows where the sun had yet to reach. Owen estimated the journey would take them just under two hours.

"I'm so excited. We could live there. What do you think? It would be a great start to our married life, a house in the country within easy driving distance of London. I wonder if there's a garden? There's sure to be." Rowena placed a hand on his knee. "I'm going on a bit, aren't I?"

"No problem. You're entitled to. I just hope you won't be disappointed.

Bramble Lane looked promising from the outset. As Owen turned the corner at the end of the road, he could see that the area was definitely one of the nicest they had seen on the drive down. Rowena had been given the keys from the solicitor and as Owen turned into the drive she took them from her handbag.

"Certainly looks good from the outside," he said, closing the car door and following her into the house.

The rooms on the ground floor were large and flooded with light; the décor was a different matter though, being circa nineteen thirties. Wallpaper, that would now be called vintage but to Owen just looked hideous, clung to every wall, flowers clashing with geometric patterns.

"Mm, I can see a use for the ninety thousand straight away, fitted kitchen, cloakroom and total refurb., of the lounge, dining and morning rooms, " Rowena said thoughtfully. " Let's see what state the upstairs is in."

Owen followed her into the master bedroom, which overlooked the front garden.

"It's just like my aunt had stepped out for a while leaving everything as it was." Rowena opened the wardrobe door. "Moth balls!" She wrinkled her nose in disgust. "A trip to the charity shop, maybe several?" She held a camel hair coat and a flowered dress up for inspection. " Such a shame. No one to look after her things and care whether she lived or died," she said sadly.

Owen took her arm. " Let's look at the other bedrooms. We'll soon get someone in to sort those out. Charity shops are crying out for good quality clothes."

There was a large bedroom at the back of the house with a bay window that overlooked the garden. Rowena walked towards the window. "Oh how lovely. Owen, look, a summerhouse – there at the end of the garden."

The garden was a bit overgrown, the lawn in need of more than simply a trim but the summerhouse looked to be in pretty good shape.

"Come on," Rowena said, pulling his arm. "Let's take a look." She held up the keys. "I wondered what this one was for."

The summerhouse looked as if it had been recently painted. The first thing he noticed was the rich scent of pine and the hand-stitched sampler hanging on one wall. The air was pleasantly warm and not a trace of damp showed on the soft furnishings. "It's as tight as a drum in here," he commented. " The roof is sound and I can see that there's an electricity point on the wall. I wonder what she used the place for?"

Rowena was opening the drawers of a small hexagonal side table. "No mystery – she used to sew - I mean embroider; there are embroidery silks, needles and material neatly arranged in every drawer. That sampler must have been one of hers."

"Home sweet home."

"I hope so. Anyway there's no reason why we shouldn't make it one."

"You really would like to live here?" Rowena kissed his cheek. " That's just great. I'm so glad you like the place."

"Who wouldn't? But I must say, I can't live with that god-awful wallpaper in the hallway."

During the next few weeks Owen was swept along on a wave of wedding fever. Rowena seemed to spend every free moment on the phone to the wedding planner at the Manor House and at the end of the second week, following his visit to Sarah Lawson, Rowena announced that she had bought 'the dress'. There were a few minor alterations to be made but the store had assured her that it would be ready to be picked up at the end of the month. Her excitement was infectious and Owen began to look forward to the event in earnest.

Forgetting his meeting with Sarah was the difficult part. He hated not being straight with Rowena but couldn't think how he could explain it all without looking as if he was trying to cover up an affair.

Peter Walmsley and Mark Furnish insisted that they all had a boys' night out the week before the wedding and so Owen reluctantly agreed to a 'booze up' for his Stag party.

Rowena and her girlfriends were spending the weekend at a Health Spa on the outskirts of the city; a weekend of pampering she called it.

Saturday night in London was typical of any in a large city. The bars and clubs were full of drinkers taking advantage of 'Happy Hours' and discounted drinks. Peter and Mark had suggested they meet in the Black Bear Club at eight. The Black Bear was tucked away in a side street and had a reputation for selling good beers and wines at reasonable prices as opposed to some of the smarter establishments selling rotgut drinks at inflated prices. Artists and businessmen were the mainstay of its clientele but on Saturday nights there was an influx of revellers drifting from the bars on the main thoroughfares. Unfortunately for Owen, on the night of his Stag party, a pop concert was being held in Leicester Square so the Black Bear was busier than normal.

"Owen, over here," Peter shouted above the din as he steered a course towards his friends. The drinks were lined up on a table in front of them.

"Made sense to buy a couple of rounds while we were at it. You can't get to the bar for love nor money." Hamish Dalton grinned. "Cheers my old mate, last week of freedom."

The drinks flowed in spite of the crowd and by the time he saw Andy Lawson Owen was well and truly drunk. He was only vaguely aware of Lawson watching him from the bar and forgot his presence almost immediately as Hamish placed another drink in his fist.

The conversation around the table now had degenerated into commenting on Owen's prowess in bed and how tasty, in order of preference, were the girls standing near the bar, each one becoming more palatable with every drink they took.

"Not interested," Owen slurred.

"Go on, last chance." Tony, a prop for the London Welsh rugby team, dug Owen in the ribs. "She'll never know."

Owen grinned, at least he thought he grinned but he couldn't be sure. "Nor interested," he repeated. "I'm off to the bog."

Somehow he managed to find his way to the Gents and propped an arm on the tiles as he stood at the stall. He was only dimly aware of the fact that he was alone, except for a tall man washing his hands in the sink.

"So, no friends to protect you here, scum bag." Andy Lawson gripped him by the shoulders and threw him back against the wall. Owen felt the cold hard surface as his head cracked against the tiles.

"Enjoying your Stag night, are you? How d'you think my little sister's enjoying herself? Dropped her like a hot cake when your tart returned from the States. She'd booked the wedding for God's sake."

Owen knew then that he must be totally out

of it. It must be a dream. He screwed up his eyes as Lawson's fist connected with his jaw and he slumped to the ground.

"She's been crying her eyes out ever since, you bastard." The punch landed in his ribs and Owen thought he heard a far off crack before he briefly passed out. He was standing when he came around, propped up by Lawson's arm, which pinioned him to the basin.

"You deserve all you get, you little shit." Owen was aware of Lawson's arm being removed as he slid to the floor. A sharp pain shot through his leg and blood pumped up like a fountain until darkness descended.

Drifting in an out of consciousness Owen heard voices and a door slam. Then something tight gripped his thigh and he drifted off again. The next thing he knew he was on a stretcher, with something over his face and a loud alarm that pierced his brain like a scalpel. He was swaying from side to side and vaguely aware that someone was talking to him.

"Won't be long now, son; just hang on in there."

The alarm was the ambulance siren; it stopped as the swaying stopped. Owen closed his eyes as he was wheeled into the Accident and Emergency Department. He wondered what had happened to him. The details were blurred but it was no dream. This was real, every ache, every cut and every bruise.

When he next awoke he was in a hospital bed, sunlight streaking down the ward like a lightening bolt.

"Well now and how are we feeling this morning, Mr Madoc? Not quite what you had planned for your Stag night I should imagine?" The nurse was on the plump side; her cheeks dimpled when she smiled; her name badge read Sister Mary Dixon. "You lot will never learn; too much drink and too much money." Her smile took the sting out of her words. "Doctor will be along in a minute. Then he'll no doubt discharge you. You've been patched up and your fiancée will be along to pick you up at ten."

"Rowena? Did someone phone Rowena?"

He hoped not. It was her Hen weekend and besides, how was he going to explain what had happened? He was dressed and sitting on a chair at the side of his bed waiting for Rowena when he saw Sarah Lawson making her way down the ward towards him.

"Ready, darling? Come along let me help you up," she said as Owen closed his eyes and prayed he was still dreaming.

Chapter 52

He didn't dare speak until he was sitting in her car. He still felt weak and found it easier to be swept along on the tide of this nightmare rather than struggle against it. Eventually as they drove in the direction of his flat he said, "Are you ready to tell me what this is all about?"

She drove on without glancing in his direction.

"Let me take you home first then I'll explain. We're nearly there."

Realising that the best course of action would be to accept his fate and wait for her explanation, he closed his eyes and spent the rest of the journey in silence.

Everything was as he'd left it, untidy and lived in. A coffee cup and plate stood on a side table, the remains of a half eaten pizza having attracted a few hungry flies. In the kitchen he knew that there would be a sink full of unwashed dishes and that his bedroom bore traces of the last night he and Rowena had spent together before she left for her spa weekend.

It was Monday morning, Rowena would be returning to her flat later in the day. He hadn't heard from her as they'd both decided that phone calls were a 'no no' and that each should enjoy themselves without worrying too much about what the other was doing. What would she think when she saw the results of his Stag night?

Sarah Lawson sat down opposite him. "Shall I make you a cup of tea or something?"

"No. I just want an explanation," Owen replied trying to keep a lid on his anger.

"I'm sorry about Andy. He got hold of the wrong end of the stick. He has a nasty temper. I'd no idea he'd come after you."

"What about the lies? He thought I'd asked you to marry me, for God's sake."

"As I said, somewhere along the line, he got things wrong."

Owen's head was thumping with a staccato drumbeat. He pressed his palm to his temple. "I still don't understand why he attacked me. The man must be insane."

"I think it was a combination of being in the wrong place at the wrong time. He'd had far too much to drink. I know it's not an excuse but the reason I pretended to be your fiancée this morning at the hospital was so that you'd see me. I thought if I used my real name you'd refuse."

"Do you blame me?"

"No, perhaps not. Anyway, I needed to see

you to plead with you not to press charges. The police have arrested Andy."

"They have?" Owen was even more confused, as far as he'd been aware they'd been alone when the attack had taken place. There were no witnesses; it would have been his word against Lawson's.

"Apparently one of your friends, Hamish someone or other grabbed Andy as he tried to leave the washroom and kept hold of him while he phoned the police."

Owen attempted a weak smile but the pain in his jaw restricted his movement. Hamish, six foot five of pure muscle was a force to be reckoned with. "And you want me to forget about all this?"

She looked down at her hands. "It's all my fault, but I don't want Andy's family to suffer; there'd be a court case, his name would be plastered all over the local newspapers and with you being so well known the Nationals and the Television News Channels are bound to get hold of it."

Owen sighed; he didn't want to get mixed up in publicity of this sort either, especially not before his wedding. He'd have to make up a story for Rowena, mistaken identity, anything that sounded reasonable and tell the same story to his friends.

"And if I do this, you'll promise to leave us alone? No more phone calls, no more pretending to be Rowena and no more nonsense about you and me being a couple."

She nodded. Her head was still lowered so he couldn't see her eyes. He picked up the telephone and rang the number of the investigating officer on the card that Sarah had handed him.

Afterwards, Owen stood at the window and looked down into the street. He saw her car pull away from the curb and once again prayed that it would be the last time he'd see her. But it suddenly occurred to him that her hair was now the same colour as Rowena's and that simple fact sent a cold shiver down his spine.

Half an hour later, his mobile rang. It was his fiancée. "Did you have a good weekend?" Rowena asked.

He grunted evasively and said that he'd missed her.

"Me too. But I must admit I feel a million dollars after all that pampering. I'll be over this evening, after I've unpacked. Then you can see what I mean."

The thought of her hands touching his body made him wince. How was he going to explain the mess he was in? After he put the phone down he went into the bedroom, stripped off his clothes and inspected the result of Lawson's attack. His face looked as if he'd gone twelve rounds with a heavyweight prize-fighter and the bruises on his body ranged from pale yellow to deep purple and as for the cut, where he'd been stabbed by a broken bottle, the scar on his leg was livid and held together by black knotted stitches. That might be easier to account for, falling back on a broken bottle, whilst drunk; it sounded feasible enough. Would it seem reasonable that a perfect stranger had suddenly mistaken him for someone else, though? Then there was why he'd chosen not to press charges; how was he going to get out of that one?

In the bathroom Owen ran a hot bath and lowered his aching body into the water. As he closed his eyes, he tried to think of an explanation that would satisfy Rowena, but he was spinning around in circles where nothing made any sense.

Chapter 53

Rowena's shock at seeing his injuries reduced her to fussing over him like a mother hen. She accepted his story about a fight breaking out in the club without question and, after making some disparaging remarks about the state some people got into when drunk, focused on the problem of how he was going to look in two weeks time. Nevertheless, Owen could see that she thought he was mad not to press charges in spite of the unwanted publicity.

"Most of the bruises should have faded by then, but those lacerations will take a time to heal. Luckily the worst of them will be hidden by your suit so our wedding photos should be OK." She stroked his cheek. "I can see I'll have to make sure you don't get into more trouble before our big day. Why don't you come over to my place and let me spoil you until then?"

Tempting as her offer was, he shook his head. "Too much to do here sweetheart; besides, remember it's unlucky to spend the night together before the wedding so I'd have to come back here at some point. Don't worry about me,

I'll be fine."

"In that case, I promise to pop over as often as possible. At least things have settled down at work and I should be able to take some time off to oversee the final arrangements."

"There you are then; you'll have enough to do."

When Rowena eventually left him alone, he took a couple of painkillers and went to bed. Putting on a brave face had left him feeling grim. He closed his eyes but his aching body wouldn't let him sleep. He kept seeing Sarah Lawson's face. Eventually he drifted off to sleep but dreamed he'd married Sarah and that he couldn't find Rowena to tell her it had all been a mistake. The distant sound of the telephone ringing woke him. He'd unplugged the bedroom extension but could hear the answer phone connecting in the living room. Andy Lawson's hesitant voice drifted towards him.

"I'd just like to say sorry, and thanks for not pressing charges. Sarah's explained and I know I overreacted." There was a beat. "I, er, well she's vulnerable and she *is* my sister. Anyway, thanks."

Owen lay back and looked at the ceiling. It was the second time he'd heard Sarah described as vulnerable; Megan had said the same thing. It wasn't a word he would have used to describe her; devious, manipulative and strong-willed sprang to mind; he wondered if he knew her at all.

He started to think about the events leading up to Lawson's attack. At first there hadn't been the slightest indication that Sarah had wanted to be anything other than a mate, although he now realised that it was naive of him not to have foreseen the problems that could have arisen by him staying over at her flat. Then there was the night of Megan's party. If only he could remember what had happened. She'd led him to believe they'd made love but for the life of him he had no idea whether that was a fact or invention on her part. However, he was certain that at no time had he ever expressed the intention of them having a relationship that was based on anything other than friendship and at no time, drunk or sober, had he ever suggested marriage; it was just too ludicrous to even consider. So why had she let her brother believe that he'd let her down and why did Lawson and Megan believe that she was vulnerable?

Two days before the wedding Rowena arrived with his wedding suit. "I thought I'd pick it up for you to save you a journey. I must admit that you look better now, thank God." She kissed his mouth and for the first time Owen didn't wince in pain. "Now everything's in order, all we have to do is sit back and enjoy it."

They were in the middle of eating their evening meal when she told him about the phone calls. "I've been having a few odd calls lately. I think someone must have mistakenly got hold of my number and when they ring they realise it's not the person they were expecting they put the phone down. I'd thought of changing it but it would cause too much hassle at the moment, so many people have my number, especially the wedding planner etc."

Owen held his breath; it couldn't be.

"I just wish whoever it is would speak and then I could put them right but after I answer the line goes dead. It's most unnerving."

"Perhaps it's as you said – a wrong number."

"That's what I thought until yesterday."

Owen waited, his heart pounding against his ribs.

"I was in the middle of packing a case for our honeymoon, just putting in things that don't crease etc., when the phone went. This time I distinctly heard the sound of a cat meowing followed by a woman's voice before the phone was put down."

"What did the woman say?"

"Well her voice was a bit muffled but I thought she said 'down Bibi or Tibby'. I'm not really sure."

A vision of a tabby cat called Bibi rubbing itself up against his legs on the night he'd slept over at Sarah's swam before him. So she was still playing games; his only hope now was that, once he was married all this nonsense would stop.

Rowena stayed over at his place that night and the following day they drove to their favourite restaurant for lunch. "This is the last time we'll see each other before tomorrow," Rowena said getting into the car.

"Why don't you let me drive?" Owen suggested.

"No problem; just rest that leg, you don't want to open up any of those scars before they heal properly."

"But…."

"But me no buts as my old Granny used to say," Rowena said as she smiled at him and drove into the traffic.

Chapter 54

Owen was awake before the phone rang. Premonitions are all very well and good after the event; people say 'I knew that was going to happen' but foresight is a gift not nearly as prevalent as the alternative. Nevertheless in spite of the sunshine and clear blue sky, even before the telephone began to ring, he knew that the day was going to end in disaster.

He picked up the phone. It was Rowena. "You're not going to believe this," she was talking quickly, running her sentences into one as if she couldn't wait to spit out the words. "Our wedding's been cancelled. I rang to confirm that the flowers had arrived. The receptionist said that I phoned earlier and told them the wedding was off. I said that they must have made a mistake and that I'd made no such phone call, but they were adamant. Owen, are you still there?"

"I don't know what to say."

"I've rung as many guests as I could, lucky we decided to make it a small 'do'. The Manor has a cancellation in three week's time and so

I booked us in then. What do you think?"

"I don't see what else we can do." Owen put his hand to his eyes to wipe away a trickle of sweat. It was a sick joke. How could he make her stop?

"The photographer is going mad. I rang him to cancel and he's insisting that we pay him in full for the day, including the cost of the album."

"That's ridiculous."

" I know. I told him that was what the deposit was for and that his had been a big enough one. But he went off on a tirade about bankruptcy for goodness sake. He said he was relying on the work to keep him afloat. He was furious saying he can't make it in three weeks time so he's going to be out of pocket."

Owen sighed. "Don't worry, sweetheart. I'll have a word with him. What I don't understand is why the Manor would cancel on just a phone call. I mean anyone could ring up and say they were you."

"That's just it. They said that I'd called in to confirm the cancellation and to collect the wedding cake."

"That can't be right, surely?"

"They sounded certain. I know it's a busy time for them and I suppose they are trying to cover up their incompetence but even so…."

Drumming his fingers on the bedside table, Owen said, "We'll get through this. Look on it as a set back, we'll sort out this mess and make sure that nothing stops us getting married in three weeks' time." As he put down the phone Owen frowned. He was determined to put an end to this right away. She'd gone too far this time. First he rang the photographer trying to explain that neither Rowena nor he had been responsible for cancelling the wedding.

"Who is then?" He was furious.

"I can't say for sure but I've got a pretty good idea that it's a woman called Sarah Lawson."

" Great. Where can I find her?"

"Won't do any good. I can't prove it was her."

"You are joking?"

"I wish."

Putting the phone down he looked up her number.

"I don't know what you're talking about, Owen. This is beginning to sound like a vendetta. I haven't cancelled your wedding, why would I?" she sounded offended.

"Where do I begin? Let's see. Oh yes, getting your brother to beat me up because he thought we were getting married, posing as Rowena to the hospital staff, and then there's the fire at my cottage…"

The line went dead. He tried to ring the number again but it was engaged. He was in no mood to leave it. Arriving at her flat he kept his finger on the bell until she finally opened the door. Her eyes were red-rimmed.

"I didn't do any of it. How could I? I'd never do anything to harm you, Owen. You must know that."

For the first time he could see what they meant. She looked vulnerable. "Should I?

"Of course, I admit that I wish things had turned out better for us after Megan's party but I'm not the vindictive person you're making me out to be."

" So you are telling me you didn't visit the Manor and cancel our wedding arrangements?"

"Is that what they said I did?"

"Not exactly; they said that Rowena did."

She wiped her eyes with the sleeve of the dressing gown like a small child, sniffed then faced him. "Well then that's your answer isn't it? Now if you don't mind, I'd like to get dressed and forget all of this"

Outside her flat Owen screwed up his eyes in the bright sunshine. Her indignation had sounded plausible. He was confused. For the first time a shadow of a doubt crossed his mind – was there the slightest possibility that Rowena had been lying and if so, why?

Their guests were notified of the change of date and time by email. Rowena still had the dress, another cake was made and Guy, a photographer friend of Mark Furnish, agreed to fill in for them. As the day approached Owen began to feel distinctly uneasy. Rowena was subdued; there was none of the frenetic anticipation that the previous Stag and Hen nights had generated.

Ten days before the event was due to take place Rowena telephoned to say she had a cash buyer for her flat. A shiver ran down Owen's spine. It was just like the film fatal attraction – he could imagine her sitting in the lounge waiting to discuss the sale, as innocent as you like.

"Owen *are* you listening?" Rowena sounded cross.

" Yes of course, that's great."

"You'll come over then?"

"What?"

"There I knew you weren't listening. I said, will you come over tonight and help me show my buyer around, discuss the finer details of the sale etc.,"

It was like he was a hamster on a wheel; he couldn't stop the train of events. He knew Sarah Lawson would be waiting for him and he had no choice but play her game.

Chapter 55

It was half past two when he rang the bell to Rowena's flat. His palms were wet and he could feel his pulse throbbing in his neck. As she opened the door she said, "She's late. She rang a moment ago to say she was stuck in traffic. So we've time for a drink before she arrives. What'll it be?"

"Stiff whiskey and soda please."

"It's like that is it?"

From the kitchen he heard the sound of ice tinkling into a glass and Rowena pouring his drink. "By the way, darling, the builders have started on Bramble Lane. We could drive down at the weekend to see how they're progressing. That's if you can spare the time. I'll have to pay them from my savings until the cheque comes through from the will."

"Sure. Why not? If you need any money just let me know."

"Thanks. I might take you up on that offer, but I'm OK. at the moment. Then there's the sale of this place – things will work out fine."

The whiskey was steadying his nerves. Life

would go on after today.

When Rowena had called to say she had a cash buyer and that the woman had insisted that it had to be *her* flat in particular, it had rung alarm bells. He just had to deal with this visit. Then make up a valid reason why she shouldn't sell to the woman and that would be that. But somewhere in the back of his mind a voice was saying – until the next time. The sound of the doorbell ringing cut into his thoughts like a lance into a boil.

"Here she is now. Do me a favour and swill out our glasses. I don't want her to think we're in the habit of boozing in the afternoon."

From the kitchen Owen could hear them talking. He tried to place the voice as belonging to Sarah but failed.

"Owen come and meet, Miss Stafford"

"Lucy, please."

So she was Lucy, this time, Owen thought taking his courage in both hands and walking into the room.

"Hullo, nice to meet you, " he said extending his hand. He knew he was grinning from ear to ear.

Lucy Stafford was a woman in her late fifties, neatly dressed, slightly overweight and with grey hair that was twisted into a knot at the base of her neck. And although he'd previously decided that Sarah Lawson had the attributes of a chameleon, he doubted that even she could successfully pull of such a transformation. His pulse rate returned to normal, as he followed in their wake, pointing out the advantages of living in the area and the amenities the flat had to offer, whilst hoping that the note of desperation in his voice was not noticeable.

Afterwards, Rowena threw her arms around his neck and kissed him firmly on his lips. "Bramble Lane, here we come," she said.

"She's going to buy then?"

"She can't wait to finalise the deal. She said she'd get in touch with her solicitors right away. Apparently her sister lives in the same block, on the same floor, that's why she wanted this flat so desperately." Rowena leant against him. "I know we've had a few hiccups along the way, but I really feel as though things are taking shape. Just the wedding to get though and we'll be out the other side, ready to start our lives together."

Her optimism was infectious. Owen walked to the off-licence for a bottle of champagne and a large box of chocolates, which they later consumed in bed and where they stayed until the pale light of dawn filtered through the bedroom curtains. He was beginning to believe her; nothing could get in the way of their happiness.

He spent the whole of Monday morning with a self-satisfied smile playing at the corners of his mouth as he worked on the mural in the Furnish Gallery. So he was totally unprepared for the appearance of Rowena at lunchtime accompanied by Sarah Lawson.

"Owen, I gather you and Sarah are friends.

When I was packing up some of my clothes earlier, I noticed that there was a message on your answerphone. I thought it might be from the wedding planner but it was from Sarah to say that you'd left your diary at her flat and she thought you might need it. So I arranged for her to meet us here."

To a casual observer there would be nothing in her words to cause alarm but Owen recognised a tone as icy as the Arctic and the unspoken question, as to why she knew nothing of his friendship with this woman or why he would have been in a position to leave his diary at her flat, hung in the air like a bad smell. His mouth fell open as he tried to compose a sentence that would not have his fiancée turning on her heel in an instant. To his surprise it was Sarah Lawson who came to his rescue.

"Er, I think friendship might be too strong a word. My brother and Owen are friends. No doubt Owen left his diary when he visited my flat with Andy."

" Thanks, I hadn't noticed it was missing," he said, wondering how she could have got her hands on it without him knowing about it.

He could tell that Rowena was still not convinced. "How is Andy, by the way?" He could feel the words sticking to his tongue like Velcro.

"Fine, he said to pass on his good wishes for your wedding. Well I must be off. Enjoy your move to your new home."

"You've got some explaining to do, I think," Rowena said following him to the wine bar on the corner.

"How does she know about Bramble Lane?" he asked.

"I told her. I didn't think you'd mind, being as you two are such 'good' friends."

"That's rubbish. She told you - it's her brother I know."

"That's not what it sounded like on the telephone. She spoke as if you were rather more than just friends."

He sat opposite her and took her hand across the table that separated them. "I'm flattered that you're jealous sweetheart but you've nothing to worry about. Sarah Lawson has a bit of a crush on me that's all. As if I would be interested in her when I have you." For the moment she was mollified but Owen wondered how long it would last and if they'd survive Sarah Lawson and her relentless persecution.

Chapter 56

The refurbishment of the Bramble Lane property was completed in record time thanks to Rowena's organisational skills and determination. Owen was still working on the mural in the Furnish Gallery when she rang to say that she'd decided to spend the weekend at the house, and was taking some of the clothes she wouldn't require until the winter in preparation for the big move.

"I'm sorry I can't join you. I'm a behind schedule and Mark is hoping to have it all finished by the beginning of next week."

"No problem. I'll probably get more done, without any distractions. I'll leave you to get back to it. Don't work to hard. I'll be in touch; love you."

She was waiting for him outside his flat. It was midnight and all he could think about was a hot shower and his bed. "Hello, Owen."

"Sarah. Look, I'm too tired for your little games tonight, if you'll excuse me."

He tried to squeeze past her to put his key in

Who is Sarah Lawson

the lock.

"It's Andy's wife – it's Hannah. She's had an accident. My car is in the garage waiting for a new part to be fitted. I've only just heard and I don't know how to get to him. He needs someone to look after the children, whilst he goes to visit her in hospital. I don't know what to do." She looked helplessly up at him and the trap closed more firmly around him.

"You'd better come in then, let me just have a quick shower and I'll run you over."

"That's very kind of you but he's not in London. The firm he works for is making cutbacks and the London flat had to go. The family still live in Birmingham, the flat was a concession."

"I see," he sighed. There was nothing he could do about it. Rowena would be able to see that surely? The woman was in a fix. He was trying to justify why he could manage to drive to Birmingham and yet could not find the time to drive to Lockford. His reasons sounded hollow, the unspoken words swirling around in his head as if in a whirlpool.

She was sitting in the chair near the window, where Rowena often sat to read. He caught his breath. It could be her; her clothes, hair, make-up, she was a couple of pounds heavier but he could see that the transformation was almost complete. The thought struck terror into his soul as he picked up his keys and followed her out of the flat.

The journey passed with little exchange of conversation, which suited him. When they arrived Owen saw that the house was a semi, built in the style of the nineteen sixties. There was no light showing at any of the windows.

"Thank you so much, Owen. I do appreciate it. Please don't wait. I'm OK. I have my key."

"I may as well see you inside."

"No, really. There's no need. I don't want to disturb the children."

"Well, if you're sure. Tell Andy I'm sorry about his wife. I broke my leg playing rugby years ago so I know how difficult it is to get around."

"Er, yes, thanks again." She was waiting for him to drive away. He could see that she had no intention of entering the house until he was gone. Well it was OK. by him; he couldn't wait to get home and to bed.

He was still asleep at ten the following morning, when Mark Furnish rang. "Just wanted to thank you, my lovely."

Owen grunted.

"Sorry, sorry, you're still in bed. I know you worked late to finish it, shouldn't' have rung, sorry again."

It was nearly five by the time he'd got back to the flat and he'd been planning to sleep forever but Mark's well-meaning phone call had made further sleep impossible. In the shower he let the water play over his tired body as his thoughts returned to driving to Birmingham in the early hours. There'd been little conversation between them until he'd turned into the street where her brother lived then she suddenly said, "When are you planning on moving to Lockford?" He'd given a non-committal reply. But the question bothered him and he began to wonder what further mischief she had in mind.

The harsh morning sunlight hurt his eyes as he stepped out of his flat for the short walk to the café where he planned to eat a hearty breakfast. He was slightly disconcerted to see Rowena walking towards him from the direction of the tube station. "You're a sight for my sore eyes," he said, kissing her cheek; her lips suddenly out of reach as she turned her head to the side.

"Really? Sore? No doubt after another night spent with Sarah Lawson?" She was furious. "What is going on, Owen? You've got an hour to convince me that you're not having an affair before I ring to cancel our wedding and this time it will most definitely be me at the end of the phone."

Chapter 57

Ignoring the café, Owen steered her towards the wine bar, found a table in a corner and, after he'd ordered the drinks, prepared to explain the mess he was in. "It all began with Andy Lawson buying Indigo Night," he said.

Rowena took a sip of her wine and left the rest untouched as Owen falteringly explained how Sarah seemed to have got the wrong end of the stick and believed there was more to their relationship than just a casual friendship. He told her of the visit to Luigi's and of his promise to spend Christmas day with her as they were both going to be alone. "I felt bad about it because she'd gone to so much trouble and then you arrived and Sarah Lawson slipped my mind."

The part he didn't mention was Megan's birthday and subsequent events. He didn't know how to explain it; she wouldn't understand, why would she? He didn't understand it himself.

"You've been a fool." She was still mad but he sensed that he was making progress.

"You're right."

"And last night?"

He held his arms wide in a gesture of supplication. "What could I do? Leave her stranded in London without a lift?"

"It might have been better, considering the situation."

"Right again. "

"Well, Owen Madoc. Looks like you've survived by the skin of your teeth this time. But promise me that this is an end to your involvement with the woman. She's trouble."

"You're not kidding." He reached for her hand and kissed her palm. "You have my word."

The following morning Owen opened his eyes reached for her hand and felt cold sheet. A note was propped up against the bedside lamp.

Darling, I've lots to do and you looked as if you needed the sleep. Will give you a ring later to discuss the sale of your flat etc., R

So, he thought, for the time being, she'd forgiven him. Nevertheless there was the night spent after Megan's party waiting in the wings to threaten his happiness.

Rowena arrived at his flat later that afternoon; a warm wind had sprung up and her hair was untidy. She was frowning as he kissed her. "Do you know that the man on the desk downstairs thought I was her?"

A shiver ran down his spine. "Who?" he asked dreading the answer.

"The Lawson woman."

Owen held her shoulders and bent towards her, "Let's agree to forget her." He made her look at him. "She can't harm our relationship, unless we let her, OK?" He could see she wasn't convinced but gave him a weak smile.

"Have you thought about selling this place?"

"I have. And you'll be glad to know that I contacted the agent this morning. I know I've let things slide lately but not any longer."

"That's good news. What about the cottage?"

Owen walked towards the window and looked out into the street where shoppers were walking away from Covent Garden. He would miss living here. "Let's keep the cottage at Fallow's End. It will be great for holiday weekends, what d'you say?"

"Sounds fine. So we're agreed, Bramble Lane and Fallow's End; they even sound like nice places to live and I for one can't wait to get away from London."

Fate has a way of altering even the best laid plans, Owen decided, when on a warm afternoon five days before his wedding, Rowena and he were enjoying a glass of wine at a table outside a bar in Covent Garden. The street entertainers were in full swing and the operatic sounds of an aria being sung close by drifted over the heads of the shoppers.

"Good Lord, it's Owen and Sarah," Duncan Jones stood on the cobbles in front of them squinting in the sunshine. "Just knew you two would get together, after that night you spent at our place for Megan's birthday bash. Good to see you again."

Owen stood up. "Duncan, I'd like you to meet my fiancée, Rowena."

She waited a moment then slowly stood up.

Duncan looked confused. " I'm so sorry, I seem to have made a mistake."

"Nice to meet you, Mr Jones. Don't apologise. It's Owen who's made the mistake by referring to me as his fiancée." She slid the ring off her finger and placed on the table. "Now if you'll excuse me, I'm afraid I'm rather busy."

Owen knew that trying to explain would be useless this time. Nevertheless, he was desperate to try but she refused to take his calls and when he arrived at her flat the concierge told him that she'd gone away and he didn't know for how long. He wondered whether this was true or whether the man had been given his instructions with regard to what he should say to him. He had no alternative but to drive down to Lockford. It was the only place he could think of where she might be.

The house in Bramble Lane looked different, smarter; the lawns and borders had been trimmed into place and the outside had been painted. Owen could see Rowena's handiwork in the swathed drapes at the lounge window and the ice sharp blinds effectively obstructing his view of the inside. Her car, a silver grey Audi, stood in the drive. He rang the bell. No answer.

"Rowena," he called through the letterbox - still no answer. "Please, I need to talk to you – to explain."

He could hear her heels tapping on the block flooring in the hall then the door opened a fraction.

"There's no need for an explanation. I wouldn't believe it, so it's a waste of your time and mine. Please, go back to London and leave me alone."

"I didn't know how to tell you. I don't remember what happened. I was drunk," he said, as she closed the door in his face.

So that was that, he thought. Sarah Lawson had managed to split them up for good at last. By the time he reached his flat, he was furious. Once inside he searched for her number but all he could find was her brother's business card. He dialled the number and heard Lawson's voice at the end of the line.

"This is Owen Madoc. I want you to tell your sister that if she contacts me again I'll slap a police injunction on her."

"I'm sorry? I don't understand. What is this all about?"

"Just tell her," he slammed down the phone and went to the cupboard to pour a stiff whiskey

Chapter 58

The M4 was busy, caravans and holidaymakers heading for West Wales clogged the middle lane, many driving at a steady fifty and refusing to pull over. Owen switched on the air con and felt a cool rush of air hit his face. Pulling out into the fast lane he left the line of caravans behind him. He intended to spend a month at the cottage. The month when he and Rowena had been due to start their new life together.

Mark Furnish had been supportive. "Relax, get away for a bit, but please, dear heart, don't forget the showing. I'm in the middle of making arrangements with other exhibitors and as soon as I get a go ahead on the date, I'll be in touch."

There was no one else who would care whether he was in London or Timbuktu, he thought with a heavy dose of self-pity. The village of Gareg Wen was busier than he'd ever seen it. Spring Bank holiday and the good weather had made it a certainty that the Anchor would be full of people requiring lunch and a cool beer and the parking situation would be impossible. Deciding to give it a miss and drive straight to the cottage, Owen turned down the lane and saw Megan Lloyd Jones with a small dog on a lead. He pulled over.

"Owen? What a nice surprise. I didn't know you were coming down." She looked uncomfortable. "I'd like to say how sorry we were to hear about you and Rowena. I do hope it had nothing to do with Duncan opening his big mouth."

He shook his head. "It was bound to happen. It's not Duncan's fault. If anyone is to blame it's me for being so stupid. Anyway," he said, changing the subject. "Is that your pooch?"

She shook her head. "No. It's the vicar's but he's broken his ankle and this poor thing doesn't get taken for a walk very often. I'm just helping out."

"Good for you. Well I must be going or I'll cause a traffic-jam. I'll see you around I expect."

"How long are you staying?"

"Not sure, couple of weeks, I think."

"Please come over, anytime, you know we'll be glad to see you."

"Thanks, I'll do that." As he drove away he thought that the last thing he wanted at the moment was company.

Waking in his cottage the following day Owen could feel the heat of the morning threading through the blinds. He put his feet over the side of his bed, yawned and walked to the window. A carpet of green fields stretched to the cliffs; the hedges were in full bud and a few early swallows were swirling in the air currents.

Dragging a deck chair and folding table on to the veranda, he drank coffee. Eating was out of the question until he'd visited the supermarket in Gareg Wen. Taking a deep breath he inhaled the scents of the morning and closed his eyes. How could he have been such a fool? He should have told Rowena about the party – if he'd explained from the start maybe she'd have understood. He was such a wimp. Sarah Lawson should have been stopped months ago. He was still in the process of beating himself up about it all when his mobile rang.

"Owen, I'm sure you haven't eaten yet and Duncan has made enough breakfast to feed the five thousand, would you be a love and come and help me out?"

It was impossible to say no to Megan and besides his stomach hadn't been filled since lunch the previous day. Walking across the field, dew-wet grass stroking his ankles, Owen decided that for just one day he'd forget all about the women in his life. Rabbits dived for their burrows as he approached and the closer he walked to the cliffs seagulls became his companions.

The cliff path was busier than he'd anticipated, holiday-makers carrying cool bags and picnic hampers took the steps leading to the beach where he could see earlier risers had bagged what they considered to be the best spots. A family occupied the cave where he'd previously spent the autumn days sketching and two young children were jumping up and down as their father attempted to build a sand boat.

Opening the gate at the bottom of the garden, Owen crossed the lawn to where he could see Megan and Duncan sitting in the conservatory.

"Good, just in time. Black coffee?"

"Please. This is very kind of you," he said, as Duncan handed him a plate piled with eggs, bacon and sausage.

"Not at all. Eat up there's plenty more." Duncan sat alongside him and waited until he had his mouth full. "Er, look, I'd like to apologise for that Sarah Lawson business."

Owen shrugged.

"The thing is we both thought you two were an item, after the party, I mean." He looked at Megan for confirmation.

"Yes, well, that's what Sarah led us to believe."

"What d'you mean?"

"She rang to thank us for the party and during the conversation she implied that you and she were now a couple. A few weeks later, she came down with some proofs and said that things had got serious between you and that you'd even talked of getting married." Megan looked at Duncan for confirmation.

"That's right. I remember saying to Megan that I thought it was all a bit sudden." Duncan picked up Owen's empty plate. "A refill?"

"No, no thanks, that's fine. What exactly did she say about us getting married?"

Megan hesitated then said, "She said that, as neither of you had any reason to wait, you'd decided to get married at the end of May. She even told us that you'd booked the venue, something about a Manor house."

Owen pressed his forehead with his hand. "I can't believe it! There's something seriously wrong with that woman. She's a complete fantasist."

"It wasn't true then?" Duncan asked.

"Of course not."

"We did wonder."

"Sarah Lawson's lies have ruined my relationship with Rowena, the woman I was to marry, at the Manor house, at the end of May."

"Good heavens." Megan covered his hand with hers and patted it. "I'm so sorry. We had no idea. What on earth could have got into Sarah?"

"That's one question, I'd like answered. Whether you believe it or not, I never gave her any encouragement intentionally. The woman just wouldn't take the hint. I was a fool to get drunk at your party, I was missing Rowena and the prospect of spending Christmas without her was getting to me. And I still have absolutely no idea what happened that night. I can't believe that I'd have no recollection of sleeping with her, if it actually happened."

Duncan frowned. "That's something none of

us will ever know; Sarah obviously can't be trusted to tell the truth."

"So you see. I can't wholly blame her for this mess up. I can't avoid my part in it all."

"What you need is a day on the water to take your mind off things. We'll call in at the Anchor later and arrange to join the old gang on a fishing trip tomorrow. The tide is full at nine. So you'll have to get up early. What d'you think?"

Owen smiled. " I think that would be just great, thanks."

Megan stood up as the phone rang. "That'll be my publishers. I'll leave you to it," she said. " Nice to see you again, Owen."

Chapter 59

The sea was relatively calm with a gentle swell as the fishing boat left the harbour and headed out along the coast. "Mackerel should be good off Wilson's point," the skipper, Jack Lewis, said, turning the boat into the open sea.

Duncan, sitting alongside Owen at the stern, said, "How are you feeling?"

"Fine. I'll be fine."

He was trying to be positive but in actual fact he felt anything but. The sun on his face the smell of the sea and the prospect of a long day fishing should have been the catalyst to lighten his mood but somehow it wasn't working. His new life with Rowena had filled his thoughts for months and now it was gone. He knew there was no chance that she'd forgive him. Sarah Lawson had got what she wanted; she'd damaged their relationship beyond repair. What did she hope to achieve by it, he wondered? Did she really believe he would run to her and forget all about Rowena?

"Penny for them?" Duncan nudged him.

"Eh?" Owen took a deep breath. " Just wondering if the fish will bite," he lied.

The Anchor was busy; a crowd had congregated outside and were drinking in the car park when, at a quarter past nine, Owen and Duncan arrived at the pub smelling of fish and salt water. Pleased with their catch, they pushed their way to the bar and ordered their drinks.

"This isn't much fun," murmured Duncan as a loud, overweight man with tattooed arms elbowed his way past them. " I think I'll call it a day. Fancy popping in for a nightcap on your way home?"

"Yes, I'd like that. If Megan can stand the smell of fish."

"She's used to it. Probably make us drink on the terrace but it's a fine night so why not?"

"Suits me."

Megan was working in her study on the top floor when they arrived. As Duncan had predicted they were banished to the terrace and were on their second 'nightcap' when she joined them.

"Good day?" she asked, sitting down.

"Excellent."

Looking intently at Owen she said, "There's something I need to tell you."

He knew it would come, just not when or what it would be. He was holding his breath, waiting.

"I had a phone call from my publishers earlier today. They wanted to arrange an appointment for me to see them to discuss the outline for the new book."

Owen exhaled with such force that Duncan raised an eyebrow and glanced at Megan, who seemed not to notice. She was twisting the cuff of her cotton Kaftan between her fingers.

"It was Sarah."

"I thought it might be." Owen put down his drink. "Right, let's have it then."

"You sound as if you were expecting trouble." Megan frowned.

"In a way. She's been like a weight around my neck for so long, I can't believe I'll ever be rid of her."

"After the preliminaries about the book were discussed, she asked if I'd seen you. I was on guard, so I said. 'Why do you ask, Sarah?' And she replied with something to the effect that you know what men are like. There was so much work arranging the wedding and now it looked as if you'd decided to get away for a bit."

"Wedding?" Owen looked confused.

"Yes. She said now that Rowena was 'out of the picture' you and she could get along with the plans you'd made without interference."

He shook his head. "It's just too ridiculous for words.

Duncan leaned forward in his seat. "I don't like the sound of this. You should get the police involved."

"How can I? They'd say it was her word against mine. There's nothing to prove one way or the other whether she's telling the truth."

"She's dangerous, Owen." Megan touched his arm. "You must be careful."

"I've got to get back. First thing in the morning, I'm going to London. This has to stop." He stood up. Duncan and Megan walked with him to the garden gate.

"You know that we are always here if you need us," Megan said, kissing his cheek.

"That's right. And I'll come up to London at the drop of a hat should you wish it." Duncan shook his hand.

The motorway was busy with rush hour traffic but he couldn't wait until later. He was trying to quell his outrage by concentrating on the road but the injustice of recent events obliterated everything else. Somehow he managed to reach the outskirts of the City without a major incident and took the well-worn route to his flat.

The acrid smell of smoke and charred wood hung like a curtain in the air as he looked up at what was left of his flat. The windows had gone, the brickwork showing blackened remnants of fire-damage. But it seemed to him that the surrounding flats had escaped with relatively minor damage. There was no sign of a fire engine just a thickset man standing in the foyer talking to the night warden. Owen opened the glass door.

"Here he is now, sir."

The thickset man stepped forward. "Chief Fire Officer Mason. I'd like to ask you a few questions if you don't mind, Mr Madoc."

Bewildered and shocked Owen nodded. "I've a few of my own that need some answers too. What on earth happened?"

"Perhaps we could find somewhere to talk?"

"In here, sir." Jack, the night warden indicated a room behind the desk, which was little more than a cupboard with two chairs and a table on which stood a small T.V.

The Fire Officer cleared his throat and began. "Apparently Miss Shaw had arranged to meet you and Miss Lawson here at eight o'clock last night? Miss Shaw arrived to find Miss Lawson smoking heavily and very upset, something about a forthcoming marriage? Anyway Miss Shaw said that she soon realised that you weren't coming and decided to leave Miss Lawson alone in the flat."

"I don't understand. I knew nothing about this meeting and how on earth did this Lawson woman get in without a key."

"The man at the desk let her in. She told him that you'd be coming along later. He said he recognised her as your fiancée."

Owen sighed.

"At about ten o'clock the night warden smelled smoke and alerted the Fire Brigade."

"What about the smoke alarm?"

"Batteries dead, from what we could see after our initial inspection."

"But I changed them a week ago." Mason frowned and coughed again. "Well, Mr Madoc you see Miss Lawson was still in the flat when the fire started and I'm afraid it was well under way by the time we arrived."

Trying to make sense of it all Owen hadn't considered whether anyone had been hurt. "Is she OK?"

"No. I'm afraid not. She was taken to St Thomas's with breathing difficulties and there are some facial burns. It looks as if she'd been smoking and had fallen asleep; all too common, in my experience."

Owen put his head in his hands. " I should go to the hospital."

"I wouldn't at present, sir. The police will want to take statements and they'll no doubt be in touch with both you and Miss Shaw. You should inform someone of where you are likely to be staying."

"How much damage is there? May I take a look?"

"Pretty extensive, I'm afraid. The fire was well contained though and fortunately hadn't spread to other properties. You can't go up there just yet, not until the Police and Fire services have finished their enquiries."

After the Fire Chief left, Owen told the warden that he'd be staying at the Travel Lodge in Covent Garden for a day or two. He was shaken and traumatised by the news; all he could think about was that it could have been Rowena and for that, at least, he was thankful.

He didn't want to think about Sarah. Remorse and Sarah no longer went hand in hand as far as he was concerned.

The room in the Travel Lodge was basic but clean. Owen picked up his phone and rang Rowena's number. Her voice sounded different, colder.

"It's me," he said

"You know then?"

"I arrived home from Wales this morning. The Fire Chief was still at the scene. He filled me in. I'm so glad you're not hurt."

Silence.

"Rowena?"

"Sarah's badly burnt."

"So I understand."

"She may be scarred for life."

"Let's not talk about Sarah. I want to know how you are."

"I thought you'd be there. I thought you'd come."

"I didn't know. I was in Gareg Wen. But I can meet you now, darling."

"It's different now. Things have changed. I'm going away."

"Where?"

"To Lockford initially then maybe to the States."

"Can I see you before you go?"

"No, I don't think so. Goodbye, Owen."

Owen heard the click as she cut the connection and he was left with nothing but the sound of silence.

Who is Sarah Lawson

Part 3

Chapter 60

It was getting dark when Richie Stevens decided to call it a day. He picked up the computer printouts that Sandy had left on his desk, stuffed them into the zipped pocket of his laptop case and locking the front door left the office. His intention was to stop at the wine bar around the corner for a quick drink then go home and sift through his paperwork.

The wine bar was full of the usual crowd of office workers on their way home and a few early drinkers. Sandy was sitting on a bar stool; she appeared to be alone and raised her glass to him as he approached. "So this is how you spend my money, is it?" he joked.

"Once in a while, boss."

"Right then, same again is it?"

Sandy looked doubtful. "I don't think so. I've got the car."

"Fair enough. Bottle of lager and an orange juice," he called to the barman.

"Did you get a chance to look at the stuff I left on your desk?" Sandy asked.

He shook his head. "Later though, I promise."

"I think you'll find some of it interesting. I certainly did."

"You did? What bits?"

Sandy shook her head. "Not a chance. I'm done for the day. Anyway I'd rather you came to your own conclusions without any spin from me."

"Point taken, Miss Smith." He raised his glass. "Just tell me this before we change the subject. What impression do *you* get of our client? Assuming you know nothing of her reasons for contacting us. Would you say she was a well-balanced individual?"

Sandy didn't answer immediately. He could see her weighing up the question. It was what he'd expect of her and it was one of the reasons he valued her opinion. "Well-balanced is not the description that immediately springs to mind. But perhaps the whole situation she finds herself in would be enough to unbalance anyone. I would describe her as being plausible. She says she's Rowena Shaw and it would be difficult not to believe her under the circumstances. Whether she's deluded or not, is a different matter."

Richie narrowed his eyes. "Have you ever thought of studying psychology?"

She laughed. "It might have escaped your notice that I have a first in the subject."

Abashed, he said, "I don't remember seeing that on your C.V. – perhaps I should retire now."

"Don't worry, it's not you. I didn't include it in my list of qualifications."

"Why ever not?"

"You might have considered me to be over qualified for the job. It's happened. And I wanted this job; there's nothing like fieldwork. I figured that the clients likely to seek the professional help of a Private Detective would have more than one or two problems to face."

"I can see I'll have to give you promotion, Miss Smith."

Sandy laughed out loud. "Chief secretary, eh?"

"Well not exactly; how does P.A. grab you?"

"Mm, the title's fine but would it involve me doing any more on the investigative side of the business?"

Richie thought for a moment. "Money's the problem. Ideally I'd like to say yes and employ an additional receptionist stroke secretary, so that you could do just that. But as you know, we're not exactly making a profit at present."

"OK then, how about this for a suggestion – my nephew has just finished his A levels and is looking for a job during the holidays until he starts college in the autumn. He could keep an eye on the desk and I'd pay him out of my wages."

He felt a knife turn in his guts. She was a good kid. "I appreciate your suggestion but I couldn't, I pay you little enough as it is."

"Let me be the judge of that. Oh and Harry is discretion itself. He wouldn't let you down."

"If he's a patch on his aunt then he'll do fine." He patted her arm.

"It's a deal then?" She looked eagerly at him and he hadn't the heart to refuse. He nodded.

"So, once Harry knows the ropes, I can begin my new job?" She raised her orange juice and clinked it against his glass.

"It's a deal." He reluctantly agreed.

It was half past nine by the time he had a chance to look at the computer printouts. Sandy had been thorough, as usual. Owen Madoc's name leapt out at him immediately. He was surprised given the newspaper coverage that he hadn't noticed the link before. He read on, mainly reports covering exhibitions of his work and interviews given with the man himself. He looked at the date – it was old news, over a year had passed. There were reports covering his proposed marriage and he was about to skip over the finer details when the name of his fiancée caught his eye. It was Rowena Shaw. It seemed she was a Public Relations consultant who worked with companies in both the U.K. and the United States. The photograph was blurred but he supposed it could be his client; it was not really clear enough for him to be sure.

He picked up the paper and inspected it more closely. The photograph showed Owen Madoc in the foreground facing the camera and his fiancée in profile. She was smiling, her hair falling to her shoulders. Apart from a superficial resemblance there was nothing more. When did they get married, he wondered, frantically searching through the rest of the material Sandy had given him? His eyes began to close before he reached a conclusion and he awoke an hour and a half later with a stiff neck and a yearning to pee. Bedtime beckoned and Richie succumbed, which was a pity. If he'd finished reading, he would have discovered the answer to his question.

Chapter 61

He'd had a disturbed night. His neck still hurt like hell. It was difficult to turn his head sideways. After a quick shower, stepping into the trousers he'd worn the previous day and pulling on a clean shirt, Richie picked up his laptop case and shoved Sandy's printouts into the pocket without giving them a second glance.

Later, as he climbed the stairs to his office he heard the sound of voices drifting down the stairwell and pushing the door open with his foot he saw Sandy standing over a youth with spiky red hair who was taking instruction from his aunt. He stood up as Richie entered the room.

"Harry, I presume," he said stretching to shake the lad's outstretched hand. "Good to meet you. Your aunt told me to expect you but I hadn't realised quite so soon."

"Is it alright?" Harry looked from one to the other.

"I don't see why not. Welcome aboard. Sandy will show you the ropes. And when you're satisfied that Harry is not going to cause us to lose any of our computerised files perhaps you'd come into my office, Miss Smith. There's something I want to discuss with my new P.A."

"I thought there might be," Sandy replied. "Quite a shock, isn't it?"

"It's certainly a surprise, though I wouldn't go so far as to say shock."

"Really?" Sandy frowned.

Two phone calls and cup of coffee later Richie opened his laptop case and removed the printouts. Five minutes later he was out of his seat and standing in the doorway. "Now, please, Miss Smith."

Sandy said, "So you hadn't read them all last night? I thought so."

He tried to shake his head and winced. "Fell asleep in the chair. So they never did get married?"

"Not as far as I can see," she said, sitting down opposite him.

"An accident, the report says. Something to do with a fire." Richie picked up the file. "At first the police suspected arson, as Madoc's cottage in Wales was burnt to the ground in a fire the previous year."

"That's true but the fire department's findings were inconclusive and pointed towards a cigarette left unattended."

"A Miss Sarah Lawson was badly injured in the fire. Now that is interesting, surely?"

"Our Miss Shaw do you think?"

"That is the question."

Harry turned out to be a carbon copy of his

Who is Sarah Lawson

aunt, efficient, helpful, and entirely trustworthy.

Within the week he'd settled into office life in Hastings Buildings as if he'd been working there for years. Richie felt confident that Sandy and he could travel to London leaving him to take phone calls and book appointments. He did however stress the importance of keeping the office diary up to date and making sure that he had their mobile numbers locked into his own phone and if he had any problems, he should ring them immediately.

During the drive Sandy made notes on a small hand held computer and by the time they'd reached the outskirts of the city she'd compiled a detailed itinerary for the duration of their visit. He knew she was wasted as an office worker and he also knew that her days working for him were numbered. She was killing time and when it suited her she'd fly away like a swallow at the end of summer but in the meantime he decided to lie back and enjoy being organised.

The Travel Lodge in Covent Garden was convenient and comfortable. Their rooms were situated on the second floor and were separated by a lift shaft.

"I wouldn't want to spend more that a day or two in there. My room's little more than a cupboard," Sandy said as she joined him in the corridor. "Where do you propose we should eat?"

"I thought we'd take a walk in the direction

of the Furnish Gallery and see if there's a restaurant near by; kill two birds with one stone."

"After we've visited Fox and Knight. We're expected there at ten thirty."

"Efficiency is your middle name, Miss Smith."

"Nearly right; it's Eva actually."

"Right then Eva actually, I hope you're in the mood for a walk."

Chapter 62

At half-past ten on the dot Wilma Forrest led them into her office. She was Assistant Editor in the firm of Fox and Knight, publishers. "Mr Stevens, Miss Smith, do take a seat. Now what can I do for you? You said on the telephone that it concerned one of our employees."

Sandy removed a notebook from her handbag.

"It's about Sarah Lawson," Richie said. "My client wishes to contact her. She's a relative and has been living abroad. It would appear that she's tried to contact Miss Lawson for some time without success."

Wilma Forrest pursed her lips. "So sad," she muttered.

He feigned surprise. "Sad?"

"Yes. Sarah did work for us. She was a very good office worker; one or two of our authors developed quite a bond with her. If she'd had better qualifications she would have made a very good assistant. She was very efficient and would drive for miles to make sure that proofs reached our authors safely. Megan Lloyd

Jones thought she was a real treasure."

"Do you mean, the crime writer, the one that was responsible for the Detective Inspector Gifford series?" Sandy asked.

"The same."

Steering the conversation back on track, he said, "You mentioned that it was 'sad' about Sarah?"

"Yes, there was a fire. She'd been visiting a friend, who was getting married and a fire broke out in the flat. Sarah was badly burned and I believe she left London to be near her brother somewhere on the South coast, although I'm afraid I don't know where exactly."

Richie stood up. "Thank you for seeing us, Miss Forrest. I'm sorry we've taken up so much of your valuable time."

"Not at all. Oh, and if you do manage to find Sarah, please tell her that we all wish her well."

Richie nodded and followed Sandy out into the sunshine.

"So Sarah Lawson was badly burned. Have you noticed your client touching a scar under her fringe, by any chance?" Sandy asked.

"Nothing escapes you, does it, Miss Smith?"

"So what d'you think?"

"It's not conclusive but it's something to consider. Now let's have lunch and follow up the next appointment on our list."

After lunch they visited the Furnish Gallery. Sandy was posing as a potential buyer. Mark Furnish hovering at her elbow. Richie watched the tableau unfold from behind the pages of a catalogue, whilst seated in a bright blue armchair in an alcove.

"I was wondering if you had any paintings by Owen Madoc on show?" Sandy asked looking over the top of a pair of tortoise-shell framed spectacles.

He admired her transformation into a sophisticated art lover, head held high, spectacles changing her slightly bohemian appearance and giving her an intellectual air. Even her walk had changed, she moved with grace and poise.

"Not at present I'm afraid. Owen's work has always been popular. In fact you'd be very lucky to get hold of an original now. He hasn't painted anything new for some time."

"Oh really?" Sandy remarked.

"Mm a tragedy in my opinion. I've tried pleading with him on several occasions but he's just not keen. He says his inspiration has gone." Mark Furnish bent his head closer to Sandy, and Richie smiled, noticing that in no time at all she'd managed to gain his confidence. "It started when his marriage plans fell apart."

"Oh what a shame. You and he were friends?"

"We were; I gave him his first break. I always knew he'd make it big."

"Do you know anyone who might be willing to sell one of his paintings?"

Mark Furnish started to shake his head. "Not to sell, no, but if you're keen to see some of his work I suggest you contact Megan Lloyd Jones out at Gareg Wen. She has a few pieces. She's such a dear that I'm sure she'd let you take a look at them. I could give her a ring if you like, to let her know you're coming. I have her phone number here somewhere"

"You would? That's extremely kind of you Mr Furnish. You don't think she'd mind?"

"Not at all." He walked to the reception desk and came back with a card, which he handed to Sandy. "When you're ready give her a ring to arrange a time." He walked with them to the door and held it open.

"By the way," he said, shaking his hand. " Would you have a contact number for Owen Madoc?"

Mark Furnish raised an eyebrow. "Not in this country, I'm afraid. Owen is living in Spain. Pity really, he had everything going for him, flourishing career, beautiful fiancée but after the fire he lost interest in most things."

Outside, he steered Sandy towards a café. "We have to talk to Owen Madoc. He's the key to unlocking this mess."

"After or before we've talked to Megan Lloyd Jones?"

"First things first, Miss Smith. Wales, then if you're up for it, a nice trip to Spain."

"All expenses paid?"

"It depends."

"On?" "Well on Harry for a start. We both can't leave the office, unless he's able to cope."

"He will be."

"You're sure?"

"Certain."

Later, driving back to their hotel Richie handed Sandy his phone. "Give Megan Lloyd Jones a ring. See when we can pop down to Gareg Wen tomorrow if possible, after we've visited Aston and Cooper. I still can't believe that you were able to get an introduction from Mark Furnish, it was more than we'd anticipated."

When they arrived back in Richie's room Sandy checked in with Harry. "He's fine. He said Rowena Shaw visited this morning but only to see if there'd been any developments. He told her that we were in London and at first she seemed a bit agitated then she calmed down, said 'good' and left."

It was ten thirty the following day and the streets of London were busy. Richie and Sandy walked to the offices of Aston and Cooper, which were in the heart of the City. Their appointment was for eleven and Martin Forbes, a junior executive showed them into his office. "I'll have to keep this short, I'm afraid – busy, busy, you know how it is. You mentioned on the phone that you wanted to discuss the whereabouts of one of our employees, a Miss Rowena Shaw?"

He smiled. "That's right. "

"I'm new here but I've made some enquiries and Miss Shaw did work for us a while back."

Sandy sat up. " When exactly?"

"A couple of months, maybe as long as a year ago, sorry I can't be more specific without going into our files and I just haven't got the time at the moment – as I said, busy, busy. She was working in the States. I think she terminated her contract with us quite suddenly from what I understand. If that's any help."

"Would you know where I could contact her? A relative is keen to get in touch."

"I don't. We have no forwarding address on file and if we had, I'm not sure it would be strictly P.C. to pass it on without her permission."

"I see. Well thank you for your time, Mr Forbes." He stood up and reaching into his pocket removed his business card. "If Miss Shaw does get in contact with you perhaps you could ask her to give us a call on this number?"

"Certainly and good luck with your search."

The next day Richie loaded the Sat Nav with details of their destination in Wales and after a hearty breakfast they left the City. The roads were fairly free of traffic and they arrived on the outskirts of Gareg Wen at a quarter past two, booked a couple of rooms at the Anchor for the night and in the morning drove down the lane to the cliff top house that belonged to the Joneses.

"That's Owen Madoc's cottage," Sandy said as they passed a For Sale sign swinging in the breeze.

"Is it indeed? You really know your stuff, Miss Smith, I'm impressed."

"It was burnt down under suspicious circumstances some time ago; the police never did find who was responsible."

Richie looked at the cottage in his rear view mirror. "Now that is interesting. Perhaps we should have a chat to the locals, for the price of a pint or two they may be willing to remember some of the details."

The house was certainly impressive. Sandy stretched as she closed the car door and followed him towards the front door.

"What a great view," she said, as the door opened.

"We like to think so," Megan smiled and stood back to let them pass. "Please do come in."

"This is very kind of you, Mrs Lloyd Jones," Richie said, following Megan into a large conservatory at the back of the house. "Your garden is splendid."

"I'm glad you like it. Now do sit down. Would you like a cup of tea?"

"Thank you and thanks for taking the trouble to answer a few of our questions. I'm afraid we weren't exactly straight with Mr Furnish, as I told you on the phone. In our business, subterfuge is sometimes a necessity."

"I must say I was intrigued. We haven't heard from Owen for some time. We were good friends a while back but well- let me put the kettle on and we can talk properly."

When she returned, she set the tray on the table, poured the tea then sat down.

"So you knew Mr Madoc, when the fire started at his flat, I understand?" Richie began.

"We did. Duncan and I were very fond of him. In fact Owen was staying in his cottage at Fallow's End the night it happened. He'd been on a fishing trip with my husband and some friends during the day and he called in here for a nightcap. But I was concerned about him."

"Oh, why was that?"

"He was still raw about Rowena cancelling the wedding."

"He wanted it to go ahead then?"

"Most certainly. It was all a mess. Sarah, the young lady who was badly burned in the fire, had a bit of a thing about Owen. So much so that she was responsible for causing nothing but trouble between him and his fiancée." She sighed. "And to cut a long story short Owen was certain that it was she who had started the fire at his cottage." Megan stood up and walked to the window. "As if that wasn't enough it seems she was also inadvertently responsible for what happened at the flat"

"How terrible, what happened?" Sandy asked.

"Well apparently Sarah had given up smoking some time before but her brother mentioned to the police that since she met Owen she'd taken up the habit again. It was thought that she'd left a cigarette unattended and it had lodged in the soft furnishings. If the fire brigade hadn't arrived so promptly who knows what might have happened."

"Was she alone?" Sandy was listening intently.

"Not initially. Afterwards Rowena told Owen that Sarah had phoned to say that he wanted them both to meet him at the flat in an attempt to sort out their problems."

"So they were all there?"

"No. Owen was adamant that he'd never said anything of the sort and was unaware that there was to be such a meeting. Rowena said she left once she realised Sarah had lied and that he wasn't going to show after all."

"It doesn't make much sense. Why would Sarah Lawson lie? What did she hope to achieve?"

"Your guess is as good as mine. Now it would seem she's paying the price, poor girl." Megan sighed. "Initially I was quite fond of her, until I found out about the trouble she'd caused. Owen couldn't move for her, she hounded him; I suppose you could say she stalked him."

"I see." Richie stood up. "Thank you so much for the tea and for the information, Mrs Lloyd Jones, it's much appreciated."

"Megan, please. You told me on the phone that you're making enquiries on behalf of your client?"

"That's right."

"Would you be able to tell me who that client would be?"

Richie stroked his chin.

"Well now, that's the big question," he replied. "Who *is* Sarah Lawson?"

Chapter 63

There was no one in the office except a young man with red spiky hair who told me that his boss and his aunt were away working on an investigation. Part of me was pleased that they were doing something positive and part of me was fearful that their efforts would turn out to be futile.

Leaving Hastings Buildings and walking down the High Street, I felt impotent rage bubbling up inside like a volcano threatening to erupt. My memory was not reliable. The events leading to my break up with Owen were unclear. I remember accusing him of having an affair but with whom was still a mystery.

A warm wind blew my hair into my face and I pushed it away irritably. My fingers touched the scar and images floated around me begging to be let in. Why couldn't I remember? The only reliable constant was that I knew who I was and I was definitely not Sarah Lawson. It was then that I saw Neil Stafford. He was coming out of Starbucks carrying a giant polystyrene mug of coffee. I hurried across the road, eager not to lose sight of him.

"Mr Stafford?"

He looked surprised.

"Sarah?"

"Could you spare me a moment?"

Glancing at the hand holding his mug, he hesitated. "I, er, I'm on my way back to work actually – coffee break but I suppose I could just as well drink it here as in the office." He pointed to a bench and we sat down. "Now then, what can I do for you?"

"When we last met you said you remembered me from my brother's party."

"Yes, that's right – Andy had a bit of a do at the golf club."

"The thing is –well - I'm afraid I've been having some memory problems."

"Mm yes, Andy told me. Rotten luck, the accident and all that."

"I wonder, could you tell me exactly what Andy said. I know it sounds odd, but it would help enormously."

He raised his mug, took a sip, winced then replied, " Let me see. He said that his sister had moved to Lockford from London after a fire in which she'd been badly burned. He mentioned something about a love affair that had ended badly. He said you'd had problems remembering much of what had happened before the fire and that a psychiatrist had diagnosed something called retrograde amnesia, which sometimes happens after a traumatic event." He attempted to drink his coffee again and this time managed to drink more than half of it before continuing.

"Apparently, he said it was all very distressing as at first you believed you were someone else."

"Who? Did he say who?" I was hanging on to his sleeve. He broke away, frowned and said. "No, look, I think you should ask Andy about this, he'll tell you far more than I can."

I smiled, trying to appear normal and not some deranged female who'd accosted him in the street. "You're right of course. I was just anxious not to rake it all up for him. I'm afraid I've been a bit of a pain lately. But you've been really helpful. Thank you so much. I'm sorry to have interrupted your coffee break." I smiled again.

He shrugged and stood up. "No problem. I hope your memory returns soon."

"So do I, Mr Stafford. So do I."

It was true that there were areas that were lost to me but it didn't alter the fact that however difficult it was to remember certain events, I wasn't suffering from a loss of identity even though the Lawson family were trying to make me believe otherwise. I knew I was Rowena Shaw and was determined to prove it.

If only Owen would answer my calls. At least he'd know me. I'd thought about going to see my old boss in London but I'd rung the office and been told that he'd moved on and was now working in San Francisco. Knowing that office staff frequently changed, I couldn't risk finding that no one there knew me either; I doubted whether my sanity was ready for that sort of revelation.

Whilst Richie Stevens was working in London, I decided that I'd take the train to Cardiff where I'd book into a hotel and then try to contact Glyn Morgan at the BBC Wales studios. He might recognise me, it was worth a try, it was no good telephoning, I'd tried that.

The train journey took nearly four and a half hours. Reading the rest of my novel had been replaced by watching the scenery pass, filling in a crossword puzzle and flicking through a trashy celebrity magazine that someone had left behind. Eventually the sunshine gave way to showers as the train pulled into Cardiff General Station. Taking a taxi to a city centre hotel, I realised that for the past couple of hours I'd not given Sarah Lawson, a second thought.

Getting away from Lockford had slackened the chains that were tying me to her, if only for a while.

Dinner that evening was taken in a dining room overlooking the Castle Grounds and for the first time in ages I began to relax, to be me, and to enjoy being somewhere no one thought they knew me.

Before I showered and dressed for dinner I switched on the six o'clock news and as I'd anticipated Glyn Morgan was definitely back from Tokyo. He was standing outside the St David's Spa Hotel interviewing the winner of the X Factor heats that had been held in Cardiff that weekend.

After breakfast the following day, I strolled out of my hotel and into the Castle Grounds. The previous day's rain had given way to bright sunshine. Feeling the warm breeze stroking my skin, I took a deep breath and walked alongside the river whilst watching an eager line of ducklings following in their parents' wake. At mid-day, I took a taxi to the television studios and at the reception desk asked if they could tell Glyn Morgan that Rowena Shaw was waiting for him in reception. Ten minutes later I heard his voice. I was standing with my back to him reading a flyer about a forthcoming series of Dr Who.

"Rowena?"

I turned around and saw him hesitate. But it was only for a second.

"My God girl, you've changed."

"You recognise me?"

"Shouldn't I?"

I could have wept. "It's been such a long time," I muttered.

"I'd recognise that arse, anywhere, my love." He pulled me to him in a bear hug and kissed my cheek. "Now let's get some lunch in the canteen then you can tell me what this is all about and what's with the new face?"

In the BBC canteen, I recognised a couple of well-known actors and a news presenter, one of whom raised his hand to Glyn as we passed his table and made for the seclusion of an unoccupied table overlooking the car park. As we finished eating, I outlined the reason for my visit.

"And there's no way you can prove you're not this Sarah Lawson?"

"Not at the moment. But I'm working on it via a Private Detective. You have no idea how difficult it's been." My cheeks were wet. I pulled a tissue out of my bag. "I didn't mean to do this. It's just such a relief that you believe me."

Glyn reached across and took my hand. "Why did you?" I asked.

"What?"

"Why did you recognise me? It couldn't be just my bum."

He smiled and patted my hand. "I'd spent most of my years at Uni, worshipping every inch of Rowena Shaw, my dear. OK the face is different, but the rest of you isn't and even the face is not that different."

"You seem to be the only one who thinks so."

"Well, put it this way. In my line of business, I've come across plenty of burn victims and some, like you, have been put back together again, almost intact."

"Burn victims?" It was as if the room was dissolving. His voice sounded a long way off. I could feel my lungs burning and hear her voice.

"Row? Are you OK? You've gone as white as the proverbial sheet."

My head was spinning. The next thing I knew Glyn was sitting at my side.

"Here drink this." He was holding a bottle of water to my lips. "I think we should go outside, lovely – get some fresh air – it's stuffy as hell in here."

Chapter 64

"You're sure you're OK?" Glyn said holding open the taxi door.

"I'm better than OK, Glyn. Thanks for everything. I'm sorry to have taken up so much of your time."

"Nonsense. I only wish I wasn't dashing off again and we could spend more time together. But remember what I said, you should take this to the police and let them deal with it. And remember now – stay in touch."

I nodded, " I promise. And I will think about the police, when the time is right."

Later, in the foyer of my hotel, I picked up some travel brochures, went to sit in the lounge and ordered afternoon tea. As I flicked though the brochures I thought about my conversation with Glyn. So the accident Andy Lawson had been referring to had actually taken place. I'd suffered facial burns. Glyn had explained that the scars, although carefully concealed by my hairline, were indicative of plastic surgery having taken place at some point. He said that by the slight reddening of the scar tissue, in his estimation, the operation would have taken place approximately a year ago.

Feeling positive for the first time since this nightmare began, I noticed that my fingers had stopped at a page showing a picturesque Welsh fishing village. There was something distinctly familiar about the photograph showing a pub and the harbour. The place was called Gareg Wen.

The more I looked at the photograph I was sure I'd been there before. Owen's face swam before me and a wave of nausea had me reaching for my teacup. A few sips and a deep breath later I felt able to read the blub underneath the photo.

Situated in the peaceful countryside of West Wales is the fishing village of Gareg Wen. Step back in time by staying at the Anchor, whose stout walls were still standing at the time of the French invasion of West Wales at the end of the eighteenth century, when local woman Jemima Nicholls tricked the French fleet into believing women dressed in national costume were a detachment of British forces. Walk the coastal paths, with uninterrupted spectacular views of the coves and bays that have inspired many of our established British writers and painters, including crime fiction and thriller writer Megan Lloyd Jones who, with her husband Duncan, has been a resident of Gareg Wen for the past ten years.

The words blurred, my pulse raced and for a

moment a hole into the past opened. I struggled to reach through and grasp fragments in complete the jigsaw of my muddled memory order to but faces and events floated away from me like feathers on a breeze.

"Would you like more tea, Madam?" the waiter asked.

"No thanks. But could you tell me where I could hire a car?"

I'd made up my mind; Gareg Wen must hold the answers to some of the questions that plagued me. Although, like most people, I knew of Megan Lloyd Jones by her reputation, I had the niggling feeling that the name meant more to me than that. So after paying my hotel bill and sliding into the hire car that was waiting in the car park, I instructed the satellite navigation system to find Gareg Wen and followed its instructions faithfully out of the city and on to the M4 heading west.

Summer it seemed had come early, trees bursting with mayflowers lined my route as I left the main motorway and headed west along minor roads. The road signs, although few and far between, were bi-lingual and a sudden memory of Owen trying to pronounce the unpronounceable made me smile. I was right then, I'd travelled this way before and with my fiancé. The word lodged in my brain like a splinter, something about it was distasteful.

Why should that be? Surely it was meant to

evoke happy memories? There must have been some.

The narrow road leading to Gareg Wen wound steeply down to the coast. In the distance I glimpsed the sea sparkling like newly minted coins and, as I drove closer, smelled the tang of salt in the breeze. It was all so familiar and yet so out of reach.

The car park of the Anchor was fairly busy but nevertheless I managed to find a parking place and went inside to book a room. As my eyes adjusted to the lack of sunlight, I saw that the holiday brochure had been spot on; it was just like stepping back in time. The décor had been sympathetically restored to an earlier period but without any lack of comfort. I walked up to the bar. "Could I book a room for a few days?" I asked a large man with greying sideburns standing behind the bar and who looked as if he was part of the furniture.

"You could be in luck, Miss. A couple just booked out this morning. We've been full up this past week, what with the good weather and summer on the way." He went to the corner of the bar, flipped open a laptop, typed in a few commands and then turned back to me. "Number three overlooking the view of the coast, do you, will it?"

"That sounds fine. I'll just pop back to the car and get my case. Won't be a sec."

"No problem. Nice to see you again, Miss Lawson."

The words followed me into the car park and I refused to let them in.

Lifting my small case out of my boot I noticed two men striding up the lane towards me. The taller of the two had his head bent in conversation with a man dressed in shorts and a blue shirt whose neck was circled by a clerical collar. They reached the front door as I approached with my case. The taller man looked up, hesitated then said, "Sarah?"

My heart sank. Not only because he'd called me Sarah but also because I was certain that I'd met him before.

Chapter 65

Warm air wrapped around them as they stepped off the plane. Sandy removed her cotton cardigan and stuffed it in her travel bag.

"Hotter than I expected," she commented following Richie across the tarmac to the arrivals lounge.

"I've organised a hire car to be picked up in the car park; it's approximately a half hour drive to our hotel so it shouldn't take long.

Later, sitting in the air-conditioned interior of the car as he drove away from the airport terminal building, Sandy said, "How did you find him so quickly?"

"I rang Megan in Gareg Wen and asked her if she had an address for him in Spain."

"And she did?"

Richie nodded whilst negotiating a slip road. "She said it was fortunate that I'd rung because, a friend of theirs had recently returned from a holiday in Los Christophe, a small Spanish village, and had met Owen Madoc in an open-air market. She said the friend recognised him immediately having met him at Megan's birthday party a while back."

"And?"

"Well, the friend struck up a conversation with Madoc who wanted to know how the Joneses were getting along and he promised to drop them a line."

"A long shot, I should think, men are always promising to write and never doing it, in my experience."

"Which is no doubt extensive," he observed with a grin. " But that's quite incorrect in this case, Miss Smith. He sent them a 'wish you were here postcard, with his address and asking them to call if they were holidaying in the area."

The car drew to a halt.

"Is this it?" Sandy asked, looking up at the small hotel Richie had booked on the Internet.

"It is. Not exactly the Ritz, I know but cheap and cheerful and not too far away from Madoc's place."

"Ideal, I'm sure," Sandy said doubtfully.

The following morning after breakfast Richie and Sandy stood in the foyer of the hotel; it was early but the temperature was already rising.

"What's the plan?" Dressed in a pale yellow sundress Sandy looked up at him through the largest sunglasses he'd ever seen.

"I suggest we walk into the village. It's not far and as it's early it shouldn't be too uncomfortable. You might want to wear that sun hat you're dangling from your fingers, though."

With a sudden gesture she plonked the hat firmly on her head. "This do?" She grinned.

"Excellent, Miss Smith. Now if you're ready, we'll be off."

The road leading to the village was not much more than a lane bordered on one side by a dried up hedge and on the other by a ditch. A man, woman and a child of about ten wobbled past on hire bicycles, the man nodding his thanks as they stood aside to let them pass.

"He lives on the outskirts of the village," Richie said, wiping his forehead with his handkerchief.

"Hot enough for you?" Sandy asked handing him a bottle of water she'd removed from the depths of an oversized bag she'd slung over her shoulder.

"Thanks. I've just realised that I'm not as young as I think I am."

"Nonsense, it's sitting behind a desk all winter, that's all."

Encouraged, Richie took a deep breath and picked up his pace. "We're almost there," he said pointing to a group of cottages in front of a small field. "Yes, there's the sign for Los Christophe. I wonder if Owen Madoc will be tempted to visit the village this morning. That would save us having to concoct a story to explain why we were visiting him."

"That wouldn't be too difficult surely. We'd only have to tell him about our case."

"Yes, but I can't help thinking it might be

better to keep quiet about our motives, at least for a while."

"Why?" Sandy looked up at him as she stopped to polish her sunglasses on the hem of her dress.

"Because I'm not sure about him and the part he's played in this case."

"I see. Let's hope you're right then. It's always possible. There doesn't appear to be much going on around here. Look, there, in the square. I think there's a market. We could be in luck."

In the shade of an awning outside a café Richie and Sandy sat drinking coffee whilst they waited. Some of the stallholders were still setting out their goods and a few early shoppers were ambling through the market place.

"Will we recognise him?" Sandy asked.

"Take another look." He handed her a copy of the photograph that had been in Rowena Shaw's album. " This face is imprinted on my brain, I've looked at it that often."

"He could look different now. This was taken a few years back." Sandy held the photo up and shaded her eyes.

"Mm, that's true but we can only hope he's not unrecognisable. His stature is average, his hair colour unremarkable, all of which could apply to almost anyone. We'll hang around here for a while and if all else fails we'll have to call on him, which I'd like to avoid if possible."

An hour later the sun had moved so that even the awning was no shelter from its searing rays.

"Let's take a walk across the square. There's a bar that looks inviting and if I'm not mistaken, from that table in the corner of the terrace, we should have a good view of the other entrance to the market place," Richie said.

"A cool beer would help too, don't you think?

"Excellent idea."

The market was in full swing by mid-day; villagers crowded the more popular stalls or haggled over prices on the periphery. Richie was feeling the effects of the heat and dehydration thanks to having drunk more than he'd intended. As a result his observation wasn't as acute as it might have been. However, no such lack of concentration affected his P.A. Sandy nudged his arm.

"That's him. I'm certain of it. Look over there. He's standing next to a tall woman with black hair wearing a red dress, you can't miss him."

He peered into the sunshine. "I'm not sure."

Sandy dragged him to his feet. "Let's take a closer look."

They walked towards a stall selling cotton skirts and blouses next to one selling fruit, in front of which the couple stood.

"Well?" hissed Sandy picking up a blue and white cotton skirt. "What d'you think?"

He nodded.

"What now?" She replaced the skirt and inspected a white blouse on the rack nearer the fruit stall.

Ignoring her question, he approached the

couple.

"Excuse me, I wonder if you could help my niece and me, as we appear to be unable to make ourselves understood."

Owen Madoc turned away from the woman. "What's the problem?" he asked.

"Sandy would like to buy this blouse but she thinks it costs too much. Could you ask the stallholder if he'd accept ten euros less for it?"

The woman in the red dress smiled. "You could try, darling but I don't think Alejo will accept a deal. I know him and he's never been known to cut his prices."

Sandy gave a rueful shrug. "Thanks. I'm no good at haggling anyway. C'mon Uncle Richie, let's see if we can find a bargain elsewhere."

"What it is to be young," Richie sighed. "Sorry to have bothered you. It's just, when I heard your accent, it reminded me of holidays spent in Wales."

"Really? I've not lived in Wales for a while; I'm surprised I still have an accent. Where did you stay, when you visited Wales?" Madoc removed his sunglasses and polished them with a handkerchief.

He could now see what he'd missed from a distance. This was definitely the man who'd been engaged to Rowena Shaw. The man, Richie was certain, who would lead them to the truth.

"Doubt if you'd know the place. It's a small fishing village on the South coast called Gareg Wen."

Chapter 66

The euphoric feeling I'd experienced after leaving Gwyn lasted until I turned the key in the lock of the featureless flat my 'family' insisted was mine. I rang Richard Stevens at his office only to be told by an unfamiliar voice that Mr Stevens and his P.A. were out of the country on business and would contact me on their return. It seemed that the young boy with red hair had been left in charge. I stressed that it was vitally important that I speak with Mr Stevens but was told that my message would be relayed to him. Biting my fingernails in frustration I wondered where I should go next in my quest to discover the truth. I massaged my forehead in an attempt to forestall a headache and ran my fingertips over the scar. Andy Lawson's words rushed back like a slap in the face. "If you continue with this, Sarah, I'll have to call Dr Kilpatrick at the Hermitage."

Perhaps it was time to take matters into my own hands. I rang directory enquiries, then rang the Hermitage and made an appointment to see

Dr Kilpatrick giving my name as Sarah Lawson.

The taxi dropped me outside the front gates. I wanted to see if there was anything about the place I recognised. To my dismay, I soon realised that there was. The curving pebbled drive leading to the front door was distinctly familiar as were the neat flower beds and close cropped lawn where patients sat on benches in the sunshine or wandered the grounds closely followed by carers or medical staff. I took a deep breath and steeling myself for what I might find pressed the bell. A young woman wearing a business suit opened the door.

"Sarah Lawson. I have an appointment with Dr Kilpatrick for two-fifteen," I said following the young woman into a reception area.

"Please take a seat, I'll call you when Doctor is ready."

I instantly recognised a Stubbs painting of a stallion with a gleaming coat. I'd sat looking at that painting before. My pulse began to race. After a short while the receptionist indicated a door on my right but she had no need, I'd known it would be there all along.

"Miss Lawson, Doctor Kilpatrick will see you now."

He was a man in his mid fifties with longish grey hair thinning at the crown. He was wearing a tweed three-piece suit, even though it was twenty degrees outside. As I passed him I detected a faint smell of sweat that had impregnated the tweed and which had been ineffectively smothered by cologne. A vision of Owen drifted into my consciousness initiated by the smell of the cologne. I felt nauseous.

"You look pale, Miss Lawson. Are you feeling ill?"

An odd question for a doctor to ask; I felt hysteria bubbling up inside. I nodded. "It's the heat, I expect. Could I trouble you for a glass of water?"

"Of course." He moved to the corner of the room where an upturned plastic water bottle dispenser sat, slid a polystyrene cup under the nozzle then handed it to me. "Relax and take small sips," he advised.

When I felt better he asked, " How have you been, Sarah?"

"Physically I'm fine, my anaemia is well controlled, Doctor but I need to clear up a few points as my memory is playing tricks and has done for some time."

"Understandably."

"Is it? You see Andy referred to the fact that I'd had an accident but he seems reluctant to explain its nature."

"Ah, I see. Well that would be because I'd advised him not to discuss the details with you."

"Why not?"

The Doctor frowned, leaned forward and bit his bottom lip. " In cases of retrograde amnesia such as yours, it's my feeling that the patient should be left to remember the traumatic incident, which was responsible for the loss of memory, independently rather than confuse the issue by extraneous input."

"What if the patient never remembers?"

"In my experience, that is rarely the case."

"But what if the patient wished to have the circumstances explained fully?" I persisted.

"What is it, Sarah?"

It was my turn to lean forward in my seat, my turn to be forceful for once. "I want you to tell me what happened. I'm not interested in case histories. This is my life Dr Kilpatrick and I'm asking you once and for all to explain, where and how I got these scars." I pulled my fringe away from my forehead and waited for his reply.

The heat of the afternoon was beginning to fade as I waited outside the gates for my taxi to arrive. I'd stopped shaking but my anger at the collusion between Dr Kilpatrick and my 'family' was not so easily dispersed. It was an outrageous and archaic concept, I reasoned. How could they agree to keep me in the dark? It was barbaric.

Eventually he'd told me about the fire in Owen's flat. Sarah Lawson was alone when it started. She'd been smoking. It appeared that a cigarette had slipped into the upholstery and she'd been taken to St Thomas's hospital suffering from facial burns and smoke inhalation. My scars were the result of facial surgery; everything pointed to me being Sarah Lawson, apart from the fact that I knew nothing would ever have induced me to smoke a cigarette. So it seemed that my visit to see Dr Kilpatrick had left me with more questions than answers.

Chapter 67

In the library, I Googled Owen Madoc with no luck other than that he was artist who spent his time living in London and his cottage in West Wales. I knew that the details were out-dated so searched again. This time I discovered a small entry in a newspaper article that read – *The artist Owen Madoc, famous for his collection entitled 'Seasons' has left the U.K. in search of inspiration in Spain. Mr Madoc stopped producing work for the esteemed Mark Furnish Art Gallery some time ago. Mr Furnish told me that he hoped to show more of Mr Madoc's work in the not too distant future.*

At the bus stop I waited in the gathering gloom. Rain clouds hung threateningly in the sky. I turned up my collar and hoped I'd escape the shower before I reached the flat. Throughout the short journey, I could think of nothing but my relationship with Owen. I remembered the plans for our wedding. But the love we once shared was something I could no longer feel. The emptiness had something to do with Sarah Lawson but I could not tie the threads together in my mind, however hard I tried.

Arthur, the old man was standing near a bench feeding the birds from a carrier bag containing scraps. He raised his hand to me as I approached. "Just made it home in time, love. Them clouds are getting lower by the minute. I'm just going to finish feeding these little beauties before I go home for a brew."

His grey hair was badly cut and deep furrows creased his brow but I could see that his clothes were clean and not too shabby. He didn't sound as if he was confused or senile, so why would a perfect stranger be involved in this charade?

"Excuse me, I wonder if you could remind me how long we've known each other." He screwed up his eyes as if thinking.

"Nigh on a year or two back, I should say. I remember you moved in after Doris died. Nice lady, kind to me, used to bake me fruit cake every Friday." He was off on a tangent.

"And I look the same, as when I moved in, do I?"

He didn't appear to think the question was unusual. "No love, especially not you young 'uns; you seem to change by the minute, change your clothes, hair, shape, you never look the same from one day to the next."

"Do you remember what colour my hair was when I moved in?"

"What's this then, eh? Twenty questions, is it?"

I smiled a tight smile that didn't reach my eyes. "Something like that."

"Well now, let me see. I do as a matter of fact 'cos it was the same colour as my granddaughter, the colour of mud. I used to tease her – muddylocks, I used to call her – my granddaughter, I mean, not you of course."

"Thank you, Arthur. Thank you very much."

"No problem, Sarah love, and how is that brother of yours keeping?"

With the smile slipping from my face like a melting icicle, I answered, "He's fine, thank you."

The name Mark Furnish bothered me; day-by-day I had the feeling that my previous life was resurfacing bit by tortuous bit. I rang directory enquiries and was put through to the Gallery.

"Furnish Gallery. How may I help you?"

"I'd like to speak to Mark Furnish please. You could tell him it's Rowena Shaw."

"Hold on please, Miss Shaw." The Entrance of the Queen of Sheba floated into my ear as I waited to see whether he'd take my call. I crossed my fingers

"Rowena?" I recognised the slightly effeminate voice immediately.

"Hello, Mr Furnish. I wonder if you could spare me a moment or two of your precious time?"

"Of course. I'm just surprised to hear you after all this time. What can I do for you, my dear?

I decided to get to the point straight away.

"Would you have an address or phone number where I could contact Owen, please?"

Silence.

"Mr Furnish?"

"Er, well yes. But you are sure you want to contact him?"

"Certain."

" I see, right then. Hang on a sec, won't be a mo,."

I could hear the click and metallic ping of a mobile phone. He was searching his directory.

"Ah, here it is. Have you a pen?"

I wrote down the address and telephone number with hands that refused to stop shaking. "Thank you," I said.

"How are you, sweetie? I must say Peter and I were gutted when you two split."

"I'm getting there, Mr Furnish."

"And what's with this Mr Furnish, all of a sudden. Don't forget to pop in and see us when you're over. I suppose you do come over from time to time."

Over from where I wondered. "From where, exactly?" The words were out before I'd had time to think about it.

He hesitated then with an embarrassed laugh said, "From the big apple, of course."

"Yes, of course. I'll do that." I tried to sound light hearted and to match my tone to his but in the pit of my stomach I felt fear, as acute as any childhood nightmare.

Before I rang Owen's number, I opened the

kitchen cupboard and poured a stiff measure of brandy into a beaker. I'd bought the spirit at the local off licence some days ago, before my visit to the Hermitage, knowing that I'd be in need of some Dutch courage.

A woman answered the phone. She sounded foreign.

"Could I speak to Owen Madoc please?"

"Who is speaking?"

"Tell him it's Rowena Shaw."

I heard her talking to him and then he took the phone.

"How did you find this number?"

"Mark gave it to me. Listen, Owen, don't hang up, I'm in trouble and I need help."

"And why should I care?"

"I don't know. That's just it. I can't remember."

"You're beginning to sound as mad as she is, now."

"Please listen. They're trying to make me think I'm someone else. They've taken my house, my identity and robbed me of my inheritance. I'm desperate, or I wouldn't have phoned you."

" I thought so. This isn't Rowena, is it? It's Sarah Lawson."

I could feel panic rising in my throat. I had to make him believe me. "Ring Glyn Morgan. He'll tell you the truth. He works for the BBC. Ask him to tell you who I am."

"Don't ring here again, Sarah or I'll have you

arrested for breaking the order."

Cradling the phone, I sank to my knees and wept.

Chapter 68

Richie and Sandy walked behind Owen and the woman in the red dress to a bar just off the market square. "It's good to meet someone who knows Megan and Duncan. I must admit that I miss Gareg Wen, although some of my time there I'd prefer to forget." Owen showed them to a table in the shade of a Eucalyptus tree, as a waiter stood aside with a nod in his direction.

After insisting on buying the drinks, Richie said, "You mentioned that you had a few problems living in Gareg Wen. I gather from Megan Lloyd Jones that there was a fire at your cottage."

Owen looked up from his beer and frowned. "Forgive me but it sounds as though you have been discussing me with Megan. If so, it's a bit odd that you and I should meet by chance, don't you think?"

He held his hands up in mock defeat. "Rumbled. I'm sorry to have resorted to subterfuge in order to talk to you but I really need to ask you a few questions and I couldn't take the chance that, if you knew why, you'd refuse."

The women had finished their drinks but before the waiter could bring more, Sandy stood up. "Connie, I wonder if you'd consider coming with me to the stall we visited earlier? I've decided to buy that skirt and I'd like another woman's opinion, also some help with the language. Shall we leave them to it for a while?"

Consuella picked up her sunglasses from the table. "Suits me. See you later boys." Her heavily accented English made the casual words sound exotic.

"Let me buy you another drink. I owe you that at least. Then I'll explain." Richie hailed the waiter and prayed that Madoc wouldn't refuse his request.

When he'd finished talking Owen bit his bottom lip, ran his finger around the rim of his glass and sighed heavily. "Do you believe that your client is Rowena?"

"I'm keeping an open mind. But I will say this – *she* believes it – of that I have no doubt. Whether it's as a result of the trauma induced by the fire or not, I can't say."

"The woman in my flat that night was Sarah Lawson. Rowena rang me and told me what had happened and that she'd left her alone. She was furious, not only with me but also with Sarah, who was playing games again. As soon as she realised that there was no possibility of me turning up she left."

"And you believed her?"

"Of course. Rowena is not, and has never been, a liar. She will always tell the truth, even if it's not pretty. Besides the fire officer's report said that a smouldering cigarette was responsible for starting the fire and I know that Rowena has never smoked."

"Perhaps she started, with the stress of the wedding being cancelled etc';"

"No, not possible. Rowena's father, whom she adored, was a heavy smoker and died prematurely thanks to lung cancer. She hated the things."

Richie raised his glass and drank deeply, feeling the ice-cold beer slaking his thirst. Whilst the sun slid through the leaves of the Eucalyptus tree making a pattern on his arms, he was thoughtful then said, "The woman's face was burned, I understand?"

"Yes, apparently it looked as if she'd been overcome by smoke and fumes and had fallen asleep on the couch. She was lucky to be alive. Much as I dislike Sarah Lawson, I wouldn't have wished that to happen, even though she started it all and I'm not just referring to the fire. But I'll never forgive her for the part she played in ruining my relationship with Rowena. Do you know I've had a couple of phone calls from her recently?"

"What did she say?"

"I don't know. I could see that the number was hers so didn't answer them."

"That phone is the one my client is using. She

told me that it contained Sarah Lawson's contacts. If she's Rowena perhaps it might be worthwhile speaking to her, should she phone again."

Owen's rueful expression followed by the shake of his head gave him his answer. He tried another tack. "My client's face is relatively free from disfigurement apart from some scars under her fringe. How could that be, if she was badly burned; surely it would be more obvious?"

Owen sighed. "The fire brigade arrived in time to prevent significant scarring so I understand. The plastic surgeon was a top man in his field and apparently her reconstructive surgery healed very quickly or so her brother told me before I left for Spain."

"I know it's a long shot but I don't suppose you've any photos of Rowena Shaw?"

Owen slipped his hand into his pocket and removed a leather wallet. "Here."

The woman in the photograph was not unlike his client but not enough to confirm that it was she. He was disappointed but realised it was unlikely to be that easy. "And your friend doesn't mind you carrying a photo of your ex around with you?"

"Connie?" he laughed. "Consuela is my housekeeper. Once a week we come to the market to shop and drink beer in this bar then I take her back to her brother's farm. She looks after my house and as you say she's my friend but there's nothing more."

"She's quite a looker."

"I'm sure her boyfriend would agree with you," Owen remarked.

"I thought I heard her call you, darling earlier."

"Connie calls everyone darling. It's her thing."

"Well it looks as if shopping's her thing too," Richie said as the girls returned armed with carrier bags. "I appreciate all the help and sorry I couldn't be more upfront from the start."

Owen held out his hand. "No problem. Good luck, I hope she doesn't cause you too much trouble; Sarah Lawson is some sick psycho."

"You're certain my client is, Sarah?"

"Positive, Rowena's been living in the States for ages."

Chapter 69

Sandy was waiting for him in the office when he arrived on Monday morning. Harry was making the tea. "There's news. Apparently Rowena Shaw's been trying to contact you. She wants you to ring her the minute you get in." Sandy's face and arms were glowing. He could see the white marks left by the necklace she'd been wearing in Spain. It was the one he'd bought her in Covent Garden. He wondered how Angie was getting along and found that the thought of her brought on a smile.

Half an hour later his client was sitting opposite him. She looked different and it took a while to realise that the change was in her expression. She seemed more confident, less confused.

"And you say that this old friend of yours recognised you as Rowena Shaw?"

"He did. I've his telephone number if you want to confirm it. It was such a relief, Mr Stevens. You can't imagine what it feels like to have no one believe you."

Richie nodded. "And you visited the Hermitage and spoke to Sarah Lawson's doctor?" Her expression changed briefly to one of exasperation. " I don't understand any of it. There was a fire and I lost my memory but only for the events surrounding the incident. Apparently I started insisting I was Rowena Shaw soon after I recovered, but no one would believe me."

He wondered whether now would be the best time to tell her and decided it would be. He began explaining how he'd managed to track down her former fiancée in Spain.

"You did? Oh that's fantastic news. Owen will know who I am. He wouldn't talk to me on the telephone. He was sure I was that woman." Her smile transformed her face so that he had a glimpse of someone quite different. He didn't relish her disappointment when he started to explain what he'd learned in Spain but now there was now no other option.

"I'm not sure how much you've been told about the accident but Owen Madoc said that prior to the fire Sarah Lawson had been making his life a misery," Richie told her what he knew.

"I see. At least I think I do. But to be honest, I'm not really sure. Bits of it have been coming back since I visited the Hermitage. I'm not certain how reliable my memory is though." She frowned trying to make sense of the fact that her fiancé had all the while been battling with a vicious stalker in the shape of Sarah Lawson.

"How much of the accident *do* you remember?" he asked.

"Nothing at all. I remember going up in the lift to Owen's flat. I remember someone opening the door but that's all until I woke up in the hospital."

"Do you remember Sarah Lawson?"

"I'm not sure. Part of me thinks I do but then the details slip away and I'm left confused. I was extremely busy in work, I do remember that, most of that year was spent in the States and when I was home I had a wedding to arrange."

The air was stuffy in the office; Richie stood up, walked over to the window and opened it wider. He looked down into the street. Shoppers scurried by accompanied by the distant hum of traffic.

"Mr Madoc said one of the reasons he was drawn to her was that she reminded him of you."

She sighed. "There must have been some facial resemblance between us, which would account for some of the reactions I've had from total strangers." She shook her head and frowned.

"What is it?" Richie walked towards her.

"I do remember something. It's nothing really." She stood up and walked over to the open window. "But I was at the Gallery and Mark Furnish mistook me for her. He laughed it off and I thought nothing of it. But it happened again a week or so later, I saw Mario, a waiter at Luigi's, who asked if I'd enjoyed the squid on Saturday night. I said I'd been in Edinburgh working for the past ten days. He looked embarrassed and said he was sorry, he'd been mistaken." She suddenly turned to face him, her smile was genuine and it changed her face completely." I do remember her. I remember Sarah Lawson!"

He was amazed at the change in her. It was impossible to believe that her reaction was not genuine.

"When I first met her she looked different. But later….."

"So what was it that made the difference? Changing her hair, make up, clothes? What was it exactly?"

"It was all of that that. She began to dress like me. On one occasion she was actually wearing the same dress, she had her teeth whitened, took trouble with her make up. But it wasn't just that. It's difficult to explain exactly."

"Do you think it could have been an attempt to emulate someone she admired? They say it's the sincerest form of flattery."

"I wish that was the case. But now I know it was definitely something more sinister than that."

"Well it certainly looks as if your memory is returning. We'll soon sort this mess out." She clasped his hand. " For the first time since this nightmare began, I believe you will."

"Thank you, Miss Shaw. I'll be in touch with

news as soon as I've completed a few further enquiries." Richie stood up and walked with her to the door of the outer office.

As the sound of her footsteps echoed down the stairwell, Sandy stopped typing and frowned. "What's up Doc?" she asked.

"The end is in sight, Miss Smith. Now let me have another look at that photograph Madoc gave us. Then ring this number and ask to speak to Glyn Morgan."

Chapter 70

The Outback Steakhouse was busy; holidaymakers keen to take advantage of the huge meals and copious amounts of liquid refreshment available indulged their appetites to the full. Rowena Miller smiled at her husband but the smile didn't reach her eyes. He was grossly overweight, which was why he liked to eat at the Outback. She'd imagined marriage to Clint Miller would be the answer. He was certainly wealthy, they had a nice house in Florida and a holiday home near the coast at Clearwater but it wasn't enough. She missed Owen.

"Eat up hun, you haven't touched your pancakes." Clint patted her hand and she fought to hide her revulsion as sauce dripped from his chin on to the napkin he'd tucked into the neck of his tee shirt.

She'd been living in Florida ever since Clint Miller had called into the New York offices of Aston and Cooper and had decided that she was the one for him. It was after Owen had moved to Spain. She couldn't face going home, not after all that had happened, so Clint Miller had seemed the best option at the time.

After they were married, it took her little over six months to realise that money wasn't everything and to think about how she was going to escape. Clint was kind, bought her everything she wanted but the sight of his large body sliding into bed next to her night after night made her want to vomit.

The trouble was she'd become lazy. The thought of losing the comfortable lifestyle and having to start all over again scared her. Clint was a shrewd businessman and in spite of his desperation to marry her had insisted that his attorney draw up a pre-nuptial agreement stating that, if his wife divorced him before they'd been together for ten years, she would not receive a penny of his vast fortune. But if the marriage lasted longer than ten years, a generous settlement, which would be agreed upon between them, would come into force.

Rowena toyed at the pancake with the tip of her fork. The thought of spending the next nine years with the man sitting opposite her was almost too much to bear.

Later, at home listening to Clint snoring alongside her, she slipped her legs over the side of the bed and walked through the double doors to the balcony. The cruiser was moored at the jetty at the bottom of the garden next to one owned by the film director, who'd made his name with the Midnight Trilogy. There was a party on board. She could hear laughter and the faint sound of music drifting towards her on the warm night air. She twisted her wedding band around her finger and took a deep breath. If only she could hear Owen's voice, it would make life more bearable. The popping of champagne corks aboard the cruiser brought back memories of her meals with Owen, the bustle of Covent Garden and London life in general. She loved strolling around the market stalls and taking the river boat down the Thames to Camden Lock and St Catherine's Dock. Nostalgic tears slid down her cheek and she wiped them angrily away remembering Gareg Wen.

"What you doing out here, honey?" Clint stood behind her, his hair ruffled from sleep.

"Nothing, just looking, I couldn't sleep. Go back to bed, there's nothing wrong."

"I think you could do with a holiday. What d'you say?"

In the darkness Rowena closed her eyes.

"Let's go to Europe. We could take in Austria, Italy, Spain; I know you don't want to go to the U.K. It would be like a second honeymoon." He sat alongside her watching the dancing lights from cruiser where the party was now in full swing.

At the mention of Spain Rowena felt her heart begin to race. "Yes. I'd like that."

Clint kissed the top of her head. "I'll get Bobby on to it tomorrow. He'll book everything.

Now come back to bed and let's get started on this second honeymoon."

There were times when Rowena missed working, not at first, meeting Clint had been the answer to her prayers then. Working at Aston and Cooper was becoming more and more difficult as there were contracts in the U.K. to fulfil. There was the little problem of Lewis Daly too. He was making life difficult, kept asking questions. After the wedding they'd moved to Florida and she'd felt safe for the first time in ages. But time had moved on. The prospect of visiting Spain and seeing Owen again filled her thoughts. Clint was out fishing. She picked up the telephone.

"Hi Bobby; it's Rowena. How are you? "

"Hey there Row, good to hear you. Excited about the trip?"

"That's why I'm ringing. Clint mentioned that we'd be taking in a visit to Spain and I've always wanted to see a place I know in the north of the country. I remember going there with my family when I was young. It's a small village approximately thirty odd miles from the French border called Los Christophe."

"Sure, no problem, as a matter of fact, I'm about to put the whole package together, so that takes care of Spain."

"Thank you so much, Bobby. Oh, and if Clint asks, we haven't had this conversation. I want to keep it surprise for him."

"What conversation?" Bobby replied.

Her excitement lasted all day. She fired up the barbecue ready for when Clint returned, had a bottle of Champagne chilling in the fridge and felt alive for the first time in ages. It was time she put things right between them, Owen Madoc had always been the love of her life and she intended to tell him so at the first opportunity.

Chapter 71

The thunderstorm took everyone by surprise. In the market square of Los Christophe Owen sheltered in the recessed doorway of a shop selling wooden toys. His hair was plastered to his head and his shirt was sticking to him. Stallholders hurried to protect their wares from the torrential rain, which was collecting in gigantic puddles in the overhead canvas awnings that threatened to collapse. Rain bounced off the cobbles and the drains refused to take more water, adding to the chaos. It was not unusual for floods in this part of Spain; Los Christophe's proximity to the Pyrenees meant that the area often suffered from flooding. It was part of its charm and reminded him of the Welsh valleys where he'd grown up.

He shook his head to remove most of the water from his hair, looked up and could see the faint glow of the sun breaking through the thunderclouds. He knew from experience that soon the cobbles would be smoking as the sun burned off the rain and peace was restored once more.

Walking across the square to the café he ordered an espresso then sat at a table outside to enjoy the fresh smell in the aftermath of the storm. Raindrops splattered at his feet from the overhead guttering. Closing his eyes he felt the warmth of the sun stroking his skin like a lover's touch and when he opened them he knew he was dreaming. Rowena was standing in front of him.

"Hello, Owen," she said and the years slipped away followed by confusion as his sun-blinded eyes adjusted. "It's me, Rowena. Don't you recognise me, darling?"

It was as if the horror from which he'd been desperately trying to escape was resurfacing. "What are you doing here?" he asked, playing for time.

"I'm here with my husband. We've been travelling around Europe. This is nearly the end of our holiday."

"I heard that you got married," the words escaped from his lips, conventional phrases that slipped from his tongue.

"And you? Are you married?"

"No. Still single."

"I still love you," she said resting a hand on his arm.

The distant roll of thunder rumbled across the plain and Owen felt the bottom dropping out of his world.

"Here you are, 'hun. I've been looking all over for you."

Owen saw her turn to face the large man who was placing an arm around her shoulders.

"Owen, I'd like you to meet my husband." Her eyes bore into his. " Clint this is Owen Madoc the artist; we were engaged once upon a time."

"Got to congratulate you on your good taste then, buddy." He held out a chubby hand then pumped Owen's vigorously. "Glad to meet you. What a coincidence. Why don't you come over to our hotel and join us for dinner later?" His grin was as wide as the Grand Canyon and Owen wondered if he had any idea what he'd got into.

"Thanks, that's very kind of you but…"

"Yes, why not?" she said. " We don't see anyone from home and I'm missing all my old friends. We are still friends, aren't we, Owen?"

In spite of himself he nodded but had the presence of mind to firmly decline their invitation. As they took their leave of him Clint Miller took a card from his inside pocket and pressed it into his hand. "Don't forget now. If you're ever if Florida, look us up."

He could feel her eyes boring into his soul as he walked across the square in the opposite direction to his cottage praying that he'd wake up from this nightmare. He forgot about the business card resting in the pocket of his shorts.

Later that day when he'd drunk enough wine to anaesthetise him, Owen made his way back home. His hands were shaking as he stood in the kitchen and poured water into a pint glass, which he downed in an effort to regain some sobriety. His encounter with the woman had unsettled him beyond measure. He wasn't sure what he should do. His head was spinning; he couldn't think clearly. He climbed the narrow staircase and sank into bed hoping that by the morning he'd have some idea. There was no way he could avoid this latest turn of events. Like it or not he had to face it. Dreams of Rowena and Sarah Lawson haunted him throughout the night. The fires that had destroyed his cottage at Gareg Wen and later his London flat burned brightly in his nightmare consuming his passion for Rowena so that he neither knew whether it had existed in anything other than his imagination.

When he awoke, he was bathed in sweat and his bed sheet was coiled like a snake around his ankles. He stepped into the shower turning the controls to cold and stood shaking off the horrors of the night so that they slid into the sewerage system along with the soap. A mug of strong black coffee, buttered toast and a telephone call to Connie, to tell her not to bother coming over and to leave the cleaning until tomorrow, left him with the rest of the day to decide what to do. He didn't dare risk going outside in case she was there waiting for him.

Paranoia haunted him until he could bear it no longer. He made up his mind. This time he wouldn't run away.

Upstairs in the spare bedroom he searched through the pocket of the shirt he'd worn when he'd met Richard Stevens and removed a card. Thankfully Connie hadn't got around to washing the small pile of clothes that were collecting in the wicker-washing basket. Then remembering the card that rested in the pocket of his shorts he held them both in his hand as he dialled Richard Stevens's number.

Chapter 72

I was almost afraid to admit it but since my visit to the Hermitage I'd had the feeling that the fog that was clouding my memory was beginning to lift. The problem was that none of it made any sense. My phone conversation with Owen, such as it was, had unnerved me. He was so angry. What had I done to make him hate me so much? However, Sarah Lawson, once a shadowy figure, was beginning to take shape. Now I could remember the phone call; she'd said that Owen was going to be in the flat and that he wanted to explain. I remember the taxi driver dropping me outside the flat. The night warden said to go on up, I was expected. And that was all – nothing else – however hard I tried I couldn't remember what happened next but it was a start and I was certain that soon, I'd remember it all. What I failed to understand was why Owen had been so sure that I was Sarah. Surely he would have recognised my voice if nothing else.

There was the sound of someone walking along the passageway followed by the ringing of my doorbell. My 'brother' was waiting on the doorstep. "Sarah, I understand you've been to see Doctor Kilpatrick," he said following me inside the flat. He sat in the ugly armchair and frowned at me. "You should have said, I'd have driven you over. Have you been having more problems?"

I smiled. " No, actually, you'll be pleased to know that I've started to remember the fire. It helped talking to Doctor Kilpatrick." I was waiting for him to react by concentrating on his facial expressions, certain that I'd be able to tell if he was lying. But to my amazement he stood up, grabbed me in a bear hug and said, "Thank goodness; perhaps now we'll hear the last of Rowena Shaw." He kissed the top of my head and I could feel tears pricking my eyelids. I didn't want to cry, I didn't want to feel anything for this man who was determined to make me Sarah Lawson.

"I'll ring Hannah, tell her the good news; this calls for a celebration; get your overnight things, we'll go out for a family meal and you can sleep at ours."

Packing my night things into a bag in the bedroom, I heard him talking to his wife, the excitement in his voice made me think that it sounded like a genuine reaction; could he fake that? I followed him to his car in a daze and as we crossed the car park we met Neil Stafford. He was holding the arm of the Grace Kelly lookalike living in the flat opposite. "Hello you two. Did you enjoy Spain, Sarah?" he asked.

Both Andy and I looked at each other in surprise. "Spain?" Andy asked.

"Oh sorry, have I let the cat out of the bag?" He dug me in the ribs. " I must say the guy you were with was all over you like a rash. I would have spoken to you but I was on a sightseeing tour and we were late getting back to the bus; too many beers in the bars of Los Christophe."

"I'm afraid you must be mistaken," I said. " I haven't been to Spain lately."

Neil Stafford took a step forward and looked at me more closely. "Must have been your double then."

My heart began to race; suddenly everything made sense. I took a deep breath to stop my voice from shaking. "They do say if we look hard enough that somewhere in the world we'll find one. Looks like you've just found mine." I slipped my arm through my 'brother's."

"Your suntan's faded pretty quickly too," Andy laughed and I forced my laughter to join his.

"I should be so lucky. Out of work and travelling to Spain. I don't think so." In the side view mirror, I watched Neil Stafford turn around and shake his head in disbelief.

Number 34 Bramble Lane was beginning to look as if it had never belonged to me. The front garden looked untidy, weeds grew in the flowerbeds and the lawn was suffering from numerous games of football being played on its, once smooth, surface. Jake and Sally ran to me as soon as I entered the house. "Aunty Sarah, we're going to the Speakeasy Diner for our dinner."

"Oh good, I think," I replied raising my eyebrows at Hannah Lawson who grinned.

"It's a new one and all their friends have been apparently. Anyway Andy's told me the good news." She kissed my cheek and I smelled Mischief.

"Is that a new perfume?" I asked.

She hesitated. "Still some gaps eh? Remember I said I liked the smell of your new perfume and you bought me some for my birthday."

I must be careful, I thought. " No sorry, can't remember. But never mind, it'll come back soon, I'm sure of it."

My optimism set the tone for the evening. The Speakeasy Diner had been designed to replicate the style of a nineteen fifties stateside diner. It was bright with red leather banquettes and Formica-topped tables. The menu consisted of Chips with everything and the kids loved it. I chose a cheeseburger with salad.

"The fries come with it," the waitress, desperately trying to maintain an American accent, lingered to take our order pencil raised above her pad.

"No fries for me," I said.

"But you love chips, Aunty Sarah," Sally said. "I do, you're right, so just this time I'll have the fries," I said. "And you can share them with me."

There was a lot I had yet to learn about Sarah Lawson if I was to maintain this façade, if only for a while longer. But I knew that the answer rested with Owen and this time I'd make him talk to me, even if I had to travel to Spain myself.

Chapter 73

The phone call left him in a quandary. How could he prove that Madoc's suspicions were correct? He glanced at the Millers' address and telephone number; there was only one way to make certain. Hoping, that the ninety thousand pounds his client would eventually collect would reimburse his trip, he rang the number and arranged with Miller to meet him and his wife the following Monday. He'd explained that he was a friend of Owen Madoc and that the artist had asked him to look them up.

"I'll be away for a day or two, Miss Smith. Unfortunately I can't afford to take you with me – this time it's Florida."

Sandy's face fell a metre or two. "That's the way the cookie crumbles I suppose, back to being the receptionist. At least I was a P.A. for a while."

Richie grinned at her hangdog expression. "You'll always be my personal assistant, Sandy and one day I hope I'll have the money to pay you what you deserve."

Realising he'd dropped the Miss Smith act, he

waited for her smart remark and wasn't disappointed. "If I'm to be your P.A, Mr Stevens, perhaps you'd better remember to address me accordingly."

"Certainly, Miss Smith."

He heard her chuckling as he left the office and walked to the Travel Agents further down the High Street.

He hated flying long distance; it always left him disorientated. The words of the novel that had previously held his attention now slid off the page and into his dreams as he slept intermittently throughout the flight. Arriving at St Petersburg-Clearwater International Airport he collected his luggage and made his way to the car park to pick up his hire car.

Thank God for air-con, he thought entering the line of traffic building up on the freeway. A swarm of persistent bees hovered over the bonnet of the car, siting on the wipers, committing suicide on his windscreen, before deciding to look for a home elsewhere. The temperature gauge on the dashboard read thirty-five degrees Centigrade and he wished he'd worn cotton trousers instead of the man-made fibre pair, which was clinging to him like Velcro. He pictured Sandy's 'I told you so face' and smiled.

The Miller's house was just as he'd expected it would be. It stood alongside others of its kind speaking of wealth and bad taste in the same breath, the architect having been unable to decide which era he was trying to re-create. The windows adhered to the modern day, whilst the porticos, balconies and large white-painted veranda could have been lifted straight from the pages of *Gone With The Wind*. A lawn trimmed with precision led down to the waterway, which he guessed wound around the properties before discharging its high-priced cargo of cruisers and yachts into the ocean. Clint Miller waved in his direction; he was hosing down the steps leading to the jetty.

"Richard Stevens, private investigator from England, I phoned last week? Your gardener said to come around the back."

"Yeah. Good to see you, Mr Stevens."

"Richie, please."

"Richie then. Come on up to the house and let's hear what brings you to my door."

They sat on the veranda beneath large ceiling fans drinking iced tea whilst he outlined his reasons for his visit.

"And you say your client knows Owen Madoc; the chap my Rowena was engaged to?"

He hesitated. "Miss Shaw was definitely his fiancée, that's true."

"And you want to ask my wife about some fire or other? I don't know whether she can be of much help, as I told you on the phone, she's been away for a few days. Only just come back as a matter of fact. I haven't even had a chance to tell her you were coming over. She'll be glad to see someone from England though, I'm sure of that – misses the old place, you see."

Richie heard footsteps crossing a wooden floor followed by Clint's wife making an appearance. He'd been warned what to expect but nevertheless it came as a shock. It was uncanny.

"Rowena 'hun. This is Richie from England, he's a P.I. and he'd like to ask you a few questions." Clint Miller stood up and kissed his wife's cheek.

She recovered well but not before he'd seen a slight tightening around her mouth and even under the tan he could see her face drain of colour. "Welcome to Florida," she said stretching out her hand.

Her voice was similar; that low breathy whisper – so easy to cultivate. Her hand was cold, in spite of the heat of the afternoon.

"I'll get us a few cool beers and a martini for my wife, while you two get acquainted." Clint disappeared through the opened French doors leaving them alone.

"What can I do for you?" she asked tucking her long legs under her on the padded seat.

"I've been hired to help my client recover her memory of events that took place in London a while ago. Apparently there was a fire at a flat owned by Mr Owen Madoc."

She sighed, took a cigarette from a packet she

removed from a flowered canvas bag at her feet and lit up. "My guilty secret, I'm afraid." She attempted a smile, which Richie noticed didn't quite reach her eyes. "It was all terribly sad. Sarah had the hots for my fiancé: she enticed me to visit his flat with what I'm sure was her intention to humiliate me further, but I soon realised that she was unhinged so I left her to it. I could go into detail about some of the sad tricks she pulled whilst trying to damage my relationship with Owen but I don't think it will help to open up old wounds, do you?" The words tripped off her tongue as if rehearsed.

"What happened when you saw Mr Madoc afterwards?"

"I beg your pardon?" The cigarette hovered mid way to her lips.

"Did you manage to explain – patch things up – that sort of thing?"

"Er, no. Actually, I didn't see Owen again. I rang him and explained that too much water had flowed under the bridge. He'd lied to me about his relationship with the Lawson woman and I couldn't forget it."

"Did you see Sarah again?"

"No. I spoke to the police, explained events prior to the fire and then decided to take up the offer of a job in New York. The further from London, the better it suited me. I managed to sell my house in Lockford, to Sarah Lawson's brother actually, which was a bit ironic."

"Luckily for me," Clint said placing the

drinks on the table between them.

Clint was a talker; Richie listened as he finished his drink and his wife finished her cigarette and lit another.

"Well, I mustn't take up any more of your time," he said. "Thank you for your help, Mrs Miller.

"No problem," she replied and as he shook her hand he noticed that the roots of her hair beneath the bleached blonde were brown.

As he drove back to his hotel he remembered Madoc's insistence that Rowena Shaw would never smoke a cigarette, no matter what stress she was under. It was another piece of the jigsaw.

Chapter 74

I've never liked Spain. I don't like the food and the scenery does not appeal to me. Throughout the taxi ride from the airport to Los Christophe, I kept thinking about what I would say to Owen. I no longer feared his rejection. If he refused to acknowledge me then I would have to deal with it. It seemed that since the fire I'd had to deal with far worse.

The flight and journey to Los Christophe was short and I was soon watching my taxi leaving the small hotel in the centre of the village wondering how long it would be before I'd be in need of another to take me home. The reception area of the Granada Hotel was little more than a hallway at the end of which stood a desk. A young man with black hair and a thin moustache, who was wearing a dark suit, smiled at me.

"Miss Shaw? We've been expecting you. I take you to your room on the first floor."

It was obvious that the place was under occupied which suited me fine. The room was pleasant, the view across the square acceptable and as I ate my evening meal in the attractively furnished dining room, I began to relax.

After dinner, I walked into the square and inhaled the warm scented air. I'd made no move to phone Owen to tell him of my arrival, but knew I couldn't put it off for long; I needed to see his reaction when he saw me. It was the end of my quest. Richard Stevens knew of my plan but we'd agreed that Andy Lawson should not be told. As far as he was concerned I was visiting a friend in London.

Walking across the square, I heard the sound of a guitar being played from the veranda of a restaurant where paella was being cooked on an open fire. It was the first time I'd ever been affected by the magic of Spain and I used it as an excuse to delay the moment that I would walk back along the road towards Owen's house. I'd passed it in the taxi earlier and found it reminded me a little of the cottage we'd shared in Gareg Wen, the memories of which were rapidly returning with each day that passed.

"Rowena?"

I turned around knowing it would be him. The light from restaurant played on his face and I knew that mine would be in shadow.

"Owen," I replied waiting for his reaction.

"I, er, I don't know what to say." The moon came out from behind a cloud and I heard him gasp. "I thought I'd be prepared for this but it's such a shock. You've got her face."

"So I gather. And she, it seems has cultivated mine together with my voice."

"How can I apologise? It *was* you on the phone, wasn't it? I should have known. I'm so sorry. She's made my life a misery for so long that I was sure she was at it again." He dropped his eyes from mine. "Besides, after the fire, you told me that you never wanted to see or hear from me again. You were adamant."

"Not me."

"Look, I can't get my head around this. Let's get a drink and talk."

The bar was quiet; at a table overlooking the square we sat and stared at each other like strangers. So much had happened since we'd last met and so much of it needed explaining.

"Where do we begin?" Owen asked placing a hand on my arm. I felt the heat of his fingers on my skin and sighed but it was a sigh of regret at what we'd lost rather than re-awakened of passion. When we'd finally discussed every aspect of the problem facing me, he took my hand in his. "How can I make it up to you? How can anyone make this terrible affair right?"

In the subdued lighting in the bar he looked much younger than I'd imagined in my dreams. Crickets playing their night-time games accompanied the sound of someone strumming a guitar from across the square, whilst my world settled around me.

"I have to live with the fact that I've been given her face and there's nothing I can do about that; it's going to be a constant reminder of what happened."

His eyes brimmed with tears, which he hastily wiped away with the back of his hand. I had the answer to my question staring back at me – there was nothing left for us – she'd won. "She must be made to pay for this. Have you spoken to the police?"

"Not recently. Richard Stevens is doing all he can. She's married and living in Florida, I understand. It's complicated."

"What about your house and the money?"

"As I said, it's complicated. But I've put my faith in Mr Stevens and I'm sure he'll find a way out of this mess."

Owen put his head in his hands. "You've been through hell and I'll never forgive myself for the part I played in it all."

" Let's walk for a while," I said, taking his arm. " It's a lovely evening."

We walked out of the square and along a lane bordered by lavender bushes, the heavily scented air wrapping around us like a satin sheet. "This is beautiful."

"I thought you didn't like Spain."

"It's growing on me." I felt his hand slip into mine. "Was that why you chose to live here because you knew I wouldn't come?" I asked.

He groaned.

"It's alright. I understand."

"You're not bitter? That surprises me."

"I've learned it doesn't help. It gets you

nowhere. As you said I've already been to hell. Hell was when no one would believe that I wasn't Sarah Lawson. But there was always just one person I wanted to convince to make me happy and that was you. The rest didn't matter."

In the moonlight I saw his jaw tighten as he drew me into his arms and kissed me. It was the kiss of a friend and both of us knew it

Chapter 75

The garden of number thirty-four Bramble Lane looked even more uncared for than on his last visit. A child's bicycle lay in the long grass bordering a hastily trimmed lawn; greenfly had attacked the rose bushes near the front door and a pile of withered petals stood where they'd fallen on the driveway.

Andy Lawson opened the door; standing in the hallway behind him was the man his client had identified as Neil Stafford. "Come in, Mr Stevens. This is my solicitor, Neil Stafford. I thought it wise to have my legal representative join us, in view of our telephone conversation."

Richie followed the pair into the lounge-room. They were alone in the house. He'd also noticed the absence of Hannah Lawson's car in the driveway. "I think, under the circumstances, that's advisable. The police will have to be contacted at some point but I feel you need to be aware of the conclusion to my investigations first."

The inside of the house was showing signs of the same chaos that had affected the garden.

Newspapers littered a coffee table, there was a layer of dust covering the surfaces and there was a faint smell of neglect. The thought suddenly struck him that what the place lacked was a woman's touch. "Maybe Mrs Lawson should hear what I've got to say?" he said.

"That won't be necessary," Neil Stafford replied.

"It's OK, Neil. It will all come out soon. Hannah and I have separated. She's taken her children and gone back to live in Birmingham." Andy Lawson looked down at his hands.

"I'm sorry to hear that." Richie opened the file he'd brought with him from the office and said, " Shall we begin, gentlemen?"

After he'd recounted his client's position, her feelings when she discovered a strange family had moved into her house and the theft of ninety thousand pounds from her bank account, he started to explain the case against Sarah Lawson. "Your sister made it her business to cause trouble between my client and her fiancé. She hounded Mr Madoc to the point of stalking him, cancelling his wedding plans, and repeatedly telephoning him."

Andy Lawson sighed and looked up.

"She then began to mould her image to that of Miss Shaw. Colouring her hair, altering her style of dress, copying her make up."

"I thought she was influenced by the London fashion scene; that she'd changed because she was living in the city."

"Not quite, Mr Lawson. Did you notice that her voice changed?"

"Sarah always had a talent for mimicry, even when she was a child." He looked again at his hands, as if the answer was written in the creases of his skin and then raised his head. "But OK, so she was playing a stupid game. Owen Madoc was an adult; he could have handled it. From what I saw of the situation he encouraged her."

His defensive attitude was only to be expected he thought; she was his sister after all. However, he was becoming more and more certain that Andy Lawson knew nothing of her plan to swop identities after the fire. But if that was so, what was he doing in Rowena Shaw's house?

"That maybe partly so but it didn't excuse her actions. She started a fire at his cottage in Wales."

"Is there any proof of that?" Neil Stafford interjected.

"We know she was in the area at the time and you must admit, at the very least, her behaviour was becoming psychotic, also the fire chief believed the fire to have been started by a lighted cigarette. The same M.O. as the one that broke out later in Mr Madoc's London flat."

"But again, no actual proof." The solicitor persisted.

" That's why I'm talking to you and not the police – yet." Richie looked down at the papers Sandy had meticulous filed. "You do both realise that after the fire, your sister, posed as Rowena Shaw by insisting to the police that she'd left Sarah alone in the flat. The situation was made easier for her as the woman the firemen rescued was suffering from burns and of course we know that the two woman were similar in appearance."

"I gave the hospital a recent photograph of my sister, for reconstructive surgery purposes." Andy Lawson said standing up and pacing the room. "This is madness. Are you asking me to believe that Sarah is now living as Rowena Shaw and the woman I've been helping to re-adjust is not my sister?"

"I am. Did you see Rowena Shaw after the fire?"

"No, why would I? I didn't know her very well. We conducted the sale via the telephone."

Richie sat up. "The sale?"

"Yes, the sale of this place. Not long after the fire, I had a phone call from Miss Shaw. She said that she'd been talking to a mutual friend and understood that I was hoping to move to the area, in order to help with my sister's recuperation, as she had a flat in Lockford." He stopped pacing and frowned. "It never occurred to me that the call wasn't genuine. Sarah had bought the flat some months before, she made the excuse that Hannah and I could use it when we brought Sally and Jake to visit their father." He sighed. "The woman I spoke to on the phone told me about this place and that she was willing to sell at a very reasonable price, for a quick sale prior to her moving to the States."

"So the last pieces of the jigsaw fall into place," he said.

"I don't understand."

"Your sister is very convincing, Mr Lawson. Tell me. When the woman you thought was you sister first recovered from her burns did she mention the name Rowena Shaw?"

"She insisted that was her name but the doctors told me that she was confused and had lost her memory. I knew that Sarah had been involved with Owen and I just thought she'd got muddled." His face coloured with embarrassment. " She'd had some mental problems of a similar nature when she was a child. She'd tried to convince everyone she was her best friend, copied her clothes, imitated her mannerisms but the doctors put it down to adolescence and said she'd grow out of it. When she insisted she was Rowena, I suppose part of me was anxious that it might have resurfaced. I didn't want to face it."

He sat down a deep frown creasing his forehead. "After the fire the psychiatrist at the Hermitage suggested that she was suffering from amnesia brought on by shock and that she'd remember who she was in time. He advised a firm hand and not to allow her to continue with the fantasy – to insist that she was Sarah."

"I see." He consulted his notes. "You accepted that this woman was your sister, without question then?"

"In view of the fact that I'd been speaking to a woman called Rowena Shaw on the telephone of course I did. There were times when I thought she was a bit strange but I put it down to her disturbed state of mind and well, after having reconstructive surgery, she was bound to look a bit different."

Neil Stafford sat forward in his seat. "This is all very well and good but do you have any concrete evidence, other than hearsay, that this woman is who she says she is?"

"That can easily be supported by comparing samples of DNA from Mr Lawson and Miss Shaw."

Lawson nodded, "Of course, anything I can do to help clear up this mess, is fine by me. Perhaps you could arrange for samples to be taken immediately. And I'll have to speak to Sarah right away, before this goes any further. Do you have a contact number, Mr Stevens?"

Driving away from the house on Bramble Lane, Richie felt little sense of achievement at solving the case. Too many people's lives had been affected and would continue to be so. Lawson was as innocent as his client in all of this and yet thanks to Sarah Lawson he'd lost his family, the home he'd paid for with the proceeds of some wise investments and the 'sister' whom he'd spent the last year trying to help. Rowena Shaw at last knew the truth but had to live with the face of her persecutor staring back at her every time she looked in the mirror. In addition to which Owen Madoc had lost the fiancée he loved. It was a mess whichever way you looked at it.

Chapter 76
Six months later

Walking along the cliff path at Gareg Wen, I feel the cold wind in my hair and stop to marvel at the ice sculptures on the foreshore. Diamond cut crystals gleam in the winter sunlight. The ground is crisp underfoot and there's more than a hint of snow in the air. I try not to think about the past and concentrate on the future, my future, not the one created for me by a mad woman.

The sale of the house in Bramble Lane seems to be progressing without a hitch and at last I'll be able to pay Richie; he's been so patient. I've come to terms with the fact that the ninety thousand and the money I had in my bank account will never be returned.

Owen and I have stayed in touch but as the months pass the threads of our relationship have weakened rather than binding us together. We can be nothing more than friends. Sarah Lawson succeeded – she damaged us beyond repair.

I've bought the cottage in Wales that we once

shared. At least the sale of Bramble Lane has allowed me to do that. It's been impossible to work in London at my old job. None of my contacts, or work colleagues recognise me and trying to explain just brings it all back again.

Dr Kilpatrick has helped me piece together the missing pieces of my memory. That Thursday, when I arrived home and found them in my house, I was sure I'd been to work. But as I walked down Bramble Lane, I saw a fire engine outside number 14 and the old lady being carried out on a stretcher towards the waiting ambulance, I smelled smoke and by the time I'd reached number 34 I knew who I was. I was Rowena Shaw and the months since the fire were as if they'd never been. The details of where I'd been until the moment I turned the key in the lock faded, the faces of the people who were supposed to be my family slid away – they were strangers who thought I was someone else.

Dr Kilpatrick explained that memory glitches were only to be expected after such a traumatic experience and that it had been down to my strength of character that I hadn't suffered a mental breakdown during those months when I'd been mistakenly identified as Sarah Lawson. All I know is that there were times when I felt my sanity hanging by a thread and if it hadn't been for Richie Stevens and Glyn Morgan perhaps I would now be an inpatient at the Hermitage.

Surprisingly Andy and I have become friends. I know he was only trying to do his best for his sister; he and I were both cheated one way and other. He's living in the flat, which he thought was mine. I did visit him once but found I couldn't stay for long; he understood, and now we meet elsewhere.

I've started to write it all down. It's a catharsis. Megan Lloyd Jones has been so helpful introducing me to her contacts, inviting me to the house she shares with her husband Duncan. She doesn't expect lengthy explanations; she knows the facts and lets me be myself.

The police still haven't found her; she disappeared after Andy telephoned her. Clint Miller has spent a fortune trying to find his wife; he's offered vast sums of money for information but neither he nor the police have succeeded.

Although I have her face, I'm sure she no longer has mine. Sarah Lawson is an enigma, a chameleon, as changeable as the weather; all I pray is that our paths never cross again.

At last this book is finished and I'm waiting for the girl from Fox and Knight to collect the proofs. I think I can hear the sound of her car's tyres crunching over the frost-covered road now.

The End

ABOUT THE AUTHOR

K.J.Rabane's main interest is in writing psychological thrillers. She also works as a supporting artist for film and television and lives near Cardiff, South Wales. Details of this book, together with her other eBooks, can be found by visiting her web page.

www.kjrabane.co.uk.

Printed in Great Britain
by Amazon.co.uk, Ltd.,
Marston Gate.